A KIDNAPPING IN NEW YORK

JACKIE WHITE

Copyright © 2024 Jackie White

The right of Jackie White to be identified as the Author of the Work has been asserted by her in accordance with the Copyright, Designs and Patents Act 1988.

First published in 2024 by Bloodhound Books.

Apart from any use permitted under UK copyright law, this publication may only be reproduced, stored, or transmitted, in any form, or by any means, with prior permission in writing of the publisher or, in the case of reprographic production, in accordance with the terms of licences issued by the Copyright Licensing Agency.
All characters in this publication are fictitious and any resemblance to real persons, living or dead, is purely coincidental.

www.bloodhoundbooks.com

Print ISBN: 978-1-917214-51-3

To my husband, who believed in me, supported me, and loved me for all these years. And now here we are.

CHAPTER ONE

GWENDOLYN

Apartment buildings hold defiantly to their odors, remembering each tenant in the pores of their walls: the Chinese takeout, the burnt toast, the fried fish, the dirty diapers, the litter boxes soiled by cats whose nine lives have long ago been extinguished. The hired help struggle, but fight a hopeless battle. Try as they might to conceal the aroma of each generation with a fresh coat of paint, the walls always win, slowly exhaling the last visceral sensations of their former tenants. Never fully fading from the building's memory.

As the elevator door creaked open to reveal the dimly lit hallway of the once grand building, I should have been focused on other, more pressing matters. Yet, anticipation contracted the muscles in my head as the immediately familiar odor infiltrated the elevator cab. The sickly sweet, slightly nauseating aroma of my past permeated my nostrils. Bringing back memories as vivid as if they had happened last week, or the week before that, instead of the two-and-a-half years since I had last stepped foot in this building. It required a conscious effort to move myself forward.

The door to apartment 19J stood impersonally amongst the

others, a large five-room high-floor overlooking the park. The waiting room wore a new yellow coat of paint, had sloughed its Berber décor for trendy vinyl, and sheathed its old chairs in gray polyester chenille. Perhaps a Botox makeover would be sufficient for me, as well.

I made sure I wasn't early, so I wouldn't have to sit around and make an already excruciating ordeal even more so. Waiting rooms, especially shrink waiting rooms, are uncomfortable on so many levels. I tried to settle my butt into the depressions left by the other fuck-ups who had waited here before me. Ditched the iced skinny mocha latte in the trash. I had managed to choke down half for breakfast. I would get another one later. For lunch.

The door to the inner office opened almost immediately. And there she was, as if time had stood still, looking exactly as she had all those many months ago. I, of course, was a completely different person.

"Gwendolyn ... Gwendolyn ..."

She whispered my name and put on the same pitiful mask everyone wore lately when speaking to me. I made a point of looking at the floor as I squeezed past her girth and stepped into the office. She turned and made a move toward embracing me. I stiffened just enough to remind her of appropriate professional boundaries. She reached out her hand. I fumbled with my bags.

"Gwen," she said again. "I was so worried–"

"Doctor Moss, please. *Please*," I said. "Has the session already begun? I haven't even had a chance to sit down."

Her mouth slipped, just a crack, and then she shut it and gestured me to the updated sofa, pretending that's what she had intended all along.

She sat. "It's just that I was so ... so shocked. And appalled. No one ever thinks it will happen to them. Or to someone they know."

I held up my hand to stop her. Wasn't it enough that I had come back? Why did she have to go rushing into it so soon? Before I was ready. I was the one paying. Wasn't this my show?

"Doctor Moss, can we just slow down for a second?" I closed my eyes. "I just need a chance to breathe. I feel like I haven't had a chance to take a breath for two weeks."

She fell silent. I opened my eyes and she nodded.

I rushed two deep breaths. I figured I owed them to her. "Thanks for seeing me on such short notice. I know it's been a while."

She nodded again.

"Over two years."

She nodded some more.

Awkward silence.

"Over two years," I said again. "And everything was going pretty well until, well, you know ... this whole *thing* happened."

"I can imagine." She nodded, as if she could. "How are you holding up?"

I didn't want to answer, but found myself answering. "I'm afraid. I'm afraid I'm on the verge of being out of control again." I searched the window for some sort of distraction, for something to focus on. But there was nothing but sky. "I'm scared and I'm nervous and I can't sleep. I'm tired all the time. With no new details, the press is finally relenting. Fresh news cycle, I guess. But I sit around all day thinking those thoughts. About the things I shouldn't do. I'm on the verge of being completely out of control. I can feel it."

I tried to smile, to minimize what I was telling her, but my lips stuck to my teeth. I rooted around in my bag for the emergency Thermos of coffee.

"Gwen ... Well, yes ... I can imagine." Again, as if she could. "I'm sure it's more stress than most people can bear. At times of extreme anxiety, we are always in danger of slipping back into our old tried and true methods of coping." She paused—a self-important pause—so I would know what she was saying was going to be insightful. "Sometimes, the most effective methods of self-distraction are the most self-destructive. But of course, you know all that already."

I hated her.

I was too exhausted to talk. I had been answering questions from the cops, from the media, from nosy neighbors, nonstop for days. I was willing to waste the $400 of insurance money just to close my eyes and sit there for the rest of the fifty minutes. As far as therapy goes, it was probably worth it. Unfortunately, she wasn't as flippant about taking their money as I was about spending it.

"I've read the newspapers. And of course, watched the television. Naturally, I've been worried about you. Concerned is a better word. I've been concerned. I know how very strong a person you are. If anybody can make it through a crisis like this, you can. And I know you will make it through. Even if it all feels overwhelming right now, at this juncture. But of course, needless to say, I was worried sick to hear about the baby. So, when you called—well, I was relieved. I welcome the opportunity to help you through this."

I turned back to the window and remembered what I was searching for. The pigeons. I watched them swoop back and forth across Fifth Avenue whenever I needed a distraction.

"It was my fault. Totally my fault."

"Your fault." She blinked. "How could it have been your fault?"

"I was there. I should have done something to stop it." I hated myself. "I could have stopped it. And I didn't."

Last night's dinner rode a wave of acrid bile, slowly bubbling up like lava, burning my esophagus, throat, mouth, and nostrils along the way. *How many more times would I have to swallow my words along with my puke? How many more times would an old meal come back to pay a revolting visit before this was all over?*

"So that makes it all my fault."

"Then tell me why it was your fault. Explain it to me. Why you think so, anyway." She shifted her considerable heft forward; psych 101 for 'I'm interested in what you're saying.'

I took a long tremulous swig of coffee, and a deep breath, to muster the strength to tell my story. Yet again.

CHAPTER TWO

Where to begin.

How far back is the beginning?

Most of the way, I decided, but not all.

"I stopped coming to see you long before I got pregnant. So, you never knew. But obviously now you do. Not only did I get pregnant, but I decided to have the baby." I shrugged with feigned nonchalance. "Once it happened, I didn't put all that much thought into it."

I'd agonized more over that decision than anything else in my life.

"Thirty-four, the old clock ticking, and then, *Surprise! You're pregnant!*"

"And the father? Has he been supportive?"

I stifled something. A laugh? A sob? "I ... I never told him. We were deeply in love." Wow. It felt good to finally say that aloud. "But before I could tell him, he left me. Just like everyone else."

I needed a minute to compose myself, to quiet the quaking within. Eventually, I cleared my throat and continued. "It was very challenging. My pregnancy. I was feeling fat and depressed and lethargic. Which made me feel more fat and more depressed and more lethargic. The vicious cycle, paying its usual unwelcome visit."

"You were having a baby and the fat cycle was in full swing?" She wagged her large head.

My face got hot.

"You *must* ease up on yourself. You *have* to give yourself a break," she said in a voice I imagine someone would use if they were your friend. "Don't you ever ease up?"

"Don't you know me at all?" I shot back. "Do you even understand me? Or have I wasted 7,000 hours of my life on this couch?"

"Ah. But if you remember, when we stopped seeing each other, you agreed to lighten up on yourself and not be such a perfectionist."

"Things change. I'm not going to be penned in by false promises."

I knew I was lashing out, using her as my whipping post, not because of anything she did, but because of everything going on in my life. That was stupid of me. And immature. Of course, I realized that. But I paid good money for the privilege.

"I waited until after I had her. Then I needed to get a handle on *my* situation. I had to start getting myself back in control. I had to get back to my old routines."

Prudence dictates that new mothers wait six weeks after giving birth to start exercising again. To give their bodies a chance to heal from the trauma of pregnancy and childbirth. But I was in great shape when I got pregnant and even ran through most of the pregnancy.

"Cassie. That's her name. But you know that, since you've been following the story. A month old when it happened. And beautiful. Even for such a little kid."

For the first time in a long time, I felt myself smile. Moss smiled back, so I frowned.

"I had already been running with her for two weeks when it happened."

The shrink raised her eyebrows. "Was she not too small to be doing that?"

"No. She was *just fine*. She slept the whole time, and she loved it." It wasn't a good thing—and I knew it—putting the need to exercise above all else. But I am who I am, and it always did make me feel superior, in a fucked-up sort of way. "I thought we had agreed a long time ago that your job is *not* to be judgmental," I snapped. "Some of the more pathetic detectives have already tried to use the 'blame the victim' scenario on me. As I tried to explain to them, I'll try to explain it to you, too."

This was not the time to mention that, although perfectly healthy, at a birth weight of five and one-half pounds, she really was tiny. Instead, I continued the patronizing tone, to be certain Moss understood that what I was telling her was indisputable common knowledge and that, as a doctor, she should be ashamed to not already know it.

I spoke slowly, deliberately, condescendingly.

The first thing I emphasized was that the thing cost me a thousand bucks. It was the best damn jogging stroller out there. I know, I did the research. Neck support, smooth ride suspension, you name it. If she fussed too much, straight against my chest in the baby carrier she went till she calmed. Then back into the stroller so I could finish my run. But I know she loved that stroller because mostly she slept. I definitely sounded like some idiotic late-night infomercial.

"Hmm." Moss pursed her lips. "I'll take this one on faith."

"It was a beautiful day," I continued, ignoring her. "Magnificent. The morning was clear, the whole city smelled clean and looked razor sharp. No ozone at all. You couldn't ask for better air to breathe."

I inhaled the stale air of her office.

I had already set up a great schedule. Cassie woke at about five. I'm breastfeeding, regaining my figure being top priority, so I was fully awake then, too. The kid was napping again by six, until about eleven, which was perfect. It gave me enough time to get in a good run with her, come back and shower. It was especially great because the early morning joggers had already finished and were on their way to work and the stay at home joggers weren't out quite yet. Compared to the craziness later in the day, the park always seemed calm during those hours. I never felt as if I was in the middle of the city.

It was perfect.

It seemed that the whole country knew what happened next. And even though only two weeks had passed, I felt like I had gone over the story a million times already.

But I understood why they wanted it that way. If years of tedious hard work in the city's Legal Aid Office had taught me anything, it was the importance of repetition. Each new telling could unearth some heretofore buried detail. Some little nugget that had fallen through the cracks might reveal itself as the missing gem. But the story was becoming increasingly confusing to me. It was becoming harder to keep the details straight. That horrific replay button was on a continuous twenty-four-seven loop. Any time I closed my eyes I would rejoin my nightmare somewhere in progress.

I attempted to focus, made a conscious effort to speak slowly, and tried not to make any mistakes.

"We left the building and entered the park the same as always, directly across the street, at 90th and Central Park West. We turned left and headed north, up those monster hills until we got to 107th, then took the path over to the East Side."

I thought back to that run, the same one I had done for over ten years, five times a week, rain or shine, sweltering hot or freezing cold. It never, ever mattered. Strangers would gawk at me with a mixture of disbelief and horror—although I liked to think of it as awe—for my audacity at thumbing my nose at the extremes in the weather. Despite everything that had happened, I couldn't help but wonder how soon it would be appropriate for me to be seen running in the park again.

I closed my eyes and I was there.

CHAPTER THREE

"We went all the way down the East Side, past The Reservoir, down the hills behind the museum, past the skating rink. We turned right along Central Park South to get back to the West Side, then finally back up north to complete the loop."

Now, not only could I see myself running, but I could feel it too. Legs aching, the weight of the jogging stroller getting heavier and heavier as I pushed it up the increasingly steep slope of the hills by the Delacorte Theater.

"The whole way north is uphill. I always get tired in that final stretch back on the West Side, in the eighties. Especially now, with the jogging stroller, because you lose your arms."

I opened my eyes a crack to look at her because I figured, obviously correctly, that a person of a certain heft would have no idea what I was talking about.

"You lose your arms," I repeated, and grasped at imaginary handlebars in the air in front of me.

She swung her face from side to side.

"I'll explain. An efficient runner uses their arms to get momentum by pumping them up and down." I realized that I had unconsciously dropped the timbre of my voice an octave and slipped into the slow, overly solicitous tone I used when I needed to convince a jury they knew everything there is to know about some obscure topic they knew nothing about.

"But when you hold on to the handles of a jogging stroller, you no longer have your arms to help pump. You lose the use of your arms as jogging tools. To keep the stroller rolling straight, you slip the tether around your wrist and hold the handlebar with both hands, suck it up, and get the whole run from your legs. That makes it a lot harder. A much more intense leg workout."

And—yes, there it was. The momentary pupil contraction, that almost imperceptible flicker of understanding that told me, like suckers on a jury, she was on board.

"Finally, there's that last big hill right before I come up to the Great Lawn. It's always been my point of exhaustion. I guess I must be switching from aerobic to anaerobic or something. So of course, that's where it happened. One of the detectives thinks whoever planned it had watched me more than once before. That they knew that's the spot where I'd have nothing left, where my strength would have all tapped out."

The white-hot tears slowly burned their way forward, percolated beneath my eyelids, and spilled like corrosive acid along the raw troughs they had previously etched down my cheeks.

"It's okay. Take your time."

She offered up the box of tissues.

I took them. Then issued a long, slow, stalling sigh. "*Me, of all people. Me, who knows better than anyone what can happen in this city when you don't pay attention to your surroundings. How I let my guard down and let this happen. How that made it all my fault.*"

I took another deep breath.

I explained to her that you can't see it from the street, there are too many trees, but when the amps are set up you can hear everything. "It's one of my favorite things in the world. Running by the Great Lawn when they're setting up for the concerts. Sound checks always happen, and occasionally the real, actual artists will even show up. It's like an unadvertised concert. And it's always the biggest names in the business. I mean, they are the only ones who can justify Central Park as a venue."

I was an inappropriate idiot, getting a charge from an ill-timed running story. It was one thing to know it. Another to care.

"That morning, they were setting up. It was all I was focused on. I hadn't heard anything about it, and was wondering who it was. They were playing, back there, hidden by the trees. I couldn't place the band. As I got closer, I listened more intently. My first mistake. I became so intent on listening that I stopped using my eyes. I was seeing, but wasn't focusing. Wasn't paying attention to what was happening around me."

I was infuriated, even then, sitting there, recounting how it had all transpired. Those stupid equipment trucks hogging up the entire right side of the road. Surely, she knew the ones I was talking about. "That insidious industrial caravan whenever there's a movie shoot or concert. They really are a monumental danger."

I glared at her.

"Those trucks force you to run way out into the middle of the street to get around them. They idle their stupid, smutty engines all day, spewing their profane, climate-destroying air pollution. Try running for a quarter of a mile past those things while holding your breath. I'm sure they must violate every clean air regulation on the books.

"The odd thing was ... and I never thought about it before that day ... They seem to never use trucks with hydraulic lifts. Instead, the roadies lay planks of wood between the road and the back of the truck to make a ramp and push their crap from inside the truck down the ramp and then use the same ramps to haul it back up again. Wire, cables, cameras, lighting, tables, chairs, whatever. In and out. Up and down. Then they're over by the stage listening to the music. None of them hang back at the trucks to keep an eye on the junk they've left strewn all over the road."

I pulled a few tissues from the box just in case. She leaned in even further. I guess she knew what was coming.

"Take a minute," she offered. "If this is too difficult."

But I was going to finish what I started.

"I remember thinking that either the band really sucked, or I was too old to appreciate the new music, when two runners materialized out of nowhere, one on either side of me. Actually, they didn't really materialize—they had been about twenty paces behind me since I passed Tavern on the Green, three quarters of a mile earlier.

"Inexplicably, I thought I was pacing them because they stayed the same distance behind me no matter how much I sped up or slowed down to take the hills. Only now, looking back, I realize that they were in great shape and were really good runners. It wouldn't make any sense that they would have the same pace as a one-month postpartum woman pushing a jogging stroller. They probably could *walk* about as fast as I was running." *Blinded, I now saw, by my own hubris.*

I looked out. My pigeons were doing figure eights.

"Before I knew what was happening, these two hulks had come up behind me and were boxing me in. In two seconds, two split seconds, they were so close, one on either side of me, that our feet were getting all jumbled up. I was tripping, stumbling over my sneakers, or their sneakers, I couldn't even tell, and my knees were buckling. I felt myself starting to actually lose my balance, to fall down. It was ridiculous, really. Something like that had never, *ever* happened to me before, and I was like, *What the hell?*—but I only thought it, I didn't have the words to say it, because now I really *was* falling and there was nothing I could do to catch my balance, because on top of everything else now I was totally freaking out because I realized that they were sticking their legs out and tripping me *on purpose* and I was panicking because there were two of them and only one of me and they were both so much bigger and stronger than I was and right then it dawned on me *what an idiot I wa*s, that I really was still too weak from just having the baby and I could barely breathe because I was scared and I was out of shape and I probably should never have been out running all those miles after all. And then one of them put his hand over mine and started prying it off the handlebar and I looked down and I realized ... I mean, I saw that they were wearing latex gloves, and that was a bad sign, a very bad sign, because that meant they had put some thought into what they were doing ... and whatever it was, whatever the hell it was, they didn't want to get caught doing it."

I looked down. The tissues were shredded in my hands.

"That's when it became surreal, like it wasn't happening to me at all, like it was happening to someone else, and I was just watching."

I was talking to myself now. It hardly mattered if Moss was there or not.

"Everything seemed to be moving so fast, but at the same time in slow motion. The guy closest to the curb. He was big, ugly. Shaved head. Stubble beard. Pockmarks on his cheek. Gang initiation scar on his forehead. His sweat smelled of garlic and cumin. I was concentrating on my feet, still trying to keep my balance, when he did it. I didn't see it coming. I was totally blindsided. He grabbed my head with his arms, wrapped them both around my head and face so tight I couldn't see, and I couldn't scream and I could barely breathe. He dragged me over the curb and away from the street, by my head. I was sure he was going to break my neck, pull my head right off my body. I didn't even have time to fight him. Then he threw me, threw me in the air, threw me across to this small patch of grass. I landed on my stomach down a little hill under the bushes. I opened my eyes. Couldn't see a damn thing, but dirt and rocks, and those prickle bushes. My head was spinning; I couldn't figure out which way was up. I was on my hands and knees, and they stung like hell. They had already begun to bleed.

"I smelled his revolting odor before I saw him. Almost blacked out when he dove into me. Knocked the air right out of my body. He flung me over onto my back like I was a rag doll. God, he was ugly. After that, I couldn't see his face anymore because he had stopped to pull a pair of pantyhose over his head. I remember those empty pantyhose legs hanging down and his big flat nose and lips smashed under the netting, I was sure he was planning to really hurt me because he thought the hose would prevent me from ID'ing him. I tried to scan my memory to see if he could have been one of the scumbags I had ever defended. I tried to remember. Did I do a crappy job? Was this retribution? Or in the scheme of things was I about to get what I deserved—raped and murdered by one of those animals I had defended and gotten set free?

"He straddled me. Sat his huge, massive body right across my hips so I couldn't move. I could barely breathe. He leaned down really close to me, and it looked like he was actually smiling under the hose. I thought for sure this was the end. One hand held my neck pinned to the ground. I decided he was being considerate; if he choked me out it wouldn't be so bad. I remember thinking, 'What the hell is he waiting for?' Then I saw his other fist coming down. Coming straight down."

My face was impassive, frozen.

"But he didn't punch me. He had a huge fistful of dirt and he ground it—crammed it—into my face and my mouth. He made a special point of sticking those massive sausage fingers down into my throat. The bitterness of the dirt and those latex gloves. The taste stung. And then, just as I braced myself to have my clothes ripped off, and to have my head beaten to a pulp, that was the exact second I realized that I wasn't holding the tether to the jogging stroller. I was over here. She was over there. I couldn't move. I couldn't breathe. I couldn't think. I was petrified. As totally and completely freaked out as I was for myself, and what was about to happen to me, it was nothing compared to that paralyzing fear in my heart when I realized Cassie wasn't with me.

"At that second, when I realized I was separated from the baby, I knew I would fight until I was dead, that nothing else mattered. I started blindly flailing with my arms and legs, trying to make some kind of contact with him so that at least I would know where the bastard was, even if I couldn't see him. But there was nothing there. Nothing to hit. Only air. He wasn't on top of me anymore. The son-of-a-bitch was gone. I couldn't figure out why, what the hell was happening. I tried to open my eyes, to get reoriented, to find the street. But I was dazed, my head was spinning.

"I couldn't stand up. I was crawling, but I saw it. There was dirt in my eyes, but I swear I saw it. The other guy, the one who had pinned me in on the outside, was pushing the jogging stroller up a plank ramp and into the back of one of those trucks. And the dirt smasher was sprinting back up to the road and around to the driver's side of the truck."

I had to pause and take a breath.

"And then it started to move ... The wooden planks dropped to the street. I heard the thud ... and just before he closed the doors in the back of the truck, the truck that now had my baby inside, I ... I saw ... I thought I saw some other bastard look right at me..." The words tasted like poison. "... *and wave.*"

My bottom lip spasmed. "And then they were gone. That's when it finally registered. They weren't after me at all. I was in the way. All they cared about was the baby. They wanted the baby. They took my baby."

The effort of the re-telling had sapped what was left of me, weakened me back to numbness. I recited the rest without intonation.

"I have no idea how much time passed before anyone stopped to help. Probably just seconds, because one or two people said they saw the whole thing happen. I was completely hysterical. I still couldn't stand up. My wrist was already swollen. Probably from when they pulled off the tether. My right cornea was scratched. I had countless lacerations and contusions. And if that wasn't enough, my mouth was still so full of the dirt that I couldn't talk." *Even now, my eyes still felt dry and scratchy, my throat was sore, and my entire body ached and creaked.*

"Soon there was a big crowd. Everyone tried to help. Someone called 911. Needless to say, my phone was in the stroller. A bicycle cop got there. Assured me they would have no trouble finding Cassie because it only took four minutes to mobilize the Amber Alert. They put a police checkpoint on every street surrounding the area.

"But that was just typical cover-your-ass crap. I knew right then, it was way too late. They don't count the time it took for the first cop to get there. Then they conveniently forget that I was completely delirious and couldn't relate what happened in any sort of coherent fashion for what felt like ages. And it took forever before he called it in to the desk sergeant. It may have taken them four minutes to mobilize the Amber Alert, but they didn't call for it for at least ten minutes after Cassie was gone.

The sons-of-bitches could have made it halfway to Rockland County by the time that alert even went out."

I looked back for my pigeons.

"I guess you already know the rest. They found the truck on CPW and 101st. No traceable prints. No baby. All that was left was one beautiful brand-new $1,000 jogging stroller."

"Do they have any idea about who could have done this?"

"Somebody who really wanted a baby. I mean, they think someone who wants to have a baby and maybe couldn't, something like that. What I'm trying to say is, they're pretty optimistic that no one went through all the trouble and risk to take her in broad daylight, at a place where there would definitely be witnesses, only to harm her. These people knew I would be there, at that time, with a baby. They even stole the contents of the diaper bag. The detectives feel confident that whoever has her is taking care of her. If you can actually call all that grounds for optimism."

I slumped down, heavy with depression, feeling as fake as those facelifted waiting room chairs.

"Gwen," she said. "I apologize, but we've actually run over. But before you go, tell me. How is the bulimia?"

"Oh." I dismissed her question with a flick of my hand. "It's great. I'm only puking like, once a day or so. If that. But I sort of think about it and think about doing it all the time. I guess it kind of could go either way."

If she had any idea what the truth really was, that I was actually back to at least seven times a day and my life was once again revolving around bingeing and the toilet bowl, she probably would have suggested another short 'visit' to one of those repugnant live-in facilities. And that was surely the last thing I could afford at a time like this.

"Once a day is admirable. Especially given the pressure you're under. But we do need to work on alleviating some of those thoughts you say are distressing you." She took out her prescription pad.

"I'm writing you some new scripts. They've come out with a whole new protocol since our last meeting. Slight alteration in the combinations, frequency, etc. We'll work on proper dosing, and monitor the side effects. We can start in the middle range and see how you feel. Then we'll talk about adjustments. And I want to start seeing you again every other day for a while..."

I don't know what else she said. I had stopped listening.

CHAPTER FOUR

ZIVI AND GISELLE

The morning sun shined brilliantly over the privileged Upper West Side neighborhood where, an hour earlier, Gwendolyn Black had been rushed in the back of an unmarked patrol car to the emergency room of Columbia Presbyterian Hospital. As she watched the traffic whizz by, she answered the questions of the detectives from the 20th Precinct regarding her brutal assault and the horrendous kidnapping of her daughter. She sat, mindlessly prodding at her raw scrapes and bruises, oblivious to the additional pain her fingers inflicted.

Those same rays glared indifferently off the concrete and rubble strewn landscape one and a half miles north, in the area of Washington Heights known as Camden Hill. Though the weather that morning was exceptionally clear for early June, the air in the lone basement apartment of 863 Wickum Avenue was stagnant and oppressive. The apartment's only window sat above the kitchen sink, opening to an air shaft in the back of the building. The bottom of the window rested evenly with the airshaft's concrete floor, so that most of the apartment was below street level. As a result, it offered minimal light even on the brightest of days. The building's antiquated boiler and hot water heater, situated just around the corner from the apartment, left the air permanently saturated in a sultry dampness.

Unlike every other apartment on the block, this one was furnished with tasteful, sophisticated, extremely expensive furniture. The couch, the chairs, the lamps, the rugs. They spoke of a time when money was not an issue for these tenants. The exception was the makeshift coffee table, dubbed the *biblioteka*, or library, in Bosnian. This particular *biblioteka* consisted of piles of textbooks, tomes, treatises, manuals and reference guides heaped together and endlessly rotated and rearranged, as one snippet of information or forgotten detail required refreshment. A sunny yellow colored the living room walls, as if that could somehow compensate for the real thing that never penetrated far beyond the lone window over the kitchen sink.

Numerous pieces of original artwork signed by the undiscovered artist G. Vaughn stood propped, sometimes three or four deep, around the perimeter of the living room. In a unique twist, each work juxtaposed seemingly inconsistent elements from unrelated schools into one comprehensive masterpiece. Renaissance and Cubism; Mannerism and Impressionism; Baroque and Minimalism. The successful marriage of these unlikely combinations was confirmation that, even on the two-dimensional plane, opposites could attract and flourish.

Unlike the visual diversity offered up in the living room, the bedroom was left intentionally stark. The painted walls and ceiling in an organic, silken milk chocolate hue accentuated its cocoon-like aura. It provided sanctuary from an often inhospitable outside world. A queen-sized mattress stretched nearly wall to wall. The bathroom was so small its door swung out into the bedroom, eternally stuck open behind the mattress.

A large green lava lamp added peaceful, hypnotic movement. The azure hue of a digital alarm clock read 11:00am.

Zivi rolled over and squeezed his eyes closed as tightly as he could. He had gotten up way too early that morning. Although he had fallen back to sleep for a short while, he was now up for good. As the mental cobwebs slipped away, he thought about what he had just done. It had been dangerous. Reckless, even. But Zivi had analyzed it from every angle. He was desperate to make her happy again. To bring her back from the dark places in her mind in which she now wandered, distraught and alone.

Yes, the more he thought about it, the more he was certain. No matter the outcome, for many reasons, it had been the right thing to do.

He propped himself on his elbow and gazed at her as she slept. Sinking as she was, deeper and deeper into a state of despondency, sleep seemed to be her single refuge. It was cruel to rouse her from her only means of escape. But he could not bear to keep the surprise to himself any longer. Not one more second.

With the tip of his finger, Zivi traced the faint blue vein delicately pulsating across her forehead, then gently drew his thumb down the perfect ridge of her nose. She pretended she was still asleep, but he saw her lips quiver as she tried to suppress a smile. Zivi leaned down, brushed his lips against hers, then gently kissed her. Enveloped her in powerful arms and slid her body on top of him. Kissed sleepy gray eyes and pale cheeks. Her blond hair spilled onto his face; he collected it behind her back, braiding it into a long loose rope that draped over her shoulder and gently brushed her breast. Slowly and methodically, he dragged his fingers along each separate vertebra, rising like a row of pebbles, forming a delicately curved path down the length of her back. He followed the path until his fingers came to rest on the firm, smooth skin inside her panties.

He had wanted to be noble and wait until she approached him. But he was only human, and he could not wait any longer. His love for her was intellectual, but it was physical, too. He needed to hold her, to protect her, to be back inside of her. He had waited long enough.

Giselle felt him getting excited.

She wanted to pull away, to whisper in his ear that she was so very sorry, that she still wasn't quite ready. But then, from somewhere deep inside, she felt the familiar longings, ones she had forgotten ever existed, slowly reawaken. Bit by bit, her resolve crumbled. The notion that this wasn't a good idea percolated deep down somewhere in her cerebral cortex, but her rational mind did not have the energy to pay it much attention. She had a vague recollection of reading online, or in one of her many books, cautioning a full six weeks before having sex again. And it had only been one. Or maybe it was two. Since all she did lately was sleep, or stare at the walls in a state of utter, down to the last fiber of her soul exhaustion, she had lost all sense of time.

Giselle closed her eyes and tried to force herself to relax, to forget what had happened, at least for the moment.

Zivi gently pulled her down toward him, slipped her breast into his mouth, slowly and expertly teasing it with his tongue.

The sensations were so intense that she literally could not breathe. A soft moan of protest followed, but it didn't matter. She tried to pull away, but he would not let her go, instead continuing the titillating torture.

Somehow, eventually, oxygen found its way back into her lungs. She managed to relax and succumb to his seduction, the boundaries between pleasure and pain beginning to blur.

She made herself small against his body and let him be her rock.

As he held her close, she felt his hips slowly grinding up into her. Her gut shouted, with sudden and renewed intensity, warning her that she was nowhere near ready for intercourse again. Neither mentally nor physically. She needed more time. To forget. To heal. To put it all behind her. Her instincts were usually right. She wanted more than anything to listen to them now. But she looked into his face, just inches away from her own, and she knew she could never deny him.

So, although she really did not want to do it, she would have preferred to wait, to let the time come when there would be no more pain, she did it anyway.

She guided him to where he wanted to be.

Afterward, they lay facing each other, her head propped on his forearm. He rested his other arm across her hip. She absentmindedly ran her fingers through his long, mussed-up hair. They looked into each other's eyes and smiled.

"Hey, *beba*. How are you today?" he whispered.

She looked up at the ceiling. "I guess I'm ... good-ish."

"Good-ish. And what's that?" he asked.

She sighed. "Kind of good. Kind of not. Kind of sad. Kind of not."

He looked doubtful.

"Oh no. That was nice. Really nice. It's just, well..." She didn't finish.

Tears welled in her eyes.

"Come here." He entwined his fingers with hers and kissed them. "Listen to me." He stared at the permanent oil paint stains under her fingernails. "I love you. I *love* you. But this. It's killing me. I'm worried about you. I, I want you to go *out*. I want you to go *outside* again. To see the sun. To get back to your life." He smiled. "To start painting again." He had told her all these things a hundred times already over the past two weeks. Today, he knew, it would be different. "The bad thing is over. Today is a beautiful day. Let's go outside and enjoy it."

"How do *you* know what kind of day it is?"

He wiped her eyes and hoisted her up so that she sat on top of him, straddling his stomach. Encircled her waist with his hands.

"Because I know everything there is to know about today," he answered.

She rolled her eyes. Buried her fingers in the curls on his chest. Furrowed her brow, deep in concentration.

"Ziv," she whispered. "What's happening to you?"

He looked down to see that two distinct puddles, two circles of murky fluid, had pooled on his chest and were now trickling through the troughs of his abdomen. The look of utter confusion on her face made him throw back his head and laugh.

He adjusted the pillows behind his head. "Look at your boobies, *beba*." He fought back a grin at her naiveté.

Giselle looked down. A thin, opaque liquid leaked from her body.

"What's happening?" There was revulsion in her voice. "*What is it?*"

"Shhh, *beba*, shhh. It's okay. Calm down." He wanted to scoop her up and protect her forever. "It is only milk."

He smiled.

"It is milk," he said again. "For the baby."

She tried to slap him. She had never done anything like that before and it caught him off guard. But as a Fifth Level Master of Systema, the discipline of Russian karate, he caught her wrist inches from his face. She snatched back her hand and turned away from him.

"How could you say that, and *smile?*" Pain rose inside her.

"I'm just saying. If there was a baby, then the baby has to eat, and you have milk to do it."

"How could you say that to me?"

She grabbed some tissues and tried to dry herself, but her breasts had an agenda all their own. Despite her disgust, milk continued leaking.

"Uggghh." It came out as a deep, desperate moan. "This is *disgusting.*"

"No. It's beautiful."

She gawked at him, unable to decipher his meaning, unable to untangle the dizzying sensations swirling around her. She had seen him pompous with those he deemed less intelligent; she suddenly felt as if she'd joined their ranks. Her hands trembled. She was afraid of what was happening to her, of this new humiliating trick her body was playing. She lowered her eyes back to her chest. Stomach muscles clenched. She was frightened that once again she could not stop what was happening from happening. She raised her eyes back to him. His mouth was smiling. She was alone. Her rock had abandoned her, too.

"Zivi," she said, trying to rally. "There is no baby. Why are you doing this?" Her memory was racing, going through the whole horrible thing yet again, one more time, in the space of a second, just to be sure the images she held so vividly were once real.

"We agreed." She was begging now, unable to stem the panic and cold sticky sweat that suddenly covered her body.

"I'm not doing anything. I'm just saying." He was so calm. So confident. She was so flustered. Inadequate. It made everything even worse.

"*Just saying,*" she repeated. "Don't you remember? We agreed. We said we wouldn't talk about..." Her throat constricted, she tasted salt, felt the burn in the back of her throat. She struggled to heave herself from the bed. "*Because there is no baby, not anymore.*" She crumpled, exhausted, against the wall.

"Things change," he said. "Things happen."

"Dead babies don't come back." What happened, she wondered, to turn him against her?

"*Beba,* listen to me." He said it softly. *Patronizingly.* She knew it. *He thought she was a dolt.*

He leaned across the bed and reached for her arm, but she spun herself away.

"I'm just saying. *What if?*"

Her breasts were leaking again, faster than before, milk now dripping through her fingers. "*What are you doing?*" she chided herself. "Please." She turned her eyes up to the earthen colored ceiling. "Please, Lord. Make it stop," she begged.

She hobbled to the bathroom.

Because of the mattress, she couldn't close the bathroom door. Not that it mattered. She had no secrets from him. Nevertheless, at that moment, she would have welcomed privacy. Giselle sat on the chipped, vintage 1800s commode. Its tank was bolted near the ceiling; it flushed by pulling a long hanging chain with a beautiful antique porcelain knob hooked onto the end. She had explained to him that it was a wonderful urban artifact and how, as soon as he refurbished it, it would realize its full historical significance. He promised he would do it. As soon as he found some time.

Right after he fixed the TV and wi-fi. She had to agree to that. Those things were certainly more of a priority. At least the toilet *worked.* The television hadn't gotten any reception for over two weeks, and the wi-fi connection was awful. That's the way it always seemed to be in this hovel. Something or other always breaking down or not working. Not the way it used to be. Like the stove. She used to have a glorious six burner state-of-the-art professional-grade range. Now? A two-coil hot plate moved out from some closet sized studio apartment. Oh, well. She still preferred this to that. Especially because it wouldn't be like this forever. The water in the toilet spun around and around noisily before it belched, spit up a little, then gurgled down the pipes.

Giselle patted herself dry, got back into bed and nuzzled onto his bicep, the one with the jailhouse tattoo. The one with the fancy 'G' in a heart emblazoned over the old gang tag, intending to conceal it.

"I need to fix that," he said, his eyes half closed, his body slouching back against the pillows.

"Yeah. And there's a couple of other things..."

"Wait." He held up his hand. "I think I hear something."

"Nice try," she said.

They lay quietly together. Time may have passed. They may have dozed. She really couldn't tell.

CHAPTER FIVE

Giselle sat bolt upright, fully awake. She focused all her attention. It had to be a mistake. She could not possibly be hearing what she was hearing. And yet ...

"Zivi." She kicked him in the shin. "Can you hear?" she mumbled. "Could it be the—no ... It can't be..." Her ears were playing tricks. "Zivi?" She was afraid to speak, so she whispered, "*Wake up.*" She grabbed the flesh on his arm, dug in her nails and twisted.

"*Oooww*," he groaned, and pried her fingers from his muscle. Then he pulled himself up and held her shoulders steady. "I did it," he whispered. "For you. For us both. This morning. I got you a baby."

"What?" Obviously, she had not heard him correctly.

He looked at her with a half-cocked grin she could not read.

But there was no escaping what was happening. The cries of a tiny infant were resonating through the isolated basement apartment. Giselle stiffened, not sure if this was all a very big, very bad joke, or if impossibly, *insanely,* he just might be telling the truth. Unfathomably, he had never looked more serious.

"What are you talking about?"

"You were so sad when the baby died, so I got you a new one. It is out there right now. Waiting for you."

"You're crazy." She found it difficult to speak. "What do you mean, *you got me a new one?* Where did you get a baby?"

Her mind was racing to make sense of what he had done, still unwilling to believe he was capable of doing what she already knew he was capable of.

The sound of crying was more urgent now.

She shook her head frantically, back and forth. Skittered away from him. "Zivi? How did you get a baby? No one just *gives* someone a baby."

She was afraid.

"Who would give *you* a baby?"

"Someone didn't want their baby," he said, smiling. Attempted to sound reassuring. "This is great!" He took her hand. "Really. It's okay. That baby is for you."

"What?"

"Gissy. Honey." He pumped out his chest with pride. "I brought you home a baby."

"No. I mean—no. That's not my—*what?*"

He studied her face. It really was quite simple. He couldn't figure out why she was having a problem understanding.

"I'm saying," he slowed his speech, "the baby out there. *It's meant for you.*"

"*What?*"

Why was she repeating herself?

"What are you talking about?" she whispered.

"You don't hear me?" He had expected her to jump out of her skin, to be crazy with gratitude and excitement. "I brought you home a baby," he said again, this time a little more enthusiastically, hoping she would pick up on the enormity of his wonderful news.

"*What?* No, you did not. That's impossible."

"Yes, I did," he insisted, smile slipping.

"*What?*" she echoed, for what seemed like the hundredth time. "No, you didn't."

He was baffled. He did not know of any man who had ever done what he had just done to prove his love. Why couldn't she just accept his generosity, with the appropriate gratitude, as he imagined any other normal person would do?

He'd try again to make her see the selflessness of his actions.

"This mother didn't want her baby."

She stared at him blankly.

He began to worry.

"Listen. There are plenty of babies out there. Someone didn't want theirs. Now I have it." He threw up his hands at the obviousness of it all.

"You're out of your mind," she said.

He looked at her, sitting there in his most comfortable lucky madras shirt. He wondered where she'd gotten it. He must have left it in the bathroom when he came home this morning.

"Yes. That's what happened." He nodded. "The mother who had this baby didn't want it."

"Zivi! Stop it!" She crossed her arms tightly across her chest. "Why are you lying to me?"

"*I am not lying to you!* People put babies out on the front steps, or leave them at a church, or at a wherever, all the time. Not everyone is like you. There are plenty of people who don't want their babies."

"Yeah, but none of those people would *ever* give their baby to *you*."

"Yes. I mean, no."

"Don't be ridiculous. You didn't get a baby from some stoop or some church or *wherever*. So, right now. Tell me what happened."

"There was an underaged girl, who couldn't keep it, and didn't want her parents to know."

"And she gave it to *you*?" Giselle glared. "Surely you don't expect me to believe a story like *that*? That ... that some girl gave her baby to you, a man with your history?"

"Giselle." Okay, this was not going well. Apparently, he hadn't thought it through quite enough. "Yes. Yes, she did," he said, trying to sound calm and logical. "She gave me her baby. *To keep*. She *didn't want* a baby. You *do* want a baby. So she gave it to me. She couldn't take care of a baby. You can take care of a baby. So, she gave it away. *To me*. And now *I* gave it *to you*. Gis, this is our baby now. We're gonna keep it like our own. Don't you understand what I'm saying? I got you what you wanted. We are now a happy family. Period. The end."

"But it's not ours. I *don't want* that baby," she whined. "I want *my* baby."

Why was she being so obstinate?

"Our baby died." She sounded in terrible pain.

He plowed ahead, pushing the story forward.

"We don't have a baby," she whispered.

"Yeah, we do. And you need to accept it, because there's no giving it back."

He had done everything. He had tried to be patient. He had tried to wait out her depression. He had done the whole supportive thing. But it was taking too long. He was done waiting. For two weeks, he had been waiting. So, now he had done the whole Američko *take action* thing. Took action to solve their problem and make her happy. Why couldn't she simply see, why couldn't she simply appreciate, what he'd just gone and done for her? The beauty of the whole situation. Even if she didn't buy his story, she had to realize that he just risked everything—his freedom, *his life*—to make her happy. Why couldn't she simply play along and embrace his brilliant solution?

"Listen to me," he insisted. "Try and understand. I have done a wonderful thing for you."

He got up and began pacing in the small bit of open floor space along the foot of the mattress. Her frightened eyes darted back and forth, from him to the open doorway, and the pathetic but insistent little wails coming from the next room.

"Okay." He took a deep breath. He would start over. He would try it again. "Our baby died. She's dead. That's a fact. I took her from you the night she died, remember? No one saw me, Giselle. No one knows you ever had that baby. No one knows she died. Think, Gissy, *think*.

"No one was here but you and me. No one saw you. No one heard you. No one hears anything or sees anything that happens in this shithole apartment. And you haven't been out of this stupid place since."

He sat on the end of the mattress.

"Not for the last two weeks. You've stayed right here. I don't even think you have left this room. I've heard about craziness like this. And I don't want it happening to you." He was annoyed, now. "You just stay in here, all the time. Stay in here and cry. *Where are you, Giselle?*" He searched her for an answer. "*What happened to you?*"

She turned to look at the wall.

It was exhausting, trying to make it all sound sane and rational.

"I didn't know what you wanted me to tell everybody about the baby." He would try again to make her understand. "If you wanted me to say anything at all. And I didn't want to ask you. Didn't want to get you even more upset. This whole time, I told everyone you're feeling sick. Nauseous, or whatever you women feel. I said to everyone that you're still pregnant. *Gis*. I said that you were too sick, too pregnant, to go out anymore. *Listen to me.* No one but me has seen you since you had the baby. No one knows, Giselle. Just think about it, yes? *No one knows you had the baby ... No one knows our baby died."*

They sat in silence.

Until she said it again. "What are you talking about?"

"I am *saying* I brought you home a baby. A gift. I am *saying* I did it because you wanted so much for us to be a family. And now. Now you have what you wanted." He smiled. "Now, we are all here. We are a family."

"No." She shook her head. "Not like that. I never said that. I don't want it like that. No."

"YES!" He had just gone out and done something crazy to show her how much he loved her. Why couldn't she accept it?

"Then you tell me the truth. Where did you get that baby? You're scaring me. Stop changing your story. *Where did you get that baby?"*

He studied his hands.

"I asked you a simple question," she pressed, her voice shaking. "Where did you get that baby?"

Did she really want to know?

"Do you really want to know?" he whispered.

She wanted the truth?

"You want truth?"

Fine.

"Fine."

Then he would give it to her.

"Then I will give it to you."

He forced himself to stay calm.

"This baby," he started, "the one screaming in other room. That baby is *our* baby. If I try to give it back, I am going to jail. If anyone finds out that is not the baby you gave birth to, then I go to prison for—for *kidnapping*. I took that baby, and if anyone finds out I am going away and I am never, ever coming back. *Ever.* They don't let people like me off for kidnapping, Giselle. Not a man with *my* record."

He opened and closed his fists, shook out his hands.

"And this one is to keep. Just like it was really ours from the beginning. There is no going back. The only thing we have is our future. No one can ever know how we got this baby, or I am going away for the rest of our lives. We will never see each other again. We will never be a family."

He stopped talking.

"There. You wanted the truth. I gave you that, too. Now you know what kind of a man I am. Are you happy? What kind of a woman are you, Giselle? Because now it's your turn. Now it's up to you." He clenched his fists. "This whole thing is up to you." Shook them out again. "Whatever you choose. It's your decision."

Giselle didn't respond. She just kept staring at the door, into the room with the screaming infant. Then she turned to stare at him.

"Zivi, listen." She was calm, almost out of body. "We'll have a baby. We'll have another baby. Just not this one. This one isn't ours."

And just like that—*ping*—the glue holding his sanity together gave way. He whirled around. Planted his feet in perfect form. Landed the right-cross, shoulder height. Sunk it squarely into the target. Felt the instantaneous sting and then the dull throb in his knuckles. Retracted his punch to admire his handiwork. A gaping hole, surrounded by a web of spidery cracks, disfigured the plasterboard wall. Precisely in the middle of the wall above the mattress. That stupid, ugly shit-brown color she took three fucking months to choose.

Giselle flinched.

Zivi shrugged. "Bummer."

His filters were disintegrating, his lucidity dissolving. He could no longer see straight. The unbearable stress of the past two weeks had broken him. He did not know what he was saying anymore. What he was doing. Why he had done what he had done. He was finished. He had done enough.

He turned and strode out of the bedroom, past the screaming, fragile life hanging in the balance on the living room floor.

A slam of the front door, and he was gone.

Gisclle sat on the bed, stunned. What in the world had just happened? They had both so wanted that child. She recalled the countless nights he'd been unable to sleep, reliving his childhood. Painfully railing against his father, a low-ranking thug in the Bosnian mafia who violated some honor-amongst-thieves edict, remedying the situation by hauling his family across the ocean to an impoverished hellhole in America, only to abandon them while he was out getting drunk and carousing. A virtueless jerk who had numerous children with countless women.

She couldn't remember exactly when it happened, but Zivi had turned it into his mantra: how the karma of the world would be set right when he himself became the opposite, when he would become the first-generation American Dream—successful businessman, beloved husband, devoted father.

For all the times his father was gone, Zivi would be there. For all the times those other men in his mother's life had used their fists, belt buckles or worse against her and against him, Zivi would use his words. How many times had he sworn that he would be the world's best father, companion, provider, lover and husband? She could not count them all. *He wanted to do it.* She stopped taking the pill.

Giselle had been on the brink of breaking into the gallery scene. Had even gotten some nibbles from a couple of trendy dealers. But when the test was positive, everything faded away. Nothing else mattered. *It would be perfect. The best-laid plan. Robert Burns.* How ironic that her favorite poem, the first one she had ever memorized, the one she loved to recite to him as they laid in bed … How ironic it was that *that* was the very sentiment which would come back to bite her in the behind. She muttered softly to herself.

> *The best-laid schemes o' mice an' men*
> *Leave us nought but grief and pain …*
> *For promis'd joy*

And suddenly she found her way back, and she was sitting on the edge of a mattress in their subterranean cave, with a brand-new hole punched in the wall ruining her hard work, and there was this insistent noise … this endless racket …

She jumped up so quickly, she tripped over his sneaker and practically fell into the living room. She knew what to expect, knew what she would see, but still she stopped short, gasped, and stumbled backward. Lying on a pale yellow blanket, screaming, was the tiniest, most perfect human being Giselle had ever seen.

She was nervous just being in the same room with it.

"Hello, angel," she mouthed more than spoke. "Hello, angel."

She reached out her hands and saw they were trembling. She didn't trust herself to lift the child without dropping it. She wiped the sweat from her palms onto her shirt, took a deep breath and tried again. She reassured herself that she was bigger and stronger than this teeny, tiny, miniature being, and surely lifting it up should not be a problem. But when she knelt closer, she realized that the bony little arms and legs, sticking straight up into the air and waving wildly, were in the way. Giselle once again backed off in frustration. She sat on her heels and started to cry.

"Please, little angel. *Please.* Please let me pick you up."

Giselle rocked back and forth on her knees as if she was praying.

"I don't want to hurt you. I promise. I promise I would never hurt you, little one."

Then she reached down, scooped the child up into her arms, held it firmly against her own body, and let out a soft sob of relief.

With the same care she would have used had she been holding the thinnest, most delicate orb of glass, she cradled that head in the palm of her hand.

Through it all, the mini crimson-colored face continued to howl.

"You're so tiny," she purred. "What's happened in your short little life, angel? Who wouldn't take care of a baby like you?"

Slowly, Giselle managed to rise to her feet. Without thinking, she gently rocked the screaming infant. Her hips slowly undulated back and forth. Translucent, matchstick fingers, light blue veins glowing from beneath parchment skin, reached desperately up to her. She shut her eyes. For a moment it was two weeks ago, and the infant she was holding was a lifeless, silent, cerulean-blue baby girl and it was Giselle who was doing all the screaming.

But this one wasn't dead. Giselle opened her eyes. This baby was frantic, crying hysterically, jerking around so wildly that it was hard to hold on to it. Tentatively, Giselle gathered its arms and legs and drew it in even closer to her body, creating a human swaddle.

"Why so sad?" she murmured. "Why are you crying so hard, little one?"

With her thumb, she softly stroked the desperate, upturned face. Gazing into those magnificent eyes, Giselle felt the emotions that had been swirling so insanely inside of her for the past two weeks, searching for an outlet, about to burst forth. And still, she held her feelings in check. As she knew she must. For this was not her child. This baby belonged to someone else. She planned on killing Zivi when he came home. How could he do this to her? Well, maybe not *kill* him, exactly.

And just as quickly her racing, hormonally challenged mind changed gears yet again. Suddenly she felt as if she had pulled her finger from some sort of mental dyke that had been blocking up her thought processes. All at once, she could imagine the many dangers: the dangers that might harm this precious miracle she held in her arms, the dangers this infant might face if returned to the life Zivi rescued it from. And she became wracked with fear. Immediately and completely, her sadness and loss for her own child was replaced with a raging sense of responsibility for this living miracle, which she alone cradled against her body. As she bent her head to kiss the baby's forehead, tears spilled from her eyes and onto the baby's cheeks and nose, running in a lazy rivulet between the perfect pink lips. The baby stopped crying just long enough to stick out its tongue and taste the salty liquid.

"*Dear God.*"

With the utter clarity that comes only on the wave of an adrenalin rush, she ripped open the top of Zivi's very favorite lucky madras shirt, sending buttons flying everywhere. She awkwardly placed her leaking breast between the tiny, upturned lips. Abruptly, the perfect miniature mouth stopped crying. It rooted around blindly, but with a seeming certainty that what it wanted, what it needed, was tantalizingly near. Slowly, the tongue found her nipple. Brushed up against it. Once. Twice. Slowly, the lips began to hold, began to *latch on*. Giselle felt her knees buckle as the Kewpie doll lips began to move, began to pull at her, began to find a rhythm, began to suck greedily.

With hobbled knees and a hunched back, she inched her way across the room and sat gingerly at the edge of the couch, as carefully as she could. The last thing she wanted was to interfere with the wonder taking place against her body. She sat stiffly. Afraid to breathe. After an agonizing few minutes the baby relaxed, snuggled closer to Giselle's bare skin, and closed its eyes. The frantic sucking had passed; it was now slow and methodical, deep and calm. Eventually, Giselle dared to soften *her* muscles too, but only slightly. Because she could not risk disturbing the rhythm. She allowed herself several deep, slow, cleansing breaths and looked down.

The baby's face, milk slowly leaking from the side of its mouth and dribbling down its perfect blush chin, was all Giselle could see. She bent her head closer. The sweet smell of its hair, brown and wispy, was all she could smell. The soothing sound of the sucking, repetitious and steady, was all she could hear. The baby's tiny fingers, unconsciously grasping and releasing Giselle's own finger, were all she could feel.

Now, the infant dozed as it ate. Giselle was dumbstruck by the child's serenity. She dared to stroke the perfectly shaped fingernails, which seemed impossibly small next to her own. She had never, in her whole life, seen or touched anything so exquisite. Had there been someone there to talk to, she would have been speechless. Giselle was suddenly certain that she was somehow transcendentally connected to the life she cradled in her arms. That somehow, this was all meant to be. She knew that after the profound grief she had been forced to bear, the universe was blessing her with the privilege of experiencing the unique, boundless, all-encompassing love of a parent and a brand-new child.

It was no longer just a wish, an abstraction, or a thing. Finally, she could relax. Because now it was finally real. This was her child. Zivi had told her so.

At that moment, there was nothing in the world but Giselle and her baby.

CHAPTER SIX

DELVECCIO AND MCMILLAN

"You believe her?" asked Detective Gary DelVeccio.

"Why wouldn't I?" answered his superior, Detective First-Grade Brian McMillan.

"I'm just asking, is all."

"What are you trying to say? Do you know something I don't?" McMillan was in a foul mood.

"No. I just know her, is all."

"So?"

"So, I don't like her." DelVeccio propped his feet on the desk and rocked his chair. "Dealt with her before. When I was in narcotics. Testified against her clients. She's aggressive as hell. A real pit bull."

McMillan shrugged. "So what?"

"She'll do anything to get her perps to walk."

"Like what?" McMillan put down the report he was holding, on the off chance DelVeccio might say something important.

"Ruthless is all. I mean, I've seen her crush the state's witness when she had nothing to go on. Make some do-gooder just trying to tell the truth look like a moron with something to hide."

"So what? All that tells me is she's good at what she does."

"Too good."

"What the hell's that supposed to mean?" McMillan was annoyed.

"Just that I don't like her method, I don't like her angle, I don't like her style, and I don't like her. She's pissed off a lot of people in the department and a lot of civilians got hurt by the no-good perps she let walk. So, now she needs our help. Well boo fucking hoo. Ya know what?" DelVeccio scoffed. "What goes around comes around."

"Are you kidding me? That bullshit's her job. I looked up her cases. Shoddy police work. Every single one of 'em. Their own frickin' fault. If you ask me, this case is obvious." Brian McMillan went back to scanning the witness statements for the hundred-thousandth time. "She deals with a lot of scum. She pissed someone off. Some real bad jackass dirtbag, who decided to get back at her. Ever think of that?"

"Maybe."

The brother-in-law detectives took simultaneous sips of stale coffee.

"What did you say was wrong with her?" asked McMillan again.

"Just wait. You'll meet her. You'll get to know her. And then *you* won't like her, either."

"Lemme get this straight. Some broad's kid is grabbed, but you don't really feel like helping her because you think she's a bitch."

DelVeccio considered it. "I never said that. I just put a huge team together."

"But that's what you *think*."

DelVeccio waved away McMillan's question. "All I did was ask you if you believed her story."

"Why shouldn't I? There were plenty of witnesses." McMillan turned his back and stared at the pigeons roosting in the eaves of the building across the street.

DelVeccio shuffled papers, searching for his phone. "Let's give her a taste of life on the other side. I'm calling Bradshaw to give her a poly."

McMillan rolled his eyes.

CHAPTER SEVEN
GWENDOLYN

Is your name Gwendolyn Black?
Deep breath in through the nose. Out through the mouth. Yes.
Do you reside at 300 Central Park West, in New York City?
Deep breath in through the nose. Out through the mouth. Yes.
Do you work for the Manhattan Legal Aid Society?
Deep breath in through the nose. Out through the mouth. Yes.
Did you jog in Central Park on the morning of June 5th?
Deep breath in through the nose. Out through the mouth. Yes.
Did you have your four-week-old daughter with you in a jogging stroller at that time?
Deep breath in through the nose. Out through the mouth. Yes.
Were you accosted during that run?
Deep breath in through the nose. Out through the mouth. Yes.
Was your daughter kidnapped at that time?
Deep breath in through the nose. Out through the mouth. Yes.
Do you know who assaulted you that morning?
Deep breath in through the nose. Out through the mouth. No.
Do you know anyone else who may have been involved in carrying out this crime against you and your daughter?

Deep breath in through the nose. Out through the mouth.
Deep breath in through the nose. Out through the mouth. No.

Do you know who was responsible for this kidnapping?

Deep breath in through the nose. Out through the mouth.
Deep breath in through the nose. Out through the mouth.

Ms. Black?

Deep breath in through the nose. Out through the mouth.

Ms. Black? Are you all right?

Deep breath in through the nose. Out through the mouth.
Deep breath in through the nose. Out through the mouth.

Do you know who was responsible for this kidnapping?

Deep breath in through the nose. Out through the mouth. Yes.

Not long ago, Gwen would have left her apartment for the mindless cross-town trek to her shrink's office without a second thought. But somehow, once again, she had forgotten that the route would take her dangerously close to the *scene*. She had vowed never to go that way again. And now here she was.

She slowed down to look. The tattered remains of the garish yellow crime tape, still knotted around prickly branches, waved to her in the breeze. Teddy bears, puppies and unicorns—some perky, others already moldered and sodden—stared blankly into space. Bouquets of roses and tulips were piled, in varying stages of decay. There was the urge to turn and run away, kick, scream and vomit. But instead her legs, with an apparent newfound ability to think for themselves, carried her from the road and down the slight embankment.

The bushes were still broken, the soil slightly darker in patches from her spilled blood. None of the perp's. The DNA had confirmed that. It amounted to nothing evidence wise. He had not deposited one drop of anything. Nothing on the ground;

nothing on her clothes; nothing under her fingernails. No bodily fluids. No shed skin. The gloves. Those latex gloves. And the idiotic pantyhose. They had done exactly what they were supposed to. The only hair torn from its scalp were clumps of her own. For all her struggling, her flailing, her kicking, there was nothing. *Nothing*. She was even a failure at evidence collection.

She laid her hand atop the coarse, unforgiving soil. She had scrubbed her fingers raw. Gotten a manicure. Nonetheless, she still felt bits of that gritty soil under her nails. She smelled the overpowering aroma of the mowed grass. It was a smell that scented candles, perfumed body lotion and soothing bath oils could not erase from her olfactory memory.

An intricate maze was cut into the earth, the remains of the ruts his sausage fingers had dug into the ground. To arm himself with the dirt he mashed into her face and shoved into her mouth. She could still taste the bitterness of the soil on her tongue as she reached her foot under the tape and pulverized those ruts into oblivion.

Slowly, wearily, she continued the cross-town journey. A paranoid vibration raised the tiny hairs on the back of her neck. Were people on video chats, or were those phones following her, pointing in her direction? Would she be trending again, later? How fucked up had society become, that a person violated was now part of the public domain, unable to process their loss privately, be it in the real world or virtually? She continued east, feigning interest in the cracks on the pavement.

At Moss's building the doorman shot off his stool and ineptly folded the *New York Post*. Was she in the paper again today? He glanced up in an embarrassed, pitiful sort of way.

"I'm sorry," he murmured as he shook his head. "It's horrible. Just horrible. We're all praying for you."

Gwendolyn looked at her feet. She had been in the

newspapers many times, for defending some of the city's most despicable criminals, but never before had so many people recognized her.

She arrived at the appointment five minutes late. The consultation room door was left slightly ajar and Gwendolyn barged in, dispensing with the customary courtesy of a soft knock.

"Good morning." The doctor looked only mildly surprised by the sudden entrance.

Gwendolyn nodded.

"How are you today?"

"How do you think?"

"I think you've been better."

Gwendolyn looked outside and saw her flock of pigeons.

They sat in silence.

"I've never been more miserable in my entire life," she finally offered. "Consumed with guilt."

"The loss of a child must be an incomprehensible burden."

"When you use the word 'loss,' you *are* using it to mean temporarily misplaced, right? Because please, whatever you do, don't suggest that I've suffered a *loss*—or that Cassie is *lost*—in the permanent sense. And that's not what the cops think, either. Everything about the timing and the methodology, the way she was taken, suggests that whoever took her went to too much trouble to turn around and hurt her. Remember, they even took everything from the diaper bag with them. I know she's fine. I'm sure of it. Whoever took her would never hurt her. So don't use the word *loss* when you're discussing this with me."

"That's good news. The police believe that the kidnappers haven't harmed Cassie. And you believe that she's okay, as well. That must be reassuring."

"I guess."

"Are they making progress?"

"I think they're no closer to tracking down the perps now than they were on the day it happened."

"What makes you think that?"

"This is what I do, what I'm good at. I've made a successful career out of figuring out what cops are thinking even before they know. And when they have zip. And right now, they have nothing. No one. Any leads they thought they had, have run cold." She shrugged. "Right now, they're just grabbing at straws."

"What straws are they grabbing at?"

"Well, for one, they finally got around to giving me a polygraph."

"How did that make you feel, taking a lie detector test when your own daughter was kidnapped?"

Gwendolyn shook her head dismissively. "They were just doing their jobs." She paused. "I told them I know who is responsible for her kidnapping."

"*You do?*"

"Of course I do. It's me. It was all my fault. If I hadn't run the same route, at the same time, every day. If I had just waited a few more weeks before I started running again. If I hadn't bagged my karate lessons so I could've just fought back a little harder. I can think of a million reasons why the whole thing was my fault."

"How did it go?"

"Complete veracity. No evidence of deception. Not that it matters, much." She pursed her lips. "Polys are notoriously unreliable. That's why they're inadmissible in court. You have no idea how many of my clients, who were guilty as sin, have beaten that thing. There are so many pathological liars out there, so many psychopaths, and so many jerks who know all the tricks of the test, that it's only the guilty-conscienced pseudo-honest who get nabbed by those things."

Gwendolyn looked out the window.

"Anyway, that took about a half hour, and the whole time all I could focus on, the only thing that really mattered at that moment, was what I was going to buy on my way home to binge on."

"Ah. The bingeing. How did you fare on that front yesterday?"

"I've been under a lot of stress lately. Maybe a couple of times," she underestimated. "It wasn't a particularly good day."

"How many times?" Moss pressed.

"I don't know. A couple of times. Why does it matter?"

"We made an agreement."

"That was a long time ago."

"Nothing's changed."

"*Everything's* changed," Gwendolyn hissed.

"That's not fair, Gwen, and you know it. We made ground rules when you started seeing me. We signed an agreement. More than four times a day for a week and we would have to address whether it would be beneficial for you to check in to a live-in facility."

Gwendolyn gasped. *"Things have changed!"*

"Nothing's changed with respect to that agreement. Those were the conditions under which I agreed to take you on as a patient."

Moss paused before she continued.

"Nothing changed with respect to what bingeing and purging multiple times a day, every day, does to your health. What it is doing to your ability to function as a healthy adult, especially with the added pressures you now face."

She paused again.

"So, would you like to tell me how many times?"

"No."

Another long stalemate, until Moss sighed and picked up a

well-worn thread of conversation. "Once again, can you remember the first time? The first time you made yourself vomit?"

Just turning twelve, breasts beginning to develop, hips getting meaty. She hated it. Hated the look, hated what it meant. Deathly afraid to become a woman. To get her period. Feeling detached from her body, being at war with it. Her body doing things without permission, morphing, changing, beginning to control her. She would have no part of it. Whatever it took. She had to remain a girl.

You are dirty. You are disgusting. You are worthless.

Gwendolyn looked up.

"I, uh, I was twelve. I didn't want to get fat." Her expression was blank, her emotions stuffed back into the closet in the bottom of her brain.

"Yes. We've discussed this many times before. How it makes perfect sense. One of the textbook times for the onset of female eating disorders. The perfect incendiary mix of bodily changes for girls who are not yet emotionally ready to become women."

Gwendolyn's pupils dilated and she stared at nothingness.

"Pre-pubescent bodies are beginning to fill out ... awkwardness and disproportionality resulting from the growth spurt preceding the onset of menstruation..."

Gwendolyn tried not to listen.

"Estrogen, progesterone and all the other mood-affecting hormones ... Grown women are still affected..."

At first, she hadn't been good at it, couldn't bring everything back up; that made her hate her body even more. Again, she felt like a total failure...

"...certain amount of weight gain is completely normal ... Many studies..."

As things spiraled out of control, they did a unit on poison control in health class, specifically accidental poisoning...

"...images in the media, television, movies, bombarding entirely unrealistic expectations of the appropriate female figure..."

If there was no syrup of ipecac in the house, she'd simply mix a few teaspoons of baking soda in a glass of warm water and drink it down...

"Not surprising that so many girls internalize outside stimuli ... distorted sense of self ... completely unrealizable ideal..."

And how in that one second, when they taught her how to vomit efficiently, her life was changed...

"...upper middle-class girls, everything done for them, believing they have no legitimate control over their lives, choices made for them, their eating habits the one thing no adult can enforce absolutely..."

What would have happened, how would her life have been different, if she had been absent on that day?

"Therefore, when you tell me what happened when you were twelve, what I hear you saying—"

"Baking soda," Gwen interrupted.

"Excuse me?"

"I use baking soda."

"I'm sorry?"

"Baking soda. In a glass of warm water. That's how I do it."

"That sounds horrible."

Gwendolyn shuddered. "You have no idea. There are tricks to being a good puker. The more disgusting the better. Like remembering all the disgusting things you see and smell every day in this city, so that you can think of them again when you shove your head into the toilet bowl."

She thought about what else she was finally willing to share.

"And the self-hatred that accompanies not being able to bring everything back up. Not only have I disrespected myself by shoving so many disgusting calories into my face, but then I can't even fix it by vomiting." She rolled her head back and looked at the ceiling. "Making me feel even worse about myself, setting up the whole pathetic cycle again."

"It sounds like a lot of work."

"If it were as easy as sticking a finger down your throat, don't you think everybody would do it?"

"Actually, no."

Gwendolyn shrugged.

"Our time is nearly up for today. Naturally, I'm praying your daughter will be back with you very, very soon. But I'd like you to do something."

Gwendolyn stood in front of the couch and waited.

"Please try to wait at least three hours after taking your meds before you throw up. It will make life easier for both of us."

Gwendolyn turned toward the door.

"Oh, and Gwen?" said the shrink.

Gwendolyn stopped, but did not turn around.

"Yesterday. How many times?"

Gwen's shoulders drooped. "Please don't ask me that question again," she said. "You know I can't give you a number. If I do, I'll just be lying."

CHAPTER EIGHT

ZIVI AND GISELLE

Two and a half hours after Zivi gifted a stolen baby to Giselle, she slouched against the back of the sofa, a terrible crick in her neck, every muscle tense. But when she opened her eyes again, all was forgotten. Nestled between her breasts was the sleeping baby.

Giselle cradled the infant against her body. A child not yet old enough to have formed permanent bonds with any other person. This baby would suffer no emotional scars because of having been transferred to her care. Giselle believed in cosmic destiny. She lived her life as best she possibly could, certain that whatever she deserved would somehow find its way back to her. She had lost her own baby and now, through a series of events that could never have been foreseen, she had been gifted a divine second chance.

And who were these birth parents, anyway? People who were so inept, so careless, so *stupid*, that they had permitted a complete stranger to rob them of their most precious possession. That was *their* fault. Shame on *them*.

So, for the time being at least, Giselle indulged in suppressing the empathy that would tear her heart apart in a second if she allowed it freedom. For the moment, she was willing to forgo even considering the nameless, faceless mother and father thrown into the frantic and devastating nightmare of having an abducted child. She chose to turn her back on whatever unknown webs of attachment were tangled around the baby she now held in her arms. She made a conscious decision to make this blissful naivety last for as long as she possibly could.

As she made these choices, Giselle was vaguely aware that she was sliding over the threshold, from accidental witness to active accomplice.

Then she slammed her mind shut.

She had a baby!

"Hello, little angel," she whispered.

Giselle gently shifted the infant to her shoulder and closed the ripped blouse as best she could. She cupped the back of the tiny head in her hand and felt the downy auburn hair between her fingers. She filled her nostrils with that innocent smell unique to newborn babies.

It was all so natural. So easy. As she rocked and sang to the baby, she knew one thing for sure. In all her life she had never been happier.

It wasn't until he sat down next to her that she realized he was home. That's how absorbed she was. Just like the old Gissy.

"Hey, babe," they both said at the same time.

He knew right then that everything would be all right.

"I love you," she said, without opening her eyes.

"I love you, too."

They sat in silence, their first as a family.

She was smiling a little now, smiling and slowly nodding with her eyes still shut, still humming.

"Giselle. Sweetie," he said softly. "I wanted our baby so

much. And I am so sorry. All I wanted to do was to be there for you. I'll never forgive myself."

"I know that."

"And the wall. I'm sorry about what I did to your wall."

"What wall?" she mumbled.

"In the bedroom."

"Forget the wall. Look at the baby."

"I know."

"Sleeping. So peaceful. And guess what?"

"What?"

"I fed the baby *my milk*." Tears slipped from her eyes. "He liked it." Then a sob. "He *liked it!* You should have seen. The milk dripped from his mouth and down his chin. The poor thing was so hungry, he was drinking like he was starving." She sighed. "I wish you could have been here to see."

He forced himself to sit quietly on the couch, to fight the urge to scoop her up and make love to her, right then and there, for the rest of the day and then forever.

"I always knew you could do it," he said.

Giselle kissed their child on the forehead. Zivi rested his hand on her knee. They sat there for a while, awed by the infant's perfection, lightly stroking the tiny fingers and toes.

"I bought some things while I was out."

"*No.*" She clucked with her tongue. "I don't need anything. And we agreed to save money."

"Who said anything about you?" he teased, sliding a huge bag emblazoned with *Bubba's Baby Superstore* in from the hallway. She almost stopped breathing. *Exactly like he knew she would.* He reached in, pulling out a package with exaggerated flourish.

"Oh," she mouthed, fresh tears welling up in her eyes. "*Diapers.* You got diapers." Her reverence was complete and honest. He knew that to her, right now, diapers were an object of high art, of functional genius. "And wipes." She ran her fingers over the plastic packaging. "Excellent. We definitely need wipes."

He loved it when she was consumed like this. It was as if he had brought her a treasure, like a brand-new set of oil paints or a fancy Italian handmade notebook.

"Zinc oxide," she said, picking up a plastic tub. "That's diaper cream," she told him, and he decided not to tell her that he already knew. She moved on to the next item. "What's this?"

"For diaper rash."

"Oh, my God." She dropped the tube as if it was contagious. "I never even considered diaper rash. What if I can't do it? The baby's getting diaper rash and I don't know what to do."

"Giselle." He tried not to laugh. "Relax. You go to the store and they help you. They helped me pick—" he waved his hands around, "all this shit. And now, if he gets diaper rash, we're covered."

He sat. "You're a natural. You already fed the kid. You're gonna be great. Tomorrow, we go to that pediatrician you picked. And you. Now you can go back to your doctor. And remember. It's only been two weeks."

"Really?"

"Really. You haven't even missed an appointment. You march right in to Doctor Epidural's office and say, '*Ha! Guess what? Did it my way after all!*'" That made her giggle. "There are tons of books about how to do everything. Go to the store and ask. Just remember," he was serious now, "you have nothing to hide. No reason for shame. This is *our* baby. You really were pregnant and now you really have a baby, and we're going out to walk around like it is the most natural thing in the world. Walk the walk and talk the talk. It's all worked out." He smiled the cutest smile he could muster. The one she could never resist.

"Think about it," he said. "How many complete idiots do we

know who have perfectly healthy kids? How hard can it be?"

She looked up at him with her big gray eyes, her jaw set resolutely. "I'm doing it." Giselle carefully placed the baby on the new changing pad, then stopped and sat back on her heels.

"What is wrong?"

"Nothing."

She pulled the tabs and slowly bent back the front of the diaper. Time stopped as they tilted their heads together to look. Her body crumpled against his.

"She's a girl," Giselle whispered. "Another chance, with another girl."

"Look at that," he whispered. "I have another girl."

"We didn't even know."

"Does it matter to you?" he asked.

"Not even a little."

"Me neither."

They stared, captivated by the perfection of their new daughter, as she flailed her skinny chicken arms and kicked the air with her skinny chicken legs.

"What do you think?" he asked. "Wanna name her Madison?"

"Oh, no. She was her own person and she deserves to have her own name. That way, we can remember her for herself. Without confusing everything."

"Yes, of course. Not Madison," he conceded.

"How about a name that starts with 'N', since 'N' comes right after 'M'."

"Absolutely. What are you thinking?"

"Nell."

"Nell it is."

"Nell. My beautiful Nellie," she cooed. "You need a diaper change, little Nellie. And then I bet you're gonna be hungry again. But I know how to fix that."

CHAPTER NINE

DELVECCIO AND MCMILLAN

"Okay, Sherlock," McMillan gloated. "It was touch and go for a hot minute, but after she explained herself, she passed the poly. What d'you have to say now?"

DelVeccio frowned. "I don't know."

"Bah!" McMillan twirled a pencil between his fingers. "When are you finally gonna admit that we may actually have ourselves a compelling, sympathetic victim?"

DelVeccio ignored the question. "I had Barkley and Hillman run a search on all her clients that are currently incarcerated. Starting with the obvious ones. The ones who maybe have a grudge. Checked out the networks they still have on the outside. I bet one of them sent henchmen after her. Cold, calculated, simple, logical. I'll close this case in a week."

"No, you won't. No drug pushing scumbag wants some baby the whole world is looking for mucking up business."

"They do if she's a super bitch. She's made some enemy that wants to stick it to her. What better way to do it? Take the broad's kid." DelVeccio smiled. "It's the quickest way to screw anybody up."

"Nah." McMillan shook his head. "That's not what

happened. Someone wanted or needed a kid. Bad. Let's have them run a check on all the local hospitals—dead babies over the past month. Hell. Run a check on the whole friggin' country, if we have to. See if any mommies have experienced a miracle."

"I doubt it. I mean, I'm not telling you not to pursue, I'm just saying. It's usually some crazy whacked-out woman with her hormones running amok, cutting babies out of bellies, stealing infants out of hospitals. Not thugs assaulting a high-profile lawyer in the middle of the day in Central Park. This has got the stink of retaliation to it."

McMillan's coffee tasted like battery acid; he never seemed to be able to get to it before it had been sitting in the pot for an hour, no, two hours minimum. "Well, if it was some disgruntled scumbag, why didn't they break something on her while they were at it?"

"I've been thinking about that." DelVeccio rocked back and forth in his chair. "Whoever is behind it just gave the order, right? The perps who carried it out couldn't care less about the woman, or her attitude."

"Maybe. I don't know. Listen, don't get me wrong. We'll follow all your clever hunches to the bitter end. But do me a favor."

"Oh, here it comes." DelVeccio grinned. "What now?"

"Indulge me."

"What d'ya want? A quart of my blood? My left nut?"

"No." McMillan stared at the adjoining roof. Watched the pigeons copulate on the filthy eaves. "I'm gonna have her followed."

CHAPTER TEN

ZIVI AND GISELLE

"I'm hungry," Giselle said. "No, not hungry. I'm starving. I'm so famished I could eat anything."

"Oh, really? You are sure you mean anything?" He came up from behind, pressed his hips against her, rested his chin on the top of her head and whispered in her ear. "Because I just happen to have something right here I know you like."

"You know what?" She took his hands off her hips. "You're disgusting. Don't you ever think about anything else? In case you haven't noticed, there's a *b-a-b-y* in the apartment."

"Oh no, just because you are a mama, don't tell me you're no fun anymore."

"Oh, I'm still plenty of fun. Don't you worry about that."

They crossed to the kitchen. Giselle, cuddling Nell, trailed behind. At the kitchen doorway Zivi paused, stomped his feet, flicked the overhead lightbulb and clapped his hands five times.

"Is it safe, oh mighty hunter?"

"One minute more, helpless damsel with child." He tiptoed to the middle of the tiny alcove kitchen. "There's a big one in the middle of the floor. Take that, you motherfucker." Zivi stomped down on the oversized cockroach that had grown either too belligerent or too lazy to join the rest of its kind skittering along the bones of the building.

"You know," he said solemnly, "if ever they drop the bomb on us, the only living thing left will be these goddamn roaches."

"I think you've shared that gem with me every single day since we moved into this palace."

"I'm just saying. They are so vulgar and so full of germs, and you can't get rid of them. We can't live like this anymore. Now that we have a kid, I mean," he called, as he shook the carcass off his fancy, extravagantly priced sneaker and flushed. "Roaches are a leading cause of childhood allergies and asthma." He was back, leaning against the kitchen doorframe. "I'll give up this job and we'll have to find a new place."

"Nothing would make me happier than moving to a place that got even *a little* sunlight, but free rent is free rent," she said. "How are we supposed to afford it? We couldn't pull it off yesterday, so what makes today different?"

"Today is completely different. For obvious reasons. I'll just go to Big TaTa and see if he has a superintendent position in another building. Since both he and I are retired, of course, it is not like he owes me favors. But maybe he'll do it for old times' sake. And if he doesn't, then I don't know. We will figure it out. Since I stopped hustling we've managed. But that was just two of us. Now it is different. Now it is three. And this really is no place to raise a baby."

He turned away. "So, I'm thinking." He took a fortifying breath and casually stared at the ceiling. "Maybe I'll go back a little bit, for a little while, you know? Until we get settled again." He held his breath. "Until I get back onto my feet."

Giselle gasped. *"What?"* She saw straight through the feigned casualness. "We've already discussed this. You know, better than anyone, there's no such thing as going back *a little bit.*"

He opened his mouth to defend himself, but there was nothing to say.

"As soon as you show up around there, Gavric will act all happy to see you—" she had already begun a weepy yet totally irrefutable tirade, "and the next thing you know he's gonna sweet talk you into running his whole distribution network again. He'll have you right back in the thick of it, even if you tell him 'no'."

"But—"

"All those crazies, strung out on whatever drugs they can get their hands on. And you know every one of them has a whole arsenal clanking around in his pants." Her voice shook with disbelief. "You've said it yourself. Gavric's so aggressive, one day his enemies aren't gonna be satisfied just hitting the street hustlers. Sooner or later, they're coming back to hit management. *You told me yourself.* It's just a matter of time."

She took a breath and pushed the hair from her face with a trembling hand. *Such drama.* He should have kept his big mouth shut.

"You're good as dead already, just talking about it." Her voice was suddenly five octaves too high. "How could you even consider it? No. No way. There is *no way* you're going back to hustling. What—what am I supposed to do this time, when you get busted? Nell will be twenty-five years old and we'll still be visiting you in prison."

"All right. You made your point. Calm down." What she said was true, which made it even more annoying.

"I'm calling that Fine Arts professor, who knows the gallery owner who went crazy when he saw my canvases. Maybe he'll give me some space or something. In the meantime, just promise me, *promise me*, you won't—"

"I promise, I promise." He feigned boredom with the conversation. But truth be told, sometimes he did miss the lifestyle. Even if most of them *were* crazy, dangerous, murderous motherfuckers.

"Here, take her and I'll see if there's anything around here that's even remotely edible."

Zivi gazed down at his daughter. He forgot all about his old cronies as he gazed intently at the flawless tiny face.

"Call me crazy, but I think she kind of looks like me."

"That's a good one," she said, her head in the refrigerator. "You talking and walking?"

"Yeah. I mean no. I mean, she has my eyes and my mouth, right?"

"Yeah. Only, you're much uglier."

"Be serious. What about my nose?" he asked. "Does she have my nose?"

Giselle ignored him. "Last night's takeout is gone. I ate it for breakfast. There is literally nothing beyond ketchup and mayonnaise in this refrigerator. If we're going to eat anything, we're going to have to go out and get it."

"Really?" He perked up. "You're ready to go outside?"

"You can't keep me cooped up in this hellhole my whole life, you know. Especially now that I'm a mommy."

He smiled. "You fell right into my trap. There's nothing I wouldn't do to get you out of this dungeon." He gave her the baby and led her to the sofa. Then he opened the front door and wheeled in an impressive new stroller.

"Oh, my God, Ziv," she gasped. "It's beautiful."

"It's the Rolls-Royce of strollers. Let's see if she likes it."

"But I want to hold her." Giselle pouted.

And with a dramatic swish, he revealed a papoose. Soon, six pounds of baby snuggled against her chest and Giselle waddled around the apartment with pride.

Then, he presented her with a small plainly wrapped box. When she peeked inside and her knees buckled, he was by her side to catch her. As he always was. On the necklace hung a baby-shoe charm trimmed in diamonds. He made sure they had made it simply, the way she liked it. Not over the top tacky, show-offy, like the other heavy hitters women liked to wear. She opened her mouth, but didn't say anything.

"Here. Let me," he said.

When she turned her back so he could fasten it around her neck, he did not need to see her face to know she was crying.

"I ... 'Thank you' is, I guess it would just be pretty lame. I mean, after what you did, everything that happened today..."

"You're right," he said, big rough fingers carefully latching the delicate double safety clasp into place. "Time to go outside and show her off."

"Yeah," she said. "Let's."

CHAPTER ELEVEN

GWENDOLYN

"*Ms. Black!*"
"*Do you know who took her?*"
"*Gwendolyn!*"
"*Are there any leads?*"
"*Where's Cassie?*"
"*Why are you back at work?*"
"*Have there been any sightings?*"
"*Gwendolyn!*"
"*How can you be here, at a time like this?*"
"*Ms. Black!*"
"*Over here!*"

Of course Gwendolyn knew she had to go back, even before the shrink suggested it. After all, what were her choices, really? To sit around a depressing apartment all day or come back to the place she loved, where she felt at home, alive and in control amid the chaos? A phalanx of obnoxious reporters outside, reproachful stares inside, but she wore her rebelliousness like a crown. She was not about to succumb to other people's judgments of her.

So here she was. Phones ringing off the hook, paper flying,

and everyone thought they needed to scream to be heard. So of course, they did. *Hubbub*. The perfect word to describe the atmosphere. Even the air was electrified. She leaned back in her squeaky city issued chair and soaked it in: the power, the pressure, the vibration, the aroma.

There was a fervor that percolated within the offices of the largest and busiest Legal Aid office in the country. This was the energy created when a group of passionate, idealistic attorneys joined together to form something larger than themselves, a tour-de-force dedicated to fighting police brutality, opportunistic judges, and the all too often blatant corruption of the judicial system. She had become one with fellow lawyers in their crusade to uphold the constitutional rights of their clients who, Gwendolyn believed, were usually despicable and almost always guilty. Well, at least they had been stripped of their so-called presumption of innocence simply by virtue of being swept up into the system that was designed to protect them in the first place. So yes, she was glad to be back. And it wasn't like she was impeding the investigation. If they needed her, they knew where to find her.

"G, the printer is jammed," a voice shouted. "I'm not gonna be able to print your doc 'til support gets here. If it's an ASAP I'll send it to Roxy's computer, but you better be sure because then I'm gonna owe her a favor."

"Marla, my phone still has the intercom," Gwendolyn shouted back. "If you ever decide to stop yelling you could try and use it."

"No can do, G. Then the whole office won't know your personal business."

"Missed you, Marl."

"Missed you too, G."

The antiquated desktop took its sweet-ass time to load up. Gwendolyn had been working on about forty open cases when she left for maternity leave. She now saw that nothing had happened in any of these defendants' lives that warranted someone requesting her password or otherwise opening a file. The only change since she had left was one of omission; in an extreme act of kindness her boss must have put a moratorium on assigning her any new cases.

Gwen rubbed her temples and sipped her latte. *To be locked up in jail.* It made her shudder just thinking about it. *Unable to exercise. Unable to choose what to eat. Unable to control any aspect of your life.* Exactly like an 'involuntary stay' at one of those live-in facilities. Her stomach turned over at the very thought of it. She couldn't imagine surviving such an ordeal. It was one of her few outlets for empathy, part of the reason she felt compelled to do everything within her power to keep her perps out of jail. The ones who just might actually be innocent, anyway. Or at least, the ones who had been framed. Or didn't deserve the harsh time they were facing.

She clicked open the first folder—Bennett, Emmett P. Docket number 54367820—and began reading, to refresh her memory.

> ... perpetrator is then alleged to have attempted to choke said undercover narcotics officer using the scarf perpetrator previously removed from his girlfriend's hair as a garrote ...

Oh, yeah. Now she remembered. *He was a bad one.* Gwendolyn had dealt with this defendant before. Pled him out on more than one prior occasion. In retrospect, she realized that he really shouldn't have gotten back out on the streets. Sometimes she was a little too good at what she did. Bennett, Emmett P. fit into the 'ticking time bomb' category. They were dangerous types. It was just a matter of time before they finally exploded and did something truly horrific. Gwen closed the folder. It all seemed so pointless. *So overwhelming. So out of control.* Her shoulders sagged from the weight of all those monkeys.

People sometimes asked why she didn't pick the other side, why she hadn't become a prosecutor, and she always deflected with some sort of evasive, hackneyed joke. But if she ever would have considered it, ever allowed herself to look deep into her soul and wonder why, the answer would have been obvious. It had been drilled into her from the time she was a little girl. These animals. The scum of the earth. They were her brethren. She was just as dirty and unworthy and worthless as they were.

She put her head down on her desk. Then, for the first time in four weeks, she wept. Honest tears. She really, really wept.

Gwendolyn lifted her eyes and glanced at the clock. *Fifteen minutes of self-pity.* She shook her head to clear the murky haze that had filled it, sighed, and turned back to repeat offender file Bennett, Emmett P., to reacquaint herself with his substantial agility. Despite being stoned out of his head, he was able to rip the trendy designer silk scarf from his girlfriend's head and twist it, bloody 13-inch hunk of her hair extension still attached, garrote style around the first narc's neck before the second undercover had a chance to subdue and finally apprehend him.

The report suggested that, not surprisingly, the cops were pretty pissed off about the way the whole thing went down. That meant that Judge Warner, the bastard they had won in the assignment lottery, was already predisposed against them. On top of that was the underaged girlfriend, whose strip search revealed belt buckle welts and cigarette burns carefully hidden below her panty line—and three glassine envelopes she claimed he made her stash where the rest of womankind secure only tampons.

All courtesy of Bennett, Emmett P. Yeah, there was no denying he was one bad son-of-a-bitch. Still, the jerk had rights.

Constitutional rights. The stuff this country was founded on. The stuff everyone in law enforcement was dutybound to uphold. *Otherwise, the next time it could be you, or worse, me...*

She scrolled through her notes. They were from her first and only interview with him on this latest offense, actually held at the defense table, two minutes before she had to present his not guilty plea. The whole day was a blur except that Gwen now remembered how Warner practically laughed in her face before he denied her request to grant bail.

The asshole.

According to what Bennett, Emmett P. had told her, which she knew was bound to be supremely unreliable, the cops went crazy on him, even after he had ceased the attempted strangulation of the narc. She opened the folder of the photos she had taken that night. He did have a welt over his left eye that was already turning yellow. And yes, there was his nose, bent and drooping. Now she remembered that he claimed the cops had kicked him in his nose. 'Belted in eye. Broken nose,' she typed into a fresh document.

Police brutality in this case was not going to amount to much, not with a defendant who was doing the narcotics-fueled super-human-strength thing while trying to strangle the arresting officer. She continued scrolling. Nothing spectacular. And then, there it was. Recollections that were as close to contemporaneous to the arrest as they were going to get. The hook she had been hoping for.

'D swears never being read Mirandas. Claims denied access to a counsel.' *Bingo.*

When would they ever learn?

She bounced her leg nervously and waited for the computer to regurgitate the choice of form pleadings to which she would fill in the substance. *This one would be easy. Piece of cake, really.* Even if Warner didn't dismiss the whole thing right now, on this motion, then failure to advise, denial of counsel, these were superb grounds for appeal. Why hadn't she played this card already, at the hearing? She racked her memory and then—*of course*. The excruciating cramps. The stabbing back pain. The contractions hitting her like a roundhouse kick to the gut. The fact that they'd had to practically carry her downstairs and into the cab that whisked her straight to the hospital. The fact that she had delivered her baby later that night.

The blank form appeared on the screen.

"Too fucking easy," she muttered, knowing she had once again beat the system at its own game.

Her fingers hovered. Something was bugging her. She opened his huge file and scrolled through his long sordid history with the law. An hour later, she was well into his history as a juvenile, when she came upon a link to a classified copy of a report from Social Services. It was marked confidential, not part of his history, available only to her because she was his attorney. The report was from nine years ago, when Bennett, Emmett P. was only fifteen years old. No doubt she had once read it, but somehow had forgotten all about it.

> In a locked closet was a crib containing a child later determined to be the defendant's son. Said child was found sleeping on a heavily soiled mattress. Said child was covered with contusions. Child was subsequently determined to be significantly malnourished. Application to sever all paternal rights to be filed.

Failure to advise? Denial of counsel? All bullshit compared to the offense he got away with nine years ago. Classified or not. She had the power and now it was payback time. She dragged his file to the bottom of the queue.

"Scumbag?" she said softly. "You ain't never gonna see the light of day. Not in *my* lifetime."

All of a sudden, she was famished. She couldn't remember the last time she had real food, a healthy meal she allowed herself to digest. She rummaged around for the takeout menus.

"*Gwen?*"

Gwendolyn jumped. The strange disembodied voice of Marla wafted unexpectedly from the intercom.

"Sorry," she shouted back. "I can't remember how to use this thing."

"Um, yeah. I'll come in and show you later," the phone whispered back eerily. "Listen, some detective just called."

"Oh?" Gwen felt the hairs on the back of her neck tingling with dread. Had they found something? She tried to chuckle, but the noise that came out of her was anything but amused. "One of my pendings?"

"Uh, no. A guy named McMillan. He's coming to see you. And G?"

Gwen couldn't respond.

"You there?"

"I'm here." Someone else's voice crawled out of her throat.

"He said it was about Cassie," the intercom warbled. "He said that they have new ideas about Cassie."

The static from the intercom made her head spin, gave her vertigo, made her feel like she was whirling out of control, even though she was sitting still. Suddenly, it seemed as if the whole office had fallen silent.

"G? He'll be here in a few minutes."

The weight of another monkey landed on her back.

CHAPTER TWELVE

ZIVI AND GISELLE

At that same moment, way uptown in Central Park, people were trying not to stare at Zivi and Giselle. It had always been that way. He was simply gorgeous and when people looked at her they always thought, *Wait just a minute—from which TV show or from which advertisement did they know her?* Now they walked, each with one hand on the stroller, giddy from joy and sleep deprivation, as they made very little progress beyond zigzagging back and forth across the sidewalk.

Giselle was just too happy for words.

Eventually they arrived at the closest playground. They chose a bench and basked in the warm sunshine. He draped his arm over her shoulders. She needlessly adjusted the pink fleece blanket swaddling their baby. Their heads lolled and rested atop the back of the bench.

"I don't know how much longer I can do this," he said.

"Do what?"

"The getting up every three hours with you all night."

"She's hungry. She wakes up. She's only got a tiny little tummy."

"I am not telling *you* to stop getting up at all hours of the night. You feed her. It's *me* I'm talking about. I can't do this anymore. I must find a job. And no one's gonna hire me if I fall asleep during a job interview. After they hire me. That's when I'll fall asleep. And don't start crying at me about it," he said knowingly. "I love you. But for now, I must get more shuteye."

And he fell asleep right there on the bench. Giselle knew he was sleeping because his arm rolled lifelessly off her shoulder and he started snoring. Then everything disappeared. She jerked her head up and forced her eyes open.

"Can't let myself..." she mumbled, right before it happened again. Everything went black; she jerked her head upright.

"Have to stop..." she whispered. This time, she may have actually fallen fully asleep for a moment or two, before Nell began to fuss and Giselle instinctively bolted to attention.

She looked around nervously, but they were the only people she could see in the park. The baby moved her head from side to side, agitated. In one continuous motion Giselle swept the wriggling bundle up, discreetly unbuttoned the fourth button of her shirt, and popped her breast into the waiting mouth.

A few short hours ago, she had firmly resolved to rein in her whacked-out emotional roller coaster. But postpartum hormones and lack of sleep were taking their toll on her resolve. Seconds later, she couldn't see through the tears. She tried to silence herself, to suffer in private dignity, but her nose was clogged and she gasped for air.

"What's the matter?" In one seamless motion Zivi sprang up, spun around and drew his elbows tight to his body, fists close to his face, in the defensive position that comes reflexively to masters in Systema.

"I'm sorry. I was trying not to wake you." She wiped her eyes with the back of her hand. "You fell asleep. I was trying to be quiet. I'm sorry." But privately, she was glad he was awake.

"Someone did something?" he asked. "Someone said something?" He looked around, but there was no one in sight.

"No. I just got a little nervous."

He sat back down on the bench.

"You have to stop the crying, *beba*. Every time you do, I'm worried someone's on to us." He stared at his hands. "I thought this was what you wanted."

"Oh Zivi, sweetie. It's *so* what I want. It's what I always wanted. I've never been so happy in my entire life."

"Well, if this is so happy," he groaned, "why are you always crying?"

His question made her feel embarrassed. Guilty. Frustrated. Jumbled.

"It's just that, well you fell asleep," she tried to explain. "And then I, then I got scared because..." Something whiny and gaspy, accompanied by fresh tears, escaped her lips.

"Hey. Shhh. I am right here." He put his arm around her, drew her close. "What could be this bad? What could be making my woman so sad? Tell me and I swear I make it all better." He wiped her tears and mucus with his sleeve.

"It's just that I got really scared. Because you fell asleep. And then I couldn't help it. I tried to force myself to stay awake, but my eyes just kept closing and my head dropped over..."

She slid to the edge of the bench.

"And I was just thinking, *Oh my God*. What if we were both sleeping, you and me," she glanced around, "right here in the park, in broad daylight and then someone came?" The words came out barely above a whisper. *"What if someone came and they grabbed Nell? What if they grabbed Nell and took her away from us?"*

"Not happening. There is no way," he said icily. "Just not happening."

He seemed so adamant. *Irrationally* so.

"Why not?"

"What do you mean, *why not*? Because it is just not happening. That's why. That shit only happens to other people. Not us. *That's* why not."

She could not believe his naivety. "What do you mean, *it only happens to other people*? This is real. It doesn't only happen to *other people*. Because YOU did it. So it *already* happened *to us*. Only it happened in reverse. What's to stop it from happening to us again, but forwards?"

"For one thing, if anyone did it, I'd kill them. Shoot them right in their motherfucking head. That is why not, for starters." He was so calm and matter-of-fact that it sounded as if he meant it. *Sometimes he scared her.*

"That doesn't help me, Ziv. Now, on top of everything else, I have to worry that whoever you did this to is gonna come looking for you and *you're* gonna get *your* head shot off."

"Are you trying to be funny?" He sounded annoyed. "Are you serious?"

"I'm totally serious. Just think about what's going on here." She poked him in the arm with her finger. "You go out and by some unbelievable, wonderful miracle, you come home with this beautiful baby. Now, in my heart of hearts I know that this isn't the actual baby I gave birth to, but I'm willing to pretend. I also know for a fact that no one gave you this baby, because you keep on telling me how you're going to jail for the rest of your life if anyone should ever find out. You make me swear on your life to never. *ever* ask any questions about where Nell came from, as if that's gonna protect me from getting in trouble or something. But you know that in my heart of hearts it's killing me. I'm really dying to know, but since I love you, I've agreed to keep my big mouth shut and not bug you. But then, when I really think about it, I gotta ask myself ... If we love Nell as much as *we* do, don't you think there's a *real* mother and a *real* father out there who love her just as much and want her back? I'm petrified that they are gonna find us and grab her back. And *then* you tell me not to worry, because if that ever happens, you'll 'shoot them in the head.' Well, Zivi, open your eyes. *You are that person.* You took Nell first. Not only am I worried about some jerk grabbing Nell back, but now I'm scared that they're gonna shoot you in *your* head for taking their baby."

"Look at me." He sighed. "You have to believe. Things are good. *They are very good.* If you believe, then other people believe, too. But if you walk around scared and crying all day long, everyone's gonna wonder what the hell is wrong with you; you'll blow the whole story wide open."

"That doesn't exactly help. I'm still worried."

"Here it is," he sounded exhausted. "Here is the solution. When we leave the apartment, we can't ever both fall asleep at the same time. Only one at a time. That way someone will always be on guard, watching her. We oughta be able to handle that, right? Deal?"

She sighed. "Deal."

"Hey, you two! What's happening?" Sabrina, the omnipresent neighborhood busybody, seemed to materialize out of nowhere.

"*Fuuuuuccckkk,*" Zivi sang out under his breath.

"Quiet," Giselle whispered, pinching his thigh.

"Hey, Sabrina. How long you been standing there?" Zivi glared at her and tried, failing miserably, to make his voice light and unassuming.

"Just got here. Whhhyyy?"

"Oh, nothinnnnng," he sang back. "Just askinnnng."

"So, busy-Gissy!" chirped Sabrina, clapping her hands. "Let's see the baby! I heard ya'll got a girl! You know, sometimes I wish I had a girl, too. Their clothes are so much cuter."

She wheeled ten-month-old Ethan over and sat down next

to Giselle. Ethan's face was almost completely covered with the sucked-on mush of what was probably once a teething biscuit. Zivi winced. Sabrina laughed.

She beamed down at her kid. "We gotta get them together and let them play, Gis. Maybe they'll hook up when they get older."

He glanced at Giselle in disgust. "I'm going for a newspaper, or something. Give you two a chance to talk."

He stood up. Glared at Sabrina. Bent over. Gave Giselle a big, long, involved tongue-kiss goodbye. Dark eyes glued to Sabrina, boring into her, trying, Giselle knew, to figure out how long she had been there and how much she might have overheard. Then he abruptly swung around and sauntered out of the park.

"Whoa. Your boyfriend is *intense*."

"Not really. He's just a little tense, with the new baby. He hasn't been sleeping much."

"Shit. Don't I know all about that. Ever since Ethan, we see less and less of Martin all the time. And all my mama says is, 'I told you so. I told you that no good son-of-a-gun would disappear as soon as his baby's born.' But I kept saying, 'No, no, no, Mama. Martin, he's just a little tense right now with the new baby.' And now here I am. Alone and bored to tears."

Giselle burped Nell and returned her to the stroller. "What about a job?"

"Not many places gonna let you bring a baby to work. And don't even say it, 'cause I can't afford daycare. That shit's expensive."

Giselle yawned.

"Where'd you go for that baby, anyway?" asked Sabrina.

Giselle froze. "What—what do you mean?" she stammered.

"Honey, what's the matter with you? Where did you go for her? Where did you have her? What hospital'd you give birth t'her in? I know you told me you were going to Lenox Hill, but my Aunt Sally works there and when I told her I heard you had a baby she said you never checked in there, ever. She *looked* for me. So, what happened? Where'd you go for her?"

Giselle shook. "I, uh, had her," she mumbled, "and then I went to, uh, Englewood."

"*Englewood*? I never heard of Englewood Hospital anywhere around here." Sabrina paused. "Oh!" She smiled. "You mean *Englewood, California!* Wait a minute. You flew to California?"

"Not Englewood, California. Englewood, New Jersey. It's just over the bridge. My father lives there. I wanted to make it easy for him to see her."

"*Giselle.* You told me your father is some loaded retired guy with his own driver that drives him wherever he wants to go. Now, you can't tell me that driver don't know his way to NYC. And the evil stepmother—I *know* you told me you were never gonna find yourself in the same state as that witch. And you're telling me you went to Jersey to be near the father you never see and the step-witch you hate?"

Sabrina faced Giselle head-on.

"Have you been drinking and drugging or something? Ya'll better not be drinking and drugging, and nursing that baby, you hear me? Cause that's dumb. *Really* dumb. I know. I take lots of classes."

"No. *No.* You know I don't do that kind of stuff. And anyway. My father's been with her for such a long time, I've learned how to ignore her."

Sabrina frowned. "Well, whatever," she finally said. "But anyway, we should take some of those classes at the Y together. They got free babysitting. Now what d'you say you named that child?"

"Nell." At least *that* wasn't a lie.

"Lemme see that baby's face already. Why you keeping her all hidden away like that?"

"I guess I just didn't want her to get cold, you know?"

"Cold? It's a friggin' oven out here today."

"Well, there is a breeze. And she has my fair skin. I don't want her getting chapped."

"First of all, that's one mighty cute baby. I *know* my Ethan's gonna be going after her. Second of all, she *does not* have your fair skin. That child has her father's coloring. And third of all, she's pretty like her mama. Ain't none of her daddy in that face."

"I don't know," said Giselle. "I think she has his eyes. And definitely his mouth. She definitely has his mouth."

"No way, sweetie. She definitely got your eyes. And that nose..."

As the illusion became more and more entwined with the truth, Giselle felt herself absorbing Nell's whole life into her own, washing away the existence of the baby's prior history. She sat up just a little straighter. She felt her complexion begin to glow, felt herself exude self-confidence.

This new truth became her.

CHAPTER THIRTEEN

DELVECCIO AND MCMILLAN

"Why's she fighting us so hard on the gang angle?" asked McMillan, yet again.

"Because she's a bitch," DelVeccio responded for the thousandth time.

"You sound like an idiot."

"'Cept I'm gonna be the one who says 'I told you so' when you finally realize something stinks."

Brian McMillan grunted. "The only thing that stinks, is that she argues with us on every friggin' theory we have. Here we are, trying to find her kid, and she's carrying on like an uncooperative witness. And by the way, I still can't figure out why we don't have suspects falling all over each other. Because I will say this. You were certainly right about one thing."

"Just one?"

"Just one. No one likes the woman."

"Except for the dirtbag recidivist population she's single-handedly sprung. *They* love her." DelVeccio chuckled. "Must be nice, having a fan club of drug pushing, gun peddling dope heads."

"You're just jealous because no one likes you."

DelVeccio feigned surprise. "I thought *you* liked me."

"Not really. I fake it since you married my sister."

DelVeccio leaned back in his chair. "I still think it was one of her cons who gave the order from the inside. Someone she pissed off, disrespected, someone who slipped through the cracks, whatever. Someone who had mountains of time to plan. Because you gotta admit, this transaction went down smooth."

"Nothing's ever perfect." McMillan twirled a pencil.

"I just want one name. One scumbag to focus on." DelVeccio started rocking.

"That part worries me." McMillan lifted a half-filled cup of coffee then put it down, unable to discern whether it was from this morning, yesterday morning, or the morning before that. "Some bastard out there has her kid. Why won't she help us narrow it down? One minute she thinks every one of those morons is a possible suspect. Then, when she thinks we might go after one of 'em, she swears that underneath it all they have a heart of gold."

"*Biiitch*," DelVeccio sang under his breath.

"Since when is not wanting to finger the wrong guy a crime?" McMillan turned and stared out the window.

"When one of those assholes she's protecting grabbed her goddamned baby. *That's* when." DelVeccio paused. "I went to the hospital. Spoke to the delivery nurse. She claims Black told *her* the father was some guy she was no longer involved with and refused to list him on the birth certificate. She told *us* her thing was drunken one-night stands. That any one of them could have been the father. She didn't ask for names and couldn't tell one face from another. Two different stories. I have three bodies dedicated to showing her picture in every bar in town."

"She didn't want to seem like a slut to the nurse and she let the guys buy the drinks at the bars?"

DelVeccio shook his head. "No one lets some stranger buy them drinks anymore. Not with the advent of date rape drugs. You know that." Then he picked up the phone and punched in Sylvia's extension.

"*Yes?*"

"Syl, get me two warm bodies to pull all the transcripts on Gwendolyn Black's trials for the last twelve months. Tell them to start looking for ... I don't know, anything that stands out, any defendant that feels slighted who maybe blames her—for anything." Then he turned to McMillan. "You okay with that?"

McMillan nodded. "That should wrap it up by morning." He made a choice, grabbed one of the paper cups and took a cold, vinegary swig. "Why'd ya think she couldn't ID any of the perps?"

"We're supposed to believe it's because the guy threw a pair of pantyhose on his frigging head. But the witnesses all said that the hose went on after she was down. She had seconds, full *seconds,* to ID the guy before that."

McMillan tried a different cup.

"Isn't it obvious she's lying?" DelVeccio pressed.

"Isn't it possible she's an innocent victim? One whose baby was kidnapped, who herself was brutally attacked, therefore she's so traumatized that she can't give a sufficient description of her attacker based on the five seconds during which she was trying to stop herself from falling on her face because the perps were trying to knock her down, before she was thrown into the bushes and had her face mauled with dirt?"

DelVeccio started rocking again. "Professional defense counsel, killer record, knows the ropes, knows what ya need to ID, what ya need for a conviction, is attacked and her kid is grabbed, and she can't even provide a description?"

McMillan stared out the window.

Sylvia came in and dropped a file on Detective Brian

McMillan's desk. "Barkley's list of all the stillborns and viables but deceased in the metro area for the past month. And John is on two."

DelVeccio stopped rocking and reached for the phone first. "Hey there, Johnny boy. How's my friend Gwendolyn Black doing? She taking you on any more marathons?"

Sylvia cracked her gum. "Brooklyn Johnny's on this, too? You guys got everyone involved."

McMillan shook his head. "Yeah, well. Pressure's on. Can't get much higher profile than this debacle." Then he turned to the window and watched the pigeons fight for space on the filthy, dropping encrusted eave, so he could think.

CHAPTER FOURTEEN

GWENDOLYN

"Sometimes even meticulously used birth control fails. I despised the pill because I retained eight pounds of water. The IUD gave me horrendous cramps and I couldn't lay off running for the weeks I needed to adjust. So, did my diaphragm slip? Did his condom have a hole?" Gwendolyn shrugged. "The minute the test was positive I made the first appointment. I made five in all. Kept three of them. The last one, I even made it onto the table, feet in the stirrups, but I just couldn't do it. The decision to not go through with the abortion was the last thing I had control over. My life, my plans, my dreams, my future, all slipped away because of that baby."

"A lot of responsibilities attached to becoming a parent," Moss noted sagely.

"I know that. I knew that. I knew it would screw me up. But I never imagined it would completely fuck me up. I got pulled away from my life, became powerless, lost my freedom."

"Could you have been feeling overwhelmed by something temporary, a pregnancy, which has a foreseeable end?"

"There was nothing temporary about it. All I could see was

the permanent isolation of being stuck with a baby I didn't want."

Gwendolyn was momentarily appalled by her own candor.

"And once you held her?"

"Maternal instincts? Still waiting. I couldn't possibly take care of this needy helpless being and maintain my workload. Not to mention running and going to the gym. And I'm only admitting that to you because you're my shrink."

"And now she's gone. Are you blaming yourself for what happened because of the feelings you just expressed?"

"No. That is superficial, clichéd thinking. I use that same insipid 'blame the victim' scenario every chance I get. But you're implying blaming the victim for her *bad thoughts*, not for her *bad actions*. That's even more spurious. I won't sign up to that kind of a guilt trip. I will admit to you, however, under the protection of the doctor–client privilege, that I probably could be more forthcoming with the detectives on the case."

"Oh?"

"I could spend more time with them. But they sicken me. They keep calling with their false leads. Gang members, ex-cons, pro-cons, pending cons. You name it, they think it. People I've met. People I haven't met. People I will meet. People I will never meet. A million half-baked theories riddled with flaws. They're driving me crazy."

Gwendolyn took a deep breath. She knew she should be thinking about Cassie.

"Where does my profound aversion to motherhood come from?"

"That's an excellent question."

"I'm so exhausted. Can't you make it easy for me? Just this one time?"

Moss sighed. "Talk about *your* mother. From a new

perspective. Instead of from the eating angle. Let's see if there's anything new to unpack."

But *really*. What hadn't she told the shrink already? That her mother was a lawyer in some small firm? That she worked part-time to stay home with Gwen and her brother? That during a hailstorm, after her father slipped outside the Guggenheim, after the car ran him over right in front of all of them, that her mother had to go back to work full time? That she felt guilty about leaving her kids all day, so she got herself remarried to the first rich man she found, just so she could go back to working half days?

But actually, it had been wonderful when it was just them. Gathered around the kitchen table, baking cookies, having the stupidest joke contest, the three of them laughing, laughing, laughing.

"We had a competition, my brother and me. Who was smarter. We had it in our heads that would make us her favorite. I don't know why we thought that; it's not like she ever loved one of us more than the other." Her brother was brilliant. "He was always better than me."

Eventually her mother decided to go back to the office full time.

Gwendolyn looked out the window and concentrated on the clouds. She could still name them. Cumulus. Stratus. Cirrus.

"Then my stepfather left."

"Did anything change?"

Gwendolyn shrugged.

But *everything* had changed. Her *mother* had changed. She was despondent. Gwen changed. She was defeated. Wished she could undo everything she had done wrong. Praying, with every fiber of her being, for her old mother to come back. Knowing it was her fault that he left. That had she done things better, more the way he wanted, he never would have gone. That she would have endured *anything* if it would bring him back so that her mother could be happy again.

"After that she couldn't function as a lawyer anymore. She couldn't concentrate. Eventually she got fired."

Her mother couldn't land another job and stopped going out. She was depressed. Agoraphobic. An empty body, sitting at the kitchen table in a dark, filthy apartment, doing nothing but *The New York Times*' crossword puzzle. Before, she could finish that puzzle every day. Sunday included. For a glorious second, her mother had been dazzling and brilliant. But by the end, even Monday's was left unfinished.

"My mother never left the apartment. She would ask me to sit down for a few minutes and look at the crossword clues with her. But I was too busy and important and condescending to help. She embarrassed me. She abandoned me. I vomited. My brother did drugs. My mother drank. We had all the bases covered."

That was when the profound aching sadness metastasized in Gwendolyn's bones.

"I asked you why you thought I couldn't form an emotional attachment to my daughter. Maybe I am afraid she will be just like me; she will abandon her mother when I need her most. And I will never let myself end up like my own mother. Even if I have to sacrifice being a mother to prevent it."

"Bonding with your own daughter is a far cry from becoming a depressed, alcoholic agoraphobe."

"For me, bonding with the child was the first step on that slippery slope. I've seen what that did to my mother. And like it or not, I am *her* daughter. And like it or not, Cassie is *my* daughter. So how do I know she won't do the same things to me that I did to mine?"

"Because you can intentionally take the other path. You

could promise that what happened to your mother will never happen to you. That you simply won't let history repeat itself. That you will do better, for yourself and for your own child."

"You don't hear me. I am desperate. I am freaking the fuck out and you are not helping me." Gwendolyn's eyes were huge. "Surely, I have some kind of personality disorder. I have *no maternal instincts*. Can't you write something on your little magic pad to make me better?"

"There's no magic bullet. Just hard work."

"Women who have free time to sit for hours in a playground have lost all their freedom and they don't even know it. They are isolated from the workforce. *What about flextime? What about part-time work?* Some women in my office took that road. You know who got all their good cases? I did. The extended leave option? *Bullshit*. You're branded as lazy, hanging around until you get pregnant again. And it's true. After the second one, they never come back. They're automatically demoted to second-class citizens in our office. I don't know how to put this kindly. What little time I had with Cassie ... wasn't pleasant. There was no rosy glow of happiness. Just the isolation blues. It was mindless, boring, repetitive stuff. Mastering the art of cleaning a baby's ass is not what I went to school for. It's not what I spent my life trying to achieve."

"But—"

"I already know what you're going to say. Eventually, she'll use the toilet. This whole playground thing only lasts for a few years."

"Exactly. And once—"

"And then what? Making dinner night after night? Homework? I need the *health club* at night. That's what *I* have to do for *my own* mental health."

"You've had Cassie for such a short amount of time. How

could you know how you would feel after one more day with her, one more week, one more month?"

"I am simply not mother material. And the mere physical act of giving birth to a child does not change that fact."

"It's not written in stone."

"Hear me out. I have a significant history of abnormal paternal experiences. I am what I am. But now the kid is missing. Something that I may have wished for on some deeply subliminal super fucked-up level. One of those nightmarish fantasies people have, but never ever want to really happen. Like killing someone or being raped, or whatever. People just think, *'What if?'* No one actually wants that shit to happen."

Gwen held up her hand and continued.

"But I am coherent enough to understand that I'm responding in a grossly inappropriate way to what would be any normal person's worst nightmare. And I am asking you—no, I am *pleading with you*— to help me. Help that does not take the form of insisting that one day soon, when you get me to see the light, I will be magically transformed into the world's greatest mother. I need help to act appropriately *today*. To find the strength to be an active participant in the recovery of my child *right now*. Please. Cut me some slack. For me, this is groveling."

"You are in denial. Denial that people change. Denial that having a child can be the most precious gift life has to offer. Denial that you, Gwendolyn, can change; you can begin to recover from your eating disorder so that something besides your own all-consuming coping mechanism can be the center of your life. But we won't accomplish all that in the next five minutes. What I *can* do to make you feel better is tell you I think it is healthy for you to start regaining control of your life. As we discussed last time, I think you should resume a full caseload at work. If anyone in the office looks at you sideways, or suggests that you are doing something inappropriate, remember you can tell them that your psychiatrist insisted on it so that you can regain some normalcy in your life. You pay me enough money. Use me as ammunition for something concrete for a change. Like being your scapegoat."

Gwendolyn tried to smile. "I already have."

"Good," said the shrink. "At least I serve some useful purpose in your life." They stared at each other. "And why don't you go for a nice long run? You need it."

Every tense, clenching muscle in Gwendolyn's body relaxed. She had gotten what she came for. *Permission.* Now, she could justify those early morning and late-night runs she had begun sneaking in. Maybe, given Moss's okay, she could even pare back on stuffing her face to the point of explosion and then puking her guts up as punishment for engaging in what for Gwendolyn was an intractable compulsion—exercising to complete exhaustion.

She felt healthier already.

CHAPTER FIFTEEN

ZIVI AND GISELLE

By the time Zivi stumbled into the living room, Giselle had Nell fed, dressed and lying on her back, mesmerized by the brilliantly colored toys dangling from the mobile above the playmat.

She leaned up to kiss him and took in the dark puffy pouches under his eyes, the sallow complexion, the tangled hair.

"Babe, you look awful."

"Stress." He raked his fingers down his face. "I just gotta get a real job. That's what's bothering me. One more day. Then everything'll be set."

"I know it will." She felt the butterflies and she believed him. He could have told her the sky was falling and she would have believed that, too. She tugged at his hair. "I'll make you coffee."

When Giselle brought him his coffee, Zivi was lying on the floor, ear to ear with Nell, both staring intently up at the whimsical animals floating above their faces. The deep, aggressive aroma wafting from the murky depths of the mug challenged Giselle's resolve at caffeine abstention.

He stood, took a tentative sip, then did a quick *heevy-jeevy* dance on the tips of his toes. "Ugh. My God, woman," he gasped. "Trust me. You're not missing anything."

Another tiny sip. "Aagghh," he moaned. "Let me be honest. Cooking is *not* your strongest asset."

Forty-five minutes later, showered, shaved and shining, he lavishly kissed her goodbye before rifling through the closet and impulsively grabbing his hoodie. It was oversized and black, emblazoned with the gang tag BRMF, for Balkan Route Motha Fuckas, his crew's insignia from back in the day. Then he strode out the door, determined not to return until gainfully employed.

Zivi hadn't held an above board, on the books job since he'd stocked shelves at the local bodega twenty-three years before, at the age of twelve. That was the year his mother's kidneys decided enough was enough. Trips to the ER, days in ICU, dialysis three times a week. It added up. Medicare and Medicaid combined were little more than a safety net full of holes. The family was a hair's breadth away from homelessness. And then she stopped responding well. *Perhaps a home dialysis machine would help*, was all that the docs could offer. But those bad boys cost a small fortune and her health was failing fast. He needed scratch and he needed it yesterday. There was a neighborhood guy, Big TaTa. Big Daddy in English. The irony was lost on neither man. In a matter of weeks, Zivi's mother was settled with her new home dialysis machine. She was hooked up. And so was Zivi. In an industry populated by morons, he was a genius. Big TaTa was no one's fool. He compensated his new, soon to be indispensable protégé, handsomely.

So far, nothing in the classifieds had panned out although, to be fair, Zivi had not made much of an effort. Everything seemed so deathly boring. He was used to the frenetic, larger-than-life existence of the upper-echelon drug dealer, exchanging substantial personal risks for commensurately impressive financial rewards. Not that it *had* to be that way. With his massive debt to Big TaTa nearly, but not totally paid off, Zivi had emerged from one of the toughest public high schools in the city with a partial scholarship to the City College of New York. He paid the balance of the tuition and supported his comfortable lifestyle by continuing to deal drugs throughout his academic career. As an unfortunate consequence, when he graduated with a 3.98 overall average in his double majors of engineering and mathematics, the diploma meant little if anything to him. Without a graduate degree and years of experience, any job would pay but a tiny fraction of the amount he had earned part-time on the streets. And additional years of schoolwork that was becoming increasingly dull and intrusive on his social calendar was not an acceptable option. Anyway, by that time, Zivi was too haughty and too world-weary to start out on the lowest rung of any job ladder.

So now, he simply started walking, putting his faith in his feet, confident they would deliver him to wherever it was that he was supposed go. He turned left off Wickum, right onto 145th, around the 168th Street/Edgecombe Avenue subway stop, made a left past his alma mater CCNY, and headed further west. When he finally stopped to look around, he was only mildly surprised to see the familiar facades of the burned out, boarded up buildings of 129th and Church Avenue. It felt like a long time since these buildings and these people had figured prominently in his life, the backdrop to his final and nearly permanent brush with the law.

The last time he strode down these roads he was making obscene amounts of money. But neighborhoods, like women, can be fickle. He had been sold out by the streets, set up and betrayed by the whispers, innuendos and echoes wafting from its empty buildings. When he was dragged away face down, cuffed and shackled like a common criminal, he faced the prospect of doing hard time—decades of it—far away from the ones who mattered most.

Somehow though, through luck, coincidence and charisma, he had managed to beat the rap and now he was back, ready to forgive this savagely Wild West Side for selling him out, if only she would have him back. Like all self-destructive addictions, she offered what he needed most. And right now, that was cash. He was willing to admit to his own indiscretions for that coveted second chance.

At the very least, he wanted the opportunity to come back and have a look around, to probe her vacant buildings for lost memories, inhale the musky perfume of excrement, blood, and drugs, wafting from her most private orifices, the back rooms protected by metal doors that enabled the hidden activities taking place within to proliferate like a virus, destroying the very body and the soul of her neighborhood. Zivi and his cronies, like new super-strains of bacteria that mutate to outwit the effects of penicillin, thrived here, despite the porous tourniquets sporadically applied by community activists and the occasional doses of heightened police presence.

Many well-intentioned souls had been seduced, corrupted, and lost their connection to the free world to her dangerous allure. Zivi had been fortunate to have escaped from her clutches intact.

The hairs on the back of his neck bristled as he felt the ethereal weight of twenty pairs of concealed eyes evaluate his presence on their block. Zivi pulled the old blue bandana from the pocket of his hoodie and tied it around his front left belt loop. The BRMF flag for 'I'm unarmed.' Then he raised his hands slightly away from his sides, stretched his fingers wide and slowly turned three times, lest protocol had changed and some grudge wielding asshole thought Zivi was reaching for a nonexistent concealed weapon. Having established himself as non-threatening, he was ready to seek out his old gang members and see which of them, in this revolving door enterprise, were still around.

He approached the chipped front steps of a seemingly vacant ramshackle four-story limestone. To the untrained eye the building was dead, a skeletal remnant of bygone days when families roamed free. But as Zivi slowly, deliberately and with practiced nonchalance climbed the front stoop, the muffled sounds of slamming doors and the thud of dropping deadbolts betrayed the human infestation within. He put his face up close to the Plexiglass window in the front door. As with all the buildings on the block, the window had long ago been smoked out with cigarette lighters. The plastic was rendered opaque, an eye clouded by thick cataracts, ensuring nothing more definitive than the soft glow of light could filter in or out. Opening the door, he stepped into the urine scented lobby and waited for his eyes to adjust to the shadowy light cast by a single filthy bulb.

His left arm was chicken winged from behind. The cold steel muzzle of a sawed-off gat crushed up against his vertebrae. The hot breath of a faceless assailant caressed his ear. "If so much as a muscle moves, I will blow your fucking brains out, yes?"

Not *exactly* the greeting he had expected. Zivi could have easily overpowered his attacker, but there was no accounting for accidents. He had seen nervous trigger fingers land healthy men in chairs, without legs, for the rest of their lives.

"Hey, hey. Whatcha doing? It's me. Zivi. Relax, *kuz*. It's only me."

"Zivi?" A voice rang out from somewhere across the lobby. "You are shitting me," it laughed. "What the *fuck* are you doing here? Ismet. Let him be, eh? This's Zivi from Živinice!"

Five massive beings materialized from the shadows of the vestibule. The biggest, a hideous switchblade scarred behemoth, slipped the safety back on his semi, slid it into the waistband of his jeans and gave Zivi a hug.

"Put the fucking gun away," he directed the sentry, whose weapon still pressed Zivi's spine. The underling quickly, but thoroughly, frisked Zivi for weapons.

"Clean, Boss."

The big guy flashed a crocodile smile. "You always were chicken-shit when it came to packing heat."

"That's why I kept *you* around."

"Ha!" The big guy laughed out loud. "That's why we were partners, eh?"

Now it was Zivi's turn to be amused. In a way, he supposed they *had* been partners. He was the brains, Osmani the brawn, working together to bring about the outlandish success of this thriving drug distribution network.

"My main man," said Osmani, walking around Zivi, giving him the once-over. "Guns mean nothing to him. He could kill you with one of those deadly *Ruski* karate chops if he wanted to."

"Osmani. What you been up to, my *kuzen*?"

"Meh. Same shit. But you? I thought you were caged for the duration. After that last bust, yes?"

"Out now." Zivi shrugged. "Laying low."

"Laying low? You shit me." Osmani grinned, brown-toothed smile slimy and obscene. "Where you living? How many *dame* you banging?"

But Zivi knew much better than to answer any remotely personal questions.

"I live nowhere, I bang nobody," he said with exaggerated innocence. "Just passing through."

"Don't sell me that shit," scoffed Osmani. "That *kuja* you had with you?" Omani snapped his fingers. "What's her name?"

Zivi flipped his wrist. "She is gone."

"That a fact? Then I track down her sweet American ass. I show her how a *real* man treats his *dama*."

Zivi's stomach lurched as he remembered how Osmani's girlfriend had once ended up in the emergency room with two teeth missing and a fractured cheekbone. Women were objects to these men. Possessions to own, use, abuse, throw away.

"*Nyet*." Zivi shook his head. "I don't come to talk old times. Now. How are things going *now*?"

"Business's good, *kuz*."

"And since Big TaTa's left? Gavric's a good boss?"

"Gavric's tuff," Osmani conceded. "Smart. Made nice with the *policajci*. Gave them a little something off'a the top, to help them not notice things, right? Now, only the guys Gavric say is okay are the ones the *policajci'll* let hang."

"*Beyet*," *shit*, Zivi brown nosed.

Both men stopped smiling and regarded each other in silence.

"Now tell me about you," Osmani pivoted. "What in the hell happened to you? I thought Gavric hand-picked you. *The great Zivi*, raising you up, straight away from me, grooming you to be his Number Two."

Zivi scowled. "Until one day, I am minding my own business, counting the cash, when one of his *deckos* come around saying Gavric wants me to keep an eye on his personal stash and leaves me with a big bag of the *Sef's* smack. Didn't think nothing of it. Anyway, what was I supposed to do? When the boss asks you to look after his personal stash, you better look after his fucking stash, yes?"

Everyone nodded.

"Then, outta nowhere, some undercovers kick in my door and bust me with seventy large and enough H for intent. Coulda sent me away till I'm 300 years old, eh? And just like that I'm heading for trial, got a date and everything. Gonna be stuck in a cage forever, yes? But months and months in, there is chaos with Gavric's stash, the whole load they ID'd me with. Said they couldn't use it anymore. Evidence is now no good." Zivi shrugged. "They still take their friggin' sweet-ass time, but since they got nothing else on me except a bunch of money, they put me out on time served. Waltzed outta that hellhole. But next time I am not so lucky. Any next times, I am fucked. No next time for me."

Assent echoed off the walls.

"But there's one thing I could never figure out, my *kuzen*." Zivi hoped, if he played his cards right, he might finally get some answers to something that had truly befuddled him, haunted him, since the day of his arrest.

"I never figure how the *policajci* got upstairs. I can't figure how they knew which door to bust in. I never found out what happened to Little Jusuf. He was supposed to be looking out for me by the front door. He never let me down before. *Never.* Most loyal son-of-a-bitch around. I pay him good scratch for that, right outta my own pocket. Never could figure out what happened, or where he went. He just disappeared."

Zivi mentally played it through, yet again.

The only lucrative thing Zivi inherited from his loathsome excuse of a father was ties to the old country. Years later, Zivi parlayed those connections to traffic product from the Balkan Route, the passage linking Afghanistan to the rest of Europe, straight to Big TaTa's door. Carefully embedding himself as the middleman, the conduit between the local organization and the overseas suppliers. Because of him, Big TaTa and later on Gavric, were able to offer their customers something reliable and different for better prices than the New York cartels, dependent on South American connections. Gavric, after he inherited the operation, agreed to honor the tradition because he wanted to keep Zivi happy. Zivi could literally keep his hands clean, if not figuratively. No contact. No manufacturing, no packaging, no selling. Zivi had used his years of faithful service to leverage himself right out of the 'dirty' part of the business.

Zivi bitterly remembered how he had perfectly set up his end of the organization so that he would never be clipped. But even after extricating himself from physical contact with product, Zivi still could not sleep. So, he took additional measures to avoid being caught. Measures which benefited everyone. Under Zivi's amateur architectural prowess, the buildings were reconfigured and renovated into modern drug-processing plants. Walls were removed, apartments joined to create factory floors where black tar heroin was turned into powder and low-grade powder cocaine was cooked into crack. All were equipped with trap doors and secret passageways. Some rooms, like Zivi's, even had pipes running from inside the building to the outside, then funneling into faux downspouts, straight into buried stash boxes.

Like Osmani's Ismet, Zivi had his own security stationed in the building whenever he was there. A buzzer system was installed so the huge, hulking fortress of a man, Little Jusuf, could buzz him if anyone unexpected, *like the policajci*, showed up. Somehow, on that day, the buzzer never rang.

The fact that he had gotten nailed was inexplicable. Zivi had turned it over in his mind until he was numb. What had happened to his sentry? Why had they busted him on the only day he had product in the room? Something did not compute.

"Yeah, tough break, *kuzen*," Osmani was saying.

"Do you know?" pressed Zivi. "We were partners. What happened that day?"

"Well." Osmani hesitated. "I did hear..."

"Hear what, *kuz?*"

"Probably nothing."

"Osmani, look at me. We used to be *partners.*"

"Okay." Osmani paused, as if he had the capacity in that pea-sized brain of his to consider his words. "It was just that Gavric started thinking you was getting too far ahead of yourself, eh?" said Osmani. "That he had to take you down a few notches."

Osmani paused. Zivi was speechless.

"Then I hear from around, not from Gavric's own mouth, you understand, that he thought his *kucka* was looking your way, yes? It's a pride thing with him, you understand?" Osmani shrugged. "And with your rep with the *dama*, he figured it must be true so he, well, he had to do what he had to do."

Osmani sucked his teeth.

"He set it up for the cops to bust your *arse* while you were minding his stash."

Zivi tried to process what he was hearing. "I never touched her. Does he think I'm crazy?" Zivi looked around for supporters. "You don't think I'm stupid enough to go after Gavric's *picka*, do you?"

"'Course not." Osmani threw his hands up in surrender. "Not me. I never believed that shit. Gavric had it wrong, is all. No one thinks you screwed around with his *dama*. Anyway, if he really thought you did it, he'd a just killed you, right? Ain't like Gavric to needlessly walk around holding a grudge. Especially when it comes to his *dama.*"

"That *motherfucker* set me up." Zivi kicked the wall. It left a dent. Plaster rained down from the pocked ceiling.

Osmani brushed dust from his shoulders. "*Brat,*" he said in a slow, menacing voice. "Respect the office."

Everyone took a step closer.

"Anyway. Your misunderstanding with Gavric? Over now."

"Water under the bridge," Zivi agreed, seething.

"Water under the motherfucking bridge." Osmani clapped Zivi on the shoulder with a vice-like grip and smiled. Zivi considered telling him about the food disgustingly caked up around his brown front teeth, but decided against it.

"Seems I need a little favor." Osmani spoke kindly; Zivi knew this was when the psychopath was at his most dangerous. "I need someone to drop off a bag with the *brat* minding the front of 128 Lasalle. Everybody here is very busy right now, and it was so kind of you to stop by, so you are the guy to do it. Besides. Gavric would like it if you did."

"Oh, no thank you." Zivi faked a laugh. "I am no runner. I haven't run shit for years now. You know that." Zivi stared at Osmani. "Like I said, I cannot do that anymore. If I get caught I am walking dead, eh? Thanks, but sorry, *kuz*. It's been real nice seeing all you again, but I gotta go."

A well-trained posse acts as a unit in response to unspoken cues from its leader. As he turned to leave, the posse did just what it was supposed to do; it closed ranks around Zivi. He found himself standing in the middle of a circle of thugs, each of whom held a powerful weapon and placed little value on human life. For the first time in a long time, Zivi felt fear. The *icy cold fingers squeezing the blood out of your heart* kind of fear.

For years, Zivi and Osmani worked together to make the operation a success. On the street, even the most well-organized enterprise meant nothing, if it did not have muscle behind it. That's why Zivi had stayed, why he had not broken off on his own. He needed the organization, specifically the enforcement branch, for protection. Osmani and his underlings kept order on the street, demanded respect and periodically flexed their muscles, just to be sure nobody forgot who they were and why they were there. If Osmani's presence was not in the back of everybody's mind, there would have been no organization.

Osmani had to keep himself busy to maintain his effectiveness. If his *članovi* liked a guy, or felt like being nice, they might merely beat the shit out of him. But if they didn't like somebody, or someone dared get out of line, it was Osmani's posse that would always let the first bullet fly.

That was the secret to the cartel's success. Users are loyal to a particular corner, or address. Whoever is stationed there is the one the user buys from. Osmani's boys made sure there was never any competition stationed on any of their blocks. *Ever.*

Zivi now understood that Gavric had set him up once already. He also realized that right now, he could not possibly get away. He was in a ridiculously bad situation and it finally dawned on him what a superbly bad idea it had been to have come back here.

CHAPTER SIXTEEN

From off in the corner, Zivi heard Ismet slip the safety from his gun.

"All right, man. Take it easy." Zivi's words hung in the still of the stifling air. "What is it you want me to do?"

Osmani slipped inside the ring of criminals surrounding Zivi. He advanced on his former partner until the two stood barely inches apart. Zivi forced himself not to look away from the jagged scars and bloodied razor burns desecrating Osmani's chin, which was deliberately positioned just above Zivi's left eye. An obvious invasion of Zivi's personal space, this was a threat.

Zivi instinctively brought his arms up, pretending to scratch his own chin and stroke his cheek. Protected his face, his throat, his solar plexus. If they moved in, at least he would go down fighting. The looming drug dealer smiled coldly. His breath was warm and moist. It smelled sour.

"That's better, *kuzen*," Osmani purred. "Not to worry. You take this bag to our *brat* at 128 Lasalle. You do that, I'll let Gavric know you were here to say *halo*. I'll say I'm sure you wasn't diddling his *dama* because no one'd be stupid enough to do that and then have the balls to show his face around here ever again. Ain't that right, *kuzens?*"

The human fortress surrounding Zivi pressed in a little closer. Muttered its assent.

"Yeah, no problem. I do that for you, Osmani."

Zivi grabbed the small brown paper bag. Responding to another unspoken order, the circle instantly dispersed and Zivi sauntered back down the crumbling steps of the deteriorating limestone walk-up.

He knew they were gathered in the doorway watching; he couldn't ditch the bag. Not yet, anyway. He faced ahead as he walked, defying the overwhelming urge to swing around and run. He turned left off 129th and out of the line of vision of the *brats* loitering in the doorway.

Just as he was about to toss the bag into someone's overturned garbage can he saw the movement out of the corner of his eye.

He tried not to break stride or do anything else suspicious. Through his peripheral vision, he could make out the unmarked police car as it silently slithered away from the curb, slinking its way behind him.

"Excuse me, sir," called a male voice from the passenger seat. "May I have a word?"

Shit, shit, shit.

Osmani had painstakingly and methodically worked his way up through the ranks as most loyal soldier. Zivi, on the other hand, had shot up the ladder in the organization. Zivi never doubted that Osmani resented him, but neither man could have benefited by setting up or otherwise ratting the other out. It would have been bad for business.

Until now. Now, Zivi was no longer a factor. He was expendable.

By showing his face back on the street, Zivi had idiotically broadcast the fact that Gavric hadn't gotten what he wanted. The one he tried to put away forever had returned. Enter Osmani. With one little bag of junk he was going to score big time, finish what the *Sef* had started.

Not that Zivi really blamed him. This was business, not personal. Hell, Zivi would probably have done the same if the situation was reversed.

What annoyed Zivi was how easily the witless Osmani had set him up. Osmani came right out and told him that Gavric had a deal with the *policajci* to lay off of his guys. But Zivi had been AWOL from the streets. These new *policajci* did not know Zivi's pedigree. To them, he was just some local street hustler who showed up sans seal of approval, by definition, someone to bust. And he was about to be busted.

"Stop, sir," the voice called with a bit more urgency. "Can you hear me, sir?"

The car eased to a stop and a plainclothes got out.

Beyet, beyet, beyet. Think, think, think.

He had to do something. His next arrest would be his last and for the first time in his life, he had something to live for.

Motherfucker, he thought.

And then he remembered. The subway entrance at the corner of 128th and Church. He hadn't seen it because the electric sign had been shot out ages ago and never replaced.

It was all in the timing.

Zivi flipped up the hood and buried himself deep within the cocoon of his oversized gang hoodie, rendering himself anonymous. He sped up until he was just ten steps from the stairway down into the subway. Then he slowed. As he had hoped, the cop approached him from behind and placed his right hand on Zivi's left shoulder. Zivi could not have planned it better. He yanked the *policajci's* wrist hard with his left hand, pulling the cop off balance. As he whipped around, Zivi used his body's momentum to help land a monstrous cross-punch square into the officer's nose. The cheek and nasal bones sounded like brittle twigs when they shattered. As the cop doubled over, Zivi grabbed the narc's hips and heaved his knee up, hard and swift, into the man's groin. The secure hold on the officer's waist insured that his body could not move, could not recoil to absorb the impact. Zivi felt his knee barrel up through the thick, fleshy soft tissue between the man's legs and pause only slightly as it split through the officer's pubic bone. For one appalling second, time stood still. From deep within the protection of the cavernous hood, Zivi stared into the other man's eyes. Then he dropped the cop, writhing and screaming, onto the filthy pavement.

Zivi didn't hang around to see what happened next. In an instant he leapt down the steps into the fetid station. Like a miraculous ghostly mirage, he saw the shadow of a subway car cast against the crumbling tile wall. People moved aside respectfully as he flew over the turnstile and onto the platform. They knew better than to get in the middle of whatever it was that was obviously going down. They seemed to wait with bated breath for the show to continue, for the pursuer, be it another drug dealer or a cop, to follow. Just as he came to the edge of the platform, the stainless steel graffiti-scarred doors of the southbound A train slammed shut in his face. Zivi raced along the platform to the conductor's window. He opened his eyes wide and pleaded.

"The wrong guy," he said. "I swear. I'm the wrong guy. They'll never believe me. Please. I'm begging you. I got a wife and a sick kid at home. They need me. I swear."

The subway doors to the train rattled open and Zivi dove in. As they started closing again, he realized he was still holding Osmani's brown paper bag. *The bag with the dope in it.* In the seconds before the doors pressed together for a second time, Zivi tossed the bag back out onto the platform. Abruptly, the wheels screamed and the train lumbered into the tunnel. Through the scratched plastic window, Zivi could just make out the partner of the disabled undercover finally arrive on the platform with his gun drawn. The civilians screamed, ducked under the benches, scattered. The train lurched forward and screeched out of the station.

He sunk down onto the bench and buried his hooded head in his hands. *That was way. Too. Fucking. Close.* Now he had to figure out how he was going to escape at the next station. By then, the *policajci* would have already radioed ahead for back-up.

At that moment, Zivi realized his drug dealing days were behind him. Way, way, *way* behind him.

Back underground at 128th and Church, the cop on the platform had no intention of calling for back-up for the next stop on the train that psychotic thug was riding. He had already made a point of taking his sweet-ass time getting down onto the platform. Hell, he didn't want to face the bastard. That perp was crazy. Probably strung out on PCP, or whatever junkies were doing these days. No cop deserved that shit, he told himself. My God, the bastard just broke my partner's dick. Sometimes those motherfuckers, they're just not worth the bother.

He turned to walk away, glad the whole thing was over, when he realized the bystanders were following him, talking to him. *The bag,* they were saying. *The paper bag. The one the guy threw down.* Someone pulled at his sleeve. Pointed. *There. Over there. Officer. Look. It's still lying on the platform.*

The cop hesitated, looked around. The crowd looked back.

He sighed. Walked over and nudged the bag with the end of his shoe. Bent down to examine it. Nudged it again. Glanced up. Was dismayed to see how many of them thought what he was doing was more interesting than staring into the empty black voids, competing to be first to see the headlights of the next incoming train as it turned the bend and emerged from the tunnel. He gingerly picked up the bag, holding it at a safe distance from his person. Then he slowly unraveled the top and peeked in. Shook it. Looked again. Then he reached inside.

"What the..."

Lying at the bottom was a half-eaten glazed donut.

The cop shook his head, as if to say *this kind of stuff happens every day.* "It's a donut. Just a donut, folks. A crazy guy with a donut. You can all go home now."

The bystanders dispersed as if nothing had happened. As he turned to see if EMS had gotten to his partner, the cop was just glad that on top of everything else, at least he wouldn't have to write up an evidence report.

Back in his decrepit limestone office, Osmani drained the dregs of his stale Turkish coffee. He swished the crumbs from the glazed donut, which had collected at the bottom of the paper cup, around his mouth. They stuck to his slimy brown teeth, ruining his tough-guy appearance.

No one had the *testisi* to tell him.

Before the doors were even half opened at the 59th and Central Park South station, Zivi was on the platform, mixing in with the crowd, racing up the stairs. During the interminable ride, he'd had more than enough time for numerous bargains with all supreme beings, if any of them would see fit to grant this one last huge escape.

Miraculously, he made it all the way out into the revealing light of day without getting collared. At the nearest souvenir table, he threw his last fifty at the vendor and grabbed an 'I heart NY' tee shirt, a pink New York Yankees baseball cap and flip-flops. He jogged to a trashcan inside the park and crouched behind the stone border wall. Swapped his hoodie and black tee for tourist kitsch, then wavered for one excruciating moment before taking the $1,750 pair of limited edition G-Factor Tomahawks off his feet. He heaved his prize possession, all the more precious because he wouldn't dare spend that kind of money today, into the basket. Once those babies hit the melted ice cream and bags of dog shit, he tossed the black hoodie on top and never looked back.

Seconds later, he emerged with his saggy jeans hiked up past his waist, nerdy tee shirt neatly and uncharacteristically tucked into his pants, long, luxurious hair strategically stashed beneath the new pink hat, and the wind whistling between his bare toes. He exchanged a twenty at a different table for a large glossy coffee table book on Leonardo DaVinci and buried his nose deep within its pages. With excruciating outward calm, he strolled north. Inside, he continued to quake.

Slowly, the knots in his neck and shoulders unwound. *Music would help.* He fished his phone from deep within his pocket. The pants fell to their familiar perch atop his hip bones. He did not bother to pull them back up.

The tune was hypnotic and guttural and strong. The sirens and alarms of the indifferent city floated away as Zivi was drawn back to a time when things were only marginally less complicated. Indifferent to American hip-hop, rap or rock, he opted instead for Tad Michaelson to growl biting angry lyrics into his ears.

    Caught in the belly of an ugly lie
Never wanted to say goodbye
Justice never fair
Bet your life; take the dare
Sun come up; what you gonna do
Stand in the shadow or allow the hue?

    Zivi chose the light. He would confess his sins and Giselle would forgive him.

CHAPTER SEVENTEEN

GWENDOLYN

She couldn't read one more word from the conspiracy theorists or those other nut-jobs who were allowed to float any moronic thing they wanted on the internet.

Gwendolyn Pays To Have Cassie Kidnapped!
Gwendolyn Sells Cassie Into Slavery!
Cassie Home: Elaborate Hoax For New Television Series!

It was Sunday afternoon and she hadn't spoken to another human being since Friday. There was no one to laugh with about the absurdity of the headlines, no one to sob with about her profound loneliness. By the time she made it to the kitchen, the walls were already spinning and the floor tilting precariously one way, then the next. She clung to the counter until her equilibrium could be trusted. She tried to make herself tea, but her hands were shaking too violently to fill the kettle. She hadn't eaten breakfast that morning and had puked up last night's dinner. She would permit herself one small portion of nutrition. An apple and ten cashews. Slowly, she sunk her teeth into the apple. Her mouth filled with saliva. Eyes closed, she tried to concentrate on the intensity of the flavor, on the texture of the crunch. But she was an audience of one, and Gwendolyn could not fool herself.

Detached, she watched herself forage through the cabinet. One sleeve of Ritz crackers. An entire box of Wheat Thins. The rest of the organic animal crackers. She was slipping below the surface.

The refrigerator held leftover Thai from two days earlier. There was no time to wipe the sauce dribbling down her chin, as she moved on to the turkey burger scheduled for tomorrow's dinner. Her stomach hurt as she forced pita and hummus down her throat. The cold broccoli smelled like a sewer. She struggled because she was too full of food to breathe. Too full of food for anything else. Only the comfort of numbness.

And still, the freezer beckoned. She was panicking. Her stomach hurt so much. She had to stop, but she could not.

Gwendolyn was drowning.

The torture of baking soda water was both evil and redemptive. However, this was the last time. She would never do it again. She was all better now. This was an unbreakable promise. From hereon in, she would be stronger than ever.

For reasons that she could not fathom, Gwendolyn told Moss about her most recent episode of bulimia. To get past the shame, she stared out the window and pretended she was telling her pigeons.

"Can you fix me?" Her voice cracked eventually, as she struggled to maintain her mask. "Because, you know, it's all very exhausting."

"Gwen." Moss's posture and expression were rigid. "Look at

me. It's time we speak seriously about the benefits of checking yourself into a facility."

"It's not a viable option." Her tongue was barely functioning.

The doctor's voice softened. "At this point I see it as one of your *only* options."

"Why would you say that?" Gwendolyn croaked.

"You spend all your energy on a futile, self-destructive, self-abusive activity. You need to apply your endless energy in a more productive manner. You need to find your daughter."

Gwendolyn opened her mouth as though to speak. Moss held up her hand and continued.

"The disease will continue to wear away at you. Eventually, you will become too weak to run or otherwise work out. That may be the only thing that will make you see things are so out of control that you have *no other choice* but to pass off responsibility for your life to the professionals. To check yourself in to a live-in facility."

"I don't want to." Gwendolyn was once again an injured child. She was struggling to breathe.

"I know. Therefore, I'm willing to go the extra mile with you, no pun intended, before we take that last step. But let me be brutally honest. If you don't work painstakingly hard, I don't see how you can avoid some time away from your present environment."

"I'll try."

"You're going to have to do better than try. And I'm not going to sugar coat it. It won't be easy, but nor would being checked in. I need not remind you that every single aspect of personal control, including all choices of physical autonomy, would be taken from you. That includes when and how much you eat and when and how much you are permitted, or more likely *not* permitted, to exercise. Privacy in the bathroom would be a thing of the past. They do not enable cheating."

Gwendolyn nodded.

"And difficulty breathing is overtly suggestive of panic attacks. I ask you again to reconsider my offer of a slightly stronger med cocktail. To get you over this hurdle. I know you've complained of a flat affect, but eventually we'll come up with the right combination."

"I know." She was finally willing to concede the point. "I can't do bulimia and the rest of my life at the same time anymore."

Gwen fished for a tissue. Moss reached out to hand her one from the box on the coffee table. Tears distorted her depth perception and Gwendolyn inadvertently grazed the shrink's hand. The gentle brush of soft skin was jarring.

But as she stuffed the pages of new prescriptions into her bag and rose to leave, she came to a decision. She was never coming back.

She was the only one riding that creaky elevator down to the lobby. Its agonizing snail's pace was perfect. Gwen pulled her arms out of the sleeves, but left the neck of her shirt intact so that it hung around her like a tiny hairdresser's cape. With speed that comes with experience in these types of situations, she deftly unhooked and slipped out of her satin bra and replaced it with the just-in-case jog bra she always kept in her bag. As soon as the arrow inched past the third floor, Gwendolyn whipped off her shirt and had the extra jogging top on before the arrow hit two. Seconds later, when the elevator bounced to an uneven stop, she stepped into the lobby, ready for a run.

The park was packed with joggers. The mid-thigh shorts she wore certainly weren't running shorts, but they weren't *so* restrictive that she couldn't put in at least five miles. She had already been out this morning before work. That would make ten in all.

Not bad for a weekday.

Because of her job, Gwendolyn was ever cognizant of the masses of evil doers roaming the streets of New York City. She was always on guard, always aware of her environment. She never ran with earbuds, or any other distraction device. But the park was packed and there was safety in numbers. It was a beautiful day. The lower loop was closed to traffic. The guys she had been noticing out of the corner of her eye for the past days or weeks were figments of her imagination. It was normal to imagine things like that after what she had been through. She convinced herself that now those vile assholes had completed their deed, had abducted her child, there was no reason for them to be watching her. She told herself all of these things, over and over again, as she did her warm-up quarter-mile. And then, even though it was against her gut, against her better judgment, she decided to do what everyone else seemed to love. She dug out her earbuds.

Four and a half miles later, it happened. She realized that she had not programmed any of those last several tunes. And then, like a micro-plane grating the fuzz from the soft skin of a ripe peach, Tad Michaelson's voice came ram-rodding its way through, violating the intimacy of her ear canal and scraping the fine hairs right off the soft skin of her eardrum.

Travel apart, yet here we are
No matter how long, no matter how far
You repel like a magnet; sting like a bee
My pollen's your nectar; but love is not free
We are cats in the alley; we snarl and we hiss

Travel the world for that one poisoned kiss.

Shit. Shit. Shit. Shit. Shit. When did he get a hold of this stupid thing? She grabbed at her heart and stumbled. Did he have to go and plant his little seeds all over her whole damned life?

Somehow, the air had gotten too thick to breathe. Gwendolyn couldn't see anymore. Everything was throbbing and pulsating and blurry. She stumbled to the nearest bench. Reached out to steady herself. Then her knees buckled and she fell hard against its cold, indifferent arms.

Someone came over to see if she was okay.

"Yeah," Gwen mumbled. "I'm okay." She closed her eyes. "I'm all right. The thing is," she pressed the heels of her hands against her temples, "I just remembered." She rubbed her forehead. "There's this call I need to make..." She hugged herself. "Should have done it already..." and rubbed her arms. "Just need to find my phone..."

She sat there shivering, even though it was 85 degrees and she had just finished running 4.8 miles.

CHAPTER EIGHTEEN

ZIVI AND GISELLE

By the time he finished dropping the deadbolts, turning the tumblers and opening the door, he knew he had awakened her from her mid-afternoon nap and she would still be groggy. But then she took one look at him and erupted in hysterical laughter. She couldn't speak, she was laughing so hard, pointing at his naked toes hanging over the end of dollar flip-flops.

"Oh, my God. I'm sorry," she gasped, pressing a hand to her diaphragm. "It's just those shoes. *Those shoes!* And that shirt. Oh, my God. Oh my *God*. I can't wait to hear *this* story. But wait. First. Did you get a job?"

His bravado evaporated into thin air.

"Uh, not really." He shook his head. "No."

"It can't be that bad." She smiled. "*It's never as bad as you think.* A very wise, very handsome, very sexy guy always tells me that when I have a problem."

"Well maybe that very wise, very sexy, very handsome, very sexy, very wise and not to mention very sexy guy, isn't always right?"

"That's not what he tells me."

"This is different. You don't want to hear this."

"We're a team, remember?" She led him to the sofa, hooked a leg over his thigh, and pressed her pelvis tight to his hips.

Not now, he thought for the first time in his life.

He owed it to her to deal with what he had done. Not tomorrow, as he would have preferred, but today, as he did not. Right now. Procrastinating was going to make it worse. If that was even possible.

It took all his self-control to gently, but firmly, disengage himself from her leg. He tried to scrape the stubble off his cheeks with his fingernails.

"Zivi."

He issued a pathetic sigh, fiddled with his Rolex, and focused his eyes on a speck of dirt on the rug.

"Well, you know I was going out this morning to get a job so we could get more money? Because of Nellie? She needs lots of things. Even though she's small. And soon she'll be bigger and then she'll need even more things. That's what they say. They say you can't believe how much stuff a kid needs. And of course, for you. You want things. Shoes. Jewelry. Well, maybe you don't really want them, but I want you to have those things, if and when you decide you want them. You deserve nice things. The best of things. And of course, the art supplies. God knows, the art supplies. We even need a second apartment—a whole studio set-up—just for art. So, like I said—"

"Zivi! You went out this morning to find a job. To earn money. I got that part already. Then what?"

"Give me a chance. I need to set the scene."

"The scene," she admonished, "is set."

"All right. So I'm walking. And I'm thinking about all the money we need and how all those jobs..." he fidgeted with his watch again, "you know..." moving on to adjusting his hair, "they really don't pay that much." Scraping at the stubble again. "At least, not at the beginning, not enough for our needs. So..."

"No." The word fell out of her, riding on the back of a slight gasp.

"I began to think. Just for a little while."

"Don't say it."

"Giselle, please. I thought, just for some extra money..."

"You didn't." She pulled her hand away from him.

"'Till I could find something better."

"Don't say what I think you're saying." She scooted her whole body back.

"Just for a little while." He groaned. "It was just an idea."

"We *talked* about this." She stood. "And you *promised* me."

He swallowed the last bit of his pride. "I am sorry. I went and talked to Osmani."

"How *could* you?" she whispered.

Why did he tell her? He had lost his touch. There would be no stopping her this time.

"You *promised* me. How *could* you?" She disappeared into the bedroom.

She was right. He had broken his promise. Zivi threw the absurd hat onto the sofa. *Good job, Einstein.* It seemed wise to lie there awhile, exactly where she had left him. To give her a chance to digest the whole thing.

Giselle collapsed on the mattress and rolled herself into a tight ball with her back to the door.

How could he?

They finally had everything. Everything they had dreamed about. An honest place. A baby. And most of all, each other.

How could he do it? How could he risk everything?

How could he be willing to throw it all away and go back to dealing drugs? She couldn't comprehend such stupidity.

Blatant, idiotic, immediate gratification, testosterone-fueled, senseless stupidity.

She had no idea how much time passed before the snake slithered across the mattress and had the audacity to put his hand on her back.

"Giselle."

"Don't *touch* me." She shook her shoulder free. "You may *not* touch me. You *lied to* me," she whisper-hissed, so she wouldn't wake the baby. "You were willing to risk prison for the rest of your life for a few more measly dollars. You betrayed me. You risked *everything we have together*. You chose money over me. Over me *and Nell*. What are we supposed to do when you get arrested? You're a bad person. *Don't touch me.*"

"*Beba*, listen to me," he whispered back. Then lay down beside her, gathered her up, and held her down tight in a full body bear hug. She fought to break free, but he was too damned strong. Even her arms and legs were pinned, so she couldn't move. "You have to listen," he whispered in her ear and his breath turned her stomach. "I didn't do anything with the drugs. I just went to talk to Osmani. It was dumb." She squirmed harder, but it did no good. "I had no job interview today," he said, ignoring her struggles. I tried, but I couldn't get one. So I just went back to 128th to talk to my brothers. That's all. I didn't even talk to Gavric. Never saw him. I just went to see my homies."

She stopped breathing. "You didn't have a job interview?"

"No. I didn't want to tell you. I was embarrassed. Ashamed. Afraid you'd think I was good for nothing. That you could do better with someone else. I thought I'd just figure out the job thing while I was walking. I swear, I really thought while walking, *I'll come up with something*. But I didn't. Instead, all of a sudden, I'm back in the hood."

"You *swear* to me?" She lay still until he loosened his grip.

"You promise you didn't touch any of his stuff?" She rolled over to face him, but she was still incensed.

"Well, not on purpose." He took a deep breath. "But here is the thing. They kinda..."

"Either you touched the stuff, or you didn't. This is not rocket science. It is *yes* or it is *no*."

"Well. It is not that simple."

"*Don't lie to me!*"

"What happened was, they put the shit in a paper bag. So I did not actually see it or touch it; no prints, no transference—"

She jumped out of the bed. "I'm taking the baby and leaving."

"No, Giselle. Listen. Pleuse."

She paused, her back to him.

"They tried to frame me."

She clucked her tongue. She was exhausted from all his stories. She started to look for socks.

"They made me do a run. And there was undercover on the block. An undercover who doesn't know me," he spewed words as fast as he could. "And the word from Gavric is that the narcs have to bust anyone they don't know. And Osmani and his crew, they forced me to do a run. With the undercover right there."

Slowly, she turned to face him. Forgot she was supposed to be escaping.

"How?" But she still wasn't ready to believe. "How could they *make you* do a run? Those are your brothers. They'd never do that. Not after all you've done for them." She turned away. "And what about you? Why didn't you just break their ribs, or knock their teeth out or something?"

"Well, actually it wasn't an option today, because they had a sawed-off gat shoved up into my back."

Her heart stopped and she forgot, once again, about the socks.

"Some new bead who didn't know me and didn't owe me anything."

She sat on the edge of the mattress.

"A gat?"

"Big mother of a gun, too. I could tell by the amount of steel pushing up against my spine."

She inched closer to him.

"Rubber grip."

She touched his arm.

"He wore a glove. So his hand wouldn't slip."

She took his face into her hands. "Osmani and his crew are *sick*. What if they shot you? What if they *killed* you? You can never go back there. Promise me. Promise *Nell. Please*."

Giselle had only met that leering, out of control psycho Osmani a few times, but she had heard all the stories.

"No, *beba*, no. They just wanted to scare me. To be sure I took that bag. They wanted me to get busted. That's all. They weren't going to really shoot me. At least I don't think so."

She stared up into his magnificent burnt sienna eyes that always twinkled with life and were ever so invincible. "What did you do?"

"I had to take it. Just in case. As I said, they had some wacko new kid holding the gun and if he had an itching trigger finger? Then what? I just started thinking about Wheelchair Wally..."

Giselle's hands shot up and clamped themselves over her mouth. She imagined the neighborhood paraplegic gunshot victim, with Zivi's precious head superimposed on the atrophied body.

"They made up some bullshit story and sent me to take the bag over to some guy on Lasalle. I'm just waiting for my chance to dump the shit, and come on back home to you and our little baby, when their motherfuckin' undercover pulls out and starts trailing me."

She gasped.

"And then this narc, he gets right up in my face and he is about to frisk me, when I turn and—"

"You didn't hurt him, did you?" Giselle knew that if he had done anything stupid like that, the city would have already launched a massive manhunt.

"I didn't do *anything* to the cop."

"Because they always protect each other and if they ever got you alone in one of their bathrooms..."

"Giselle! I *said*—"

"I'm just saying..."

"And *I* am just saying."

"But if you *did*..."

"But I didn't..."

"Okay."

"All right."

"Go easy on me, I've had a very bad day."

But she still had not decided whether or not she believed him.

"I did not do anything to the cop. Besides stand there and pray. I said, 'If you just help me get out of this one last mess I swear, *I swear*, I'll never do anything bad ever again.' And then, I'm telling you, it was like He heard me. Because the subway appeared right out of nowhere. And I just about flew down the steps because the undercover was right behind me yelling, '*Stop or I'm gonna shoot!*' But the only thing I was about to do was get my butt back home to you guys."

"Oh, my *God*. And did he?"

"Did he what?"

"Shoot."

"Oh, yes. He was shooting. And people were running everywhere to get out of the way. And then, just when I get to the platform, the train was pulling out of the station. So I ran as fast as I could, ditched the bag of dope in a garbage can, closed my eyes and did my best ever jump right onto the back of that train, just in time as it pulled around the bend. And when I open the door and fell into the car, I still heard that cop shooting at me from way back on the platform."

"Thank God you're safe." She started to get up, but he pulled her back down.

"Not yet safe. I know the way these cops think. They're calling for back-up at the next station. So I spent whole time thinking and praying, and apologizing for all the hurt I may have caused in the world, and all the bad things I did in my life."

"How long did *that* take? Was it the local or the express?"

"Not funny, Gissy. This was no laughing matter. They were really trying to get me. I came this close," he held his fingers an inch apart, "to being killed."

"I know. I'm sorry," she said, falling back in love with him, almost forgetting what he had done.

"So when we pulled into the station, I saw that some cops are hanging out on the platform. Definitely. Undercover."

"*Really?*"

"*Yes*. I had to hide behind people and sneak upstairs just to get out of there alive. Then I wasted what little money I have on all this shit." He waved his hands. "So they can't ID me. And then I hightailed it back here as fast as I could."

He lay down on the bed and propped the back of his head up on his forearm.

"And *now* I am home. *Now* I am safe."

She stood over him. She did not know whether to be relieved that he had escaped this latest idiotic escapade unscathed, or to tell him she'd had enough. She had done this already—survived the ups and downs, lived on the roller coaster of gut-wrenching fear that accompanied being the significant other of someone in his treacherous profession. She was tired of it. Outgrown it, really.

"Ziv, you look me right in my eye and tell me once and for all your drug dealing days are over. Because I can't do this anymore. My heart just can't take it." Her voice rose. "I can't be with someone who goes out in the morning and may never ever come back again. I can't live like that. I won't do it. Not anymore. It's your choice." The baby stirred and Giselle lowered her voice. "It's either me and Nellie, or your brothers and the drugs."

CHAPTER NINETEEN

"*Beba*, I'm telling you. This thing that happened today. It was a sign. I am never, *ever*, selling or touching drugs again for as long as I live. I did my time. I am *never* going back there. I swear it."

"Okay."

"Good."

"Because if you ever did…"

"*Giselle*. I'm telling you, that part of my life is over. I promise. There is nothing that'll ever come between you and your man again. Not drugs, not nothing. I swear to it."

She flopped down next to him. "You know what I still don't get?"

"What?" He took her hand.

"Why would Gavric tell Osmani to set you up? Gavric loved you like a true blood brother."

"I have no idea." He slid her hand inside his pants. "Now come over here and show your man how glad you are that he is home in one piece."

He tried to pull her on top of him.

But she refused to budge. "I thought you and Osmani got along fine at the end. The whole thing doesn't make sense."

"*Beba, pleeaasse*. Can we drop it?" He guided her hand up and down, up and down. "It doesn't matter. I'm back and it is over. That's what's important."

"No. No, it's not over. They can't go and do something like this to one of their own. It's not right."

"Honey, listen to me." He was pleading. "I cannot trust anybody in this whole wide world except you. It is you and me. That is all there is. Just you, me and little ol' Nellie. You guys are my life. This right here, in this apartment? *This* is my life now. You two are my future. Nothing—not drugs, not anybody, *nothing*—will ever come between us again. I swear."

Finally, she smiled.

"I have an idea. Start packing. Because we're moving. Someplace that is not so damn claustrophobic." His magnificent dark eyes were twinkling again. "Somewhere with real windows and no bugs. Somewhere that smells clean. This place was okay for two of us for a little while, but we can't let Nell live in this dump. And I'll find a real job. A real, honest, on the books, pay your taxes job."

"Really?" God, she loved him.

"I'm telling you. Today, it was a sign. The new me is right here in front of you. Come over here." He pulled her on top of him. "I'm introducing you to the new Zivi."

He closed his eyes and was kissing her now. Apparently, the subject, as far as he was concerned, was closed.

But not so for Giselle.

"Baby?"

"Gis, you're *killing* me here. What is it?"

"I was just thinking. Why would the cops shoot at you in a crowded subway station?" She started touching him just the way he liked. Slow and steady, firm but not too hard.

He groaned with pleasure. Leaned back. Relaxed.

"They're not supposed to shoot into a crowd. It's too dangerous."

"I guess Gavric must have told them, *no interlopers on his turf. No matter what.* So they shot at me."

He ran the tips of his fingers back and forth across her breasts.

"No, that doesn't make sense. I don't think Gavric would say that."

Zivi pretended to shoot himself in the temple, rolled his eyes back into his head, and feigned death.

"He would never give his blessing to something like that," Giselle continued, ignoring the histrionics. "You remember how broken up he was when his little boy was killed a couple of years ago. I can't believe he'd risk it again." She pulled on him a little too hard. Just to be sure he was paying attention to her, not enjoying himself too much. Not yet, anyway.

"Easy, girl," he gasped, sinking his head further into the pillow.

"*Well?*" She tugged again.

"Look. I honestly do not know. Gavric is an ice-cold prick and I would very much like to stop talking about him. Because there is only one thing I am sure of, and that is that I have just had a *very* hard and *very* difficult day. I am *extremely* stressed. And tense. So all I am asking, no *begging*, is for you to stop talking about Gavric and everything else for the next twenty minutes. It would make me very happy if you just take off your clothes and get on top of me. I promise you. *That* is the right thing to do."

"Yeah, well since when did you become the boss of me?" She tried her best to sound indignant.

"Ummmm, *beba*, I'm not sure," he mumbled. "You tell me."

She didn't answer. She couldn't. Because her mouth was busy doing other things.

His pants lay crumpled on the edge of the mattress. When one of his cell phones sprang to life with its loud, pulsating beat and vibration, her teeth sank into his stiff, sensitive flesh. He screamed. She looked up at him, questioningly.

"It's all right," he said, gasping for air. "Ignore it. Don't stop. I'll get it later."

She returned to what she was doing. What she was so very good at. But the hateful gadget continued to disrupt her concentration.

She glared at it, releasing the suction.

"*No ... Please... don't... stop...*" he begged.

But she had already turned away from his spreadeagled body and was rummaging through the pockets of his pants. By the time she found the right one, it had stopped ringing.

She stared at the caller ID. "*No!*"

"*What?* Come *on, beba.* We are so close. Just one more minute. You can't stop now."

"It's your drug dealer people!"

"It is not," he groaned. "How could that possibly be?"

"Because it says right here, *public payphone.* Who else would be calling you from a public payphone?" She scowled at him. Did he think she was some kind of idiot?

"Public payphone?" He somehow managed to push himself up into a sitting position. "Shit. *Goddamn mother ... Quick!* Giselle! *Give me the phone!*"

"No." She spun away. "You said you weren't talking to them anymore."

As she was deciding what to do with it, the hideous thing started ringing all over again. And before she had time to think, he leapt up and grabbed it out of her hands, shoving her aside.

He limped to the kitchen and twisted himself over the sink for reception. He tried speaking quietly, but holding the phone up to the window made that impossible.

The apartment was small and Giselle heard every word.

"I told you never to call me on this number."

He looked at his watch.

"It's not enough time."

The voice on the other end was yelling. "What is the matter with you?" Zivi shouted back. "Are you fucking crazy?" But the phone was already dead. He hobbled back into the bedroom and grabbed his pants. He couldn't scramble into them quickly enough. Snatched the few spare dollars and the loose change strewn across the mattress. Threw on an old pair of shoes and practically ran to the door.

Giselle sat, frozen. Was Zivi, *her* Zivi, really running away from a perfectly good blow job? Something was very, very wrong.

"Zivi? What's ... What's going on?"

Was he running out to meet Osmani? Gavric? Who else could make him jump like that? What other bosses did he have?

He stopped short. Ran back to the bedroom. "*Listen.*" Was all out of breath. "I want you to listen to me. Everything is gonna be okay," he panted. "Don't worry."

He was speaking so fast.

"But I gotta run out. No time to explain now."

She could barely understand him.

"Just do me favor. Remember one thing. I love you. You are my life. No matter what happens, you must believe that. You are the one I love. I *promise*."

"What are you ... Wh-where are you going?"

"So sorry," he called back as he fled. "I'll make it up to you. I swear. Don't worry. It's not about the drugs."

But it obviously was about the drugs. There was nothing else it could be.

CHAPTER TWENTY

DELVECCIO AND MCMILLAN

DelVeccio was panting. "Hey. She made a call after her jog, then got into a cab." I'm at 44th and Park. She's heading into Grand Central. Stay close to the phone."

"You think you got something?"

"Maybe. Her cabbie was driving like a lunatic on the way over here." DelVeccio exited his own taxi and was absorbed by the rush hour crowd.

"Think she saw you? Was she trying to shake you?"

"She didn't see me."

"Maybe she's just going somewhere."

"I caught her in the zoom. She looks bad, Brian. Really bad."

"That's good, isn't it? This is what you wanted. 'Bad' is how a person's supposed to look after their kid is snatched."

"Yeah, but she had some kind of breakdown during her run. And now she could be headed out of town—Metro North—why else would she take a cab to Grand Central? If she were just taking the subway downtown she would have hopped on the B or the C at 96th and kept going."

"Bags or suitcases?" asked McMillan.

"Just the typical tote."

"Then maybe she's going nowhere."

"That's why I'm worried. Why was she out there? She never runs at this time of day. She knows all the tags. They could have left a message. It could have been anything I would have missed —a ... a string in a tree," DelVeccio flailed his arms, "a ... a ... carved trunk, anything. I think they may have made contact. That's why she was rushing to get here."

"Not to catch a train."

"I don't think so."

McMillan held his breath. "Is she carrying anything that could hold a ransom?"

"I don't think so," said Gary DelVeccio. "But ya know what? I can't really tell."

CHAPTER TWENTY-ONE

GISELLE

What he had just done should have been the last straw. She wanted it to be. She told herself it was. She knew that she owed it to herself.

Last time, the last three times really, were different. He was right. She *did* enjoy the lifestyle. But she was much younger then. In those days they were the free-spirited, early twenties bohemian artist on the cusp of breaking into the gallery scene and the secretly well-educated late-twenties hunky drug dealer, embracing life together and living it to its largest.

Giselle did not have the strength to go through the inevitable again. Because there was no doubt in her mind he would go down, it was just a matter of *when*. The last time he went to prison, she barely survived. It broke her. Her heart could no longer work properly. A weight upon her chest prevented it from functioning. Each beat sent a spasm of pain, which could only be eased by hours upon hours of fitful sleep. Somehow, she had made it through, but his actions today tore away all the old scabs. She had no strength left to conquer the relentless, debilitating fear that each time he walked out the door he might simply never return.

The sun shifted, the light from the single window dimmed, and Giselle was suddenly ravenous. She 'tsked' her tongue. Somehow, Zivi had never installed more than a hot plate in the apartment. As a result, although she loved to cook, since moving into the current space she never could. And, although the situation used to be tolerable, now it was completely unworkable. The constant demands of breastfeeding left her parched, famished and scrambling for food in frequent and unpredictable intervals. Suddenly, her life seemed to revolve around eating. Between the three of them, someone was always doing it—usually she or Nell but, on occasion, Zivi too could be found rummaging for some form of physical sustenance.

She would grab a bite with a friend. Immediately. Before the walls of the cave began closing in around her. She called around, but no one was home. She scrolled through the numbers again. There was only one person left, the one person she had omitted the first time through. Giselle was appalled at herself that she would even consider it, but she really needed to hear an adult voice, so her finger hit 'send' and seconds later the phone was ringing.

"Hey, Gissy honey. How're you?"

"Hey, Sabrina," she half sighed. "I'm running out with Nell and grabbing something, so if you're not busy—"

"Girlfriend, it's like you're reading my mind."

"Great," said Giselle, with a feeble attempt at enthusiasm. "Papa Vinny's in twenty?"

"See ya then."

Giselle secured Nell, who was already fussing, into the baby carrier strapped to her chest and pushed the empty stroller to the elevator. "Please, sweetie, if I feed you now, we'll be an hour late for Sabrina and Ethan."

Giselle searched the diaper bag for the favorite pacifier. Predictably, it was nowhere to be found. Instead, she offered the baby four or five others; each time, Nell locked her lips tight and spun her head away from the offensive phony.

Back in the apartment, Nell screamed for food. Giselle, unable to see directly below the baby strapped to her chest, tripped over an end table, sending the lamp to the floor. She was too frayed to pick it up; her one desperate priority was to hunt down the singular pacifier Nell deemed worthy.

One last time, in complete exasperation, she plunged her hand back into the mysterious depths of the diaper bag. Her fingers brushed against something familiar. The binky. *The binky.* She dramatically pulled the pacifier from its hiding spot, yanking her cell phone out right along with it. It fell noiselessly onto the carpet and lay unseen, hidden by the overturned lamp. She popped the binky into Nell's open mouth and hurriedly locked the door behind them.

As the elevator doors rumbled closed and lifted the two to street level, Giselle's cell phone struggled, its battery dying, to emit the latest song Zivi had programmed into the ringtone. But in truth, it could have been blaring all the music of the New York Philharmonic, because there was no one in the apartment to hear it.

Flushed and sticky, Giselle traded the humidity of the day for the dry swelter of Papa Vinny's. The arid heat of the place, fed by four large pizza ovens, was stifling. A thin layer of flour dusted the counter and hung suspended around the pizza station, before dissipating into the hot fragrant air. One inadequate air conditioner, inexpertly wedged into a jagged hole cut into the wall above the front door, dripped water and complained loudly. As a large dollop of condensation splashed onto Giselle's cheek, she proudly noted that Zivi could have installed that unit a thousand times more professionally and tinkered with it until it hummed with cooling precision. Then she remembered she was furious with him.

Exhausted from the tremendous effort it had taken to get there, Giselle stumbled into the booth next to Sabrina, Ethan and Martin, and braced herself for the imminent verbal onslaught. She tried to recall what on earth she was thinking when she had made this dinner arrangement.

Her stomach growled angrily. "Sorry I'm late."

"No prob," said Sabrina. "We just had to start without you, is all. Ethan was hungry. He loves his 'za, that's for sure. He's happy happy once he gets his pizza."

Ethan was completely absorbed in picking up and squishing, with his little grease-laden hands, every piece of cut up pizza on his plate. Then his attention turned to pulverizing each bit into his face, clothes and hair. Anywhere but his mouth. Sabrina looked at her son in wonder, as if she had never seen anything so adorable in her whole life.

"Bet you never seen anything so adorable in your whole life as that boy with his food. I could just eat him up all by myself. Look! Look how he just missed his mouth! Look, Giselle! Isn't he just the *cutest?*"

"The cutest," agreed Giselle, nodding. *Note to self*, she thought. *Keep all opinions regarding Nell's adorable eating habits private.*

Sabrina reached across the table and tapped her boyfriend's hand. "Martin," she said. He appeared not to hear. She tapped harder. "Martin! I was just showing Giselle how cute Ethan is when he's eating."

"What?" Martin's eyes were glued to the television set hanging above the food prep area.

"I was just telling Giselle..." Sabrina gave him a swift kick under the table to get his attention, but it still didn't work.

"*Martin!*"

"*What!?!*"

"I was just telling Giselle to watch Ethan eat!"

"Sabrina, please. I'm watching the game." He distractedly picked Ethan up off the bench and sat his son on his lap. Giselle watched as he gently stroked his little boy's head. Then Ethan began grinding the remaining pieces of pizza into his father's arm. Martin, riveted to the TV, seemed oblivious.

Sabrina rolled her eyes and turned back to Giselle. "So, how ya been, girlfriend? I'm glad you called. It got me thinking. We should start hanging out more, you and me, getting together for dinner and what not, you know? Martin, he's never around, and I bet we got a lot in common, you and me, you know?"

Nell suddenly grew tired of her binky, spat it out, and started wailing for her mother's breast. Giselle used the commotion as an excuse not to answer. Nell shrieked impatiently.

"It's okay. I'm right here," whispered Giselle.

Cradling Nell's head in her hand, Giselle slowly and carefully brought the baby to her chest. Nell's lids slid shut and Giselle felt the baby's body dissolve from a tense, rigid ball into a soft, relaxed bundle. Giselle, too, closed her eyes, spending the next few minutes in her most favorite meditative place: visualizing love flowing from her own body and into her baby.

"Sabrina, why'd you never feed my baby like that?" demanded Martin.

"What're you talking about? Nobody hangs on my titty like that." Sabrina shook her head. "I already told you, I'm not fond of you going after me like that. Why, can you imagine me, Sabrina..."

The bus boy delivered Giselle's dinner and she searched for some distraction from their idiotic bickering. The TV set caught her eye. The post-game show was winding up, and an announcer was previewing the stories from the local news, coming up right after the next round of commercials. She was just able to catch part of one of the last headlines.

"...continue to update you on the police progress in finding the missing baby snatched so brutally from its mother three months ago in Central Park..."

The blood drained from Giselle's face. Did she hear it right? Of course she did. There was no mistake. Zivi stole Nell. *Of course* he did. The baby *had* to have come from somewhere. *Of course* she did. There was a mother, a father, a family out there somewhere, looking for her. And if they were looking for her, of course the police were involved. *Of course* they were. That's why Zivi had worked so hard to convince her that Nell was now theirs. Because they had to be convincing. They *couldn't* mess up. The police were out there. *Looking*. Looking for liars. Looking for baby thieves. And if they got caught, they would both go away to prison. *Of course, of course, of course*. Giselle had almost forgotten the truth, she had played the 'she's ours now' game so well. But how *could* she have? How *could* she have done that? What in the world had she been thinking? But now, after all this time, how could she ever give Nell back? But wait. *Wait*. The announcer said *'progress.'* Were the police closing in on them? Was one of them right here, right now, in the pizzeria? Were any of these people undercovers, watching her, waiting for her to slip up? Giselle looked around wildly. The blood thumped in her temples. The moisture vanished from her mouth and she couldn't swallow.

In a daze, she turned her attention back to the TV. Took a bite of her pizza. They had lowered the volume, but she could just make out what the reporter was saying.

"...violently taken from her as she was finishing her usual morning jog in Central Park on June 5th."

Then a woman came on the screen, eyes red and swollen

from crying, gasping for breath between quiet sobs. In her hands she held a picture of a newborn Nell, just as she had looked when Zivi brought her home. Giselle recognized the woman immediately. They had been in the courtroom together.

It was Gwendolyn Black. Zivi's lawyer.

"All I want is my baby back. I don't know who could have done this to me. Please, I beg you, come forward and give me my baby back. If anyone knows anything. If *anyone* knows who could have done this. *Please.*"

Giselle knew. She knew who did this terrible thing. She knew everything. She and Zivi. They had taken the baby. *His lawyer's baby.* The shock of the revelation made Giselle suck in a sharp gulp of air. The flour floating up from the pizza station got caught in her throat. She began to cough.

All it took was a split second. The pizza in her mouth, the bite she had forgotten to chew, got swept back into her windpipe. And there it stuck. She couldn't breathe. She willed herself not to panic. The noise of her own heart beating and the pounding sensation of the blood coursing through her temples was deafening.

Giselle looked at Sabrina, who was looking at Martin, arguing with him about something else. Giselle's eyes began to water. Her fingers and toes tingled. She knew she had to put Nell somewhere safe before she blacked out. She couldn't believe how clearly she was thinking. Not on the table. *She could fall off.* Not on the bench. *She could fall off.* Giselle felt her eyes losing focus and the lump of pizza hopelessly blocking even the tiniest trickle of air from reaching her lungs. She pulled Nell off her breast and shoved her into Sabrina's arms. Giselle pleaded with her eyes for Sabrina to take care of her baby. Sabrina's mouth stopped moving mid-sentence and her jaw hung open.

"Gis, what are you...?" And then Sabrina must have seen what was happening.

Giselle felt herself sliding down the back of the bench.

"Martin! Help Giselle! She's choking!" screamed Sabrina.

Through eyes half rolled into the top of her head, Giselle could just barely see that Martin was stuck, wedged into the booth beneath Ethan. Frightened by his panicking mother, the toddler held fast to the table with one hand, and to his father's shirt with the other.

The air was getting thicker now, almost viscous. Her eyes filled with water. She had the sensation of her whole body becoming submerged. Giselle tried to move her arms, but it was as if she was deep below the surface and the weight of the water was too heavy to push away. She heard someone, maybe Martin, yell, *"Get an ambulance,"* but the words were garbled and muted, as if they too floated through her underwater world.

"Take her!" Giselle thought she heard Sabrina yell, but she couldn't see anymore. Everything was black. She hoped her precious daughter was safe; she felt embarrassed for leaving the baby in such a way. As she began her final descent, slipping under the table, Giselle was ready to relax and release herself to the unexpected serenity, to the calm darkness of oxygen deprivation. And just as she lost consciousness, Giselle felt the painfully sharp thrusts grabbing her from behind, violently jolting her diaphragm up and in, up and in, up and in, under her ribcage.

Sabrina had one arm around Giselle's shoulders and was gently caressing her hair with the other.

"She's fine. Just needs to rest some," Sabrina was saying.

Giselle struggled to focus her gaze across the table. Nell was perched skillfully and comfortably in Martin's arms, sucking peacefully on Ethan's bottle of apple juice. Ethan sat next to them, mesmerized by the interloper cradled in his father's arms. One bottle of juice won't hurt, Giselle thought, as she closed her eyes and sank back into Sabrina's body.

Seconds later, EMS burst through the door.

"She was choking, but now she's fine." Sabrina stared at the two paramedics. "Don't you think you boys are a little late? I had to do the Heimlich on her myself. If we'd waited for you two to show up, she'd be dead by now."

"Please," broke in one of the paramedics. "If you don't mind, I'd like to ask her a few questions."

Sabrina shrugged.

"Do you know what happened?" the paramedic asked Giselle.

"I ... The TV... The pizza..." An ocean of tears spilled down her face. Giselle couldn't continue.

Annoyed, the medic turned back to Sabrina.

"Go ahead. What happened?"

"Well, we're all eating pizza. And the news comes on. And they start talking about the baby. The one that was kidnapped. And then Giselle here, she heard the story, and she being a new mama and all, everything hits you hard when you get a new baby. Because that's when she choked on the 'za." Sabrina lowered her voice. "That's her baby right there. She was born like, like two weeks after that other baby was." Sabrina shrugged at the obviousness of the situation. "I think she just freaked out when she heard about it and that's how she choked."

"Is that what happened?" he asked Giselle.

Giselle nodded. She felt sick.

"Sweetheart," said Sabrina, patting Giselle's hand. "They don't know anything about that baby kidnapper. Isn't that right?" Sabrina asked no one in particular. "Police telling everyone to hold their little ones tight, though." She shook her head in disgust. "Right in the daylight hours, that crime happens and they have no suspects. How can that be? A monster like that, still on the loose."

"No suspects..." Giselle repeated quietly.

"*Disgusting*," Sabrina said, "To take a baby like that from its mama's arms. And the police, they got no one, nada, nothing..."

The paramedics gave each other a look. "Are you okay?" they asked impatiently. "You don't need to go to the hospital, do you?"

Giselle shook her head. "I'm fine. Thanks," she whispered, afraid to breathe, afraid to do anything that might make them stay and ask more questions.

They turned and headed to the counter. Ordered a couple of slices before they left.

"Sabrina," Giselle said. "You saved my life."

"No problem, girlfriend." Sabrina smiled and blushed down at her dinner. Martin smiled at her proudly.

Giselle grabbed a bunch of napkins and dried her face while she tried to work out the details in her head. First, why hadn't anyone put it together that Nell was the lawyer's missing baby? The woman even held up a picture of Nell when she was a tiny infant. Why hadn't anyone looked at that picture and then looked at Nell and put the two together? Giselle looked over at the baby happily gumming Ethan's bottle as Martin gently rocked her in his arms. Like all babies, Nell's face changed dramatically from week to week. Could it be that her face had changed so much that other people really could not tell that the two were one and the same?

Maybe.

The truth was, Zivi was right. There was absolutely no reason to suspect them. Giselle had been pregnant. Nell was about the same age that their own baby would have been, had she lived. Even her nose was sort of a miniature Zivi nose. She could easily pass as their baby.

Then Giselle's thoughts touched on something else. How could *she* not have heard about that lawyer's baby being kidnapped before today? Stuff like that was always front page of the newspapers, especially the tabloid ones. Giselle thought about that. When was the last time she saw a newspaper, anyway? Not since ... Her hand flew up to her mouth. Not since Zivi brought Nell to her. She never bought the newspaper, he always did. And she suddenly realized Zivi hadn't brought one home in weeks. And she, she *herself*, had taken to crossing the street to avoid walking past newsstands. She'd been afraid, on an unconscious or perhaps even conscience level, that she would accidentally see headlines regarding Nell—of which, now that she allowed herself to think about it, there must have been many.

And the TV. Giselle's mouth slipped open. The day before Nell came, the TV hook-up had gone down in the entire building. A few hours later, Zivi had fixed the connection for all the upper floors, but not for them. He kept saying that he was waiting for a backordered part before he could bring the signal back underground to their apartment ... Slowly, the fog that had settled on her brain began to lift. He did something. He *did* something to the TV so she wouldn't find out.

And what about her phone? There were no apps. *It had no apps!* No news apps, no headline apps, no local alerts. Giselle could barely swallow. She never realized, her brain drowning in hopelessness after Madison, floating among the clouds ever since Nell. All the despair, unconsciousness, excitement, sleep deprivation. She hadn't even realized. Her news apps were gone. *All of them. Gone.* A gasp escaped from her throat.

"Gissy? You okay?" asked Sabrina. "You want me to get those guys back here?"

"No. No," she managed to sputter. "I was just thinking. That's all."

"I bet. Almost choking to death can make a person think a lot of things."

Giselle nodded. Then she reached out her hands toward Martin. "I can take her back now."

"It's okay. You eat. She ain't complaining. I can hold on to her for a few more minutes." He smiled.

She nodded and smiled back. It was a weak smile, but it was the best one she could muster.

For the rest of the meal, they all sat in silence. Even Sabrina had run out of things to say.

As she ate, Giselle realized she was scared. She was in over her head. She needed a fresh start. She needed a clean break.

"Sabrina?" Giselle's voice cracked. "Do you think you and Martin could help me out with one more thing? Can you help me carry some boxes back to my apartment?"

"'Course we can, sweetie. There's no way I'm letting you go home alone after what just happened. I'm not letting you out of my sight."

Giselle was grateful; she was completely exhausted, so weak in fact, that this time she strapped Nell into the stroller instead of the pack.

"You know, Gis," Sabrina was saying, "my mama, to this day, she always telling me to chew my food real good. And I say, Mama, what's the matter with you? You don't have to tell me that. Nothing's gonna happen to me. I'm a grown woman. But you know what? She's right. Accidents happen *by accident*. That's why they're called accidents in the first place. Now, take Martin. If you wanna talk about chewing, that's one *huge* accident just waiting to happen..."

CHAPTER TWENTY-TWO

ZIVI AND GWENDOLYN

Hordes of well-heeled professionals streamed into Grand Central Terminal. Indigenous New Yorkers instinctively followed Urban Darwinian Code, ensuring the greatest odds of maneuvering the granite caverns of the station in one piece and with all personal belongings intact. Survival depended upon suppressing demonstrations of weakness, e.g. gawking, loitering, or otherwise revealing oneself as lost, vulnerable or, worse yet, a tourist.

Natives wore 'street face,' a slightly annoyed, defiant expression. Moreover, real New Yorkers carried all manner of shopping bags, totes or purses tightly against their bodies. All clasps firmly secured by zipper or buckle. Velcro, magnets, or other half-hearted suburban fasteners were nothing more than invitations for trouble.

Finally, the Code incorporated the principle of selective deafness. A seasoned commuter will never hear, much less stop to answer, a ringing payphone. So, when one of the last such remaining antiquated communication devices, specifically the fourth from the right of the northeast entrance of Grand Central Terminal, sprang to life, no one picked it up.

Until Zivi burst through the streaming crowd and grabbed the receiver. Instinctively, the crowd shifted to give him the room he needed to conduct his nefarious affairs because, under Urban Darwinian Law, anyone receiving calls on a public payphone is, by definition, up to no good.

"*Yes*," he panted, "I am here."

Silence.

"*Hello?*"

Silence

"Are you there?"

"You *motherfucker*," she hissed.

Her throaty, icy voice was so full of venom that it made Zivi smile. He hadn't heard her orneriness for almost a year. He could just about feel her forked tongue searching and prodding for him through the telephone line.

"Hey, cookie! What is up?" he asked, with the exaggerated enthusiasm she hated.

"Don't give me what's up," she snapped. "How the hell could you do this to me?"

"Do what, pussycat?" Teasing her used to be one of his favorite pastimes.

"Zivi, don't give me that shit or I swear I'll kill you." She was so angry her voice was trembling. "I'm not kidding. I'm at the end of my rope and I'm not prepared to take any more of your crap."

"*Oooohh.* And here I thought everything was *just peachy*. But no. Instead, you are mighty pissed off, yes?" He smiled.

"I'm *pissed off??* Pissed off doesn't even *begin* to explain the way I'm feeling." He knew her ears were all hot and prickly; he could hear it in her voice.

"All right. All right. I am just busting chops. Just having a little fun. That is not a crime now too, is it?"

No answer.

"So, what *is* up?" he needled. "Why did you call me? It wasn't exactly, uh, how do I say it, the best of timing."

"Poor you," she snarled. "Things haven't exactly been the best of *timing* for me either, lately."

"All right, all right, cupcake. Chill out." He was enjoying this. "I am just making conversation, you know. Lightening mood."

He thought he heard her growl.

"How has the past year been treating you? Do much running lately?"

"I didn't call you to talk about my running."

Zivi laughed. "I *bet* you didn't."

"Cut the small talk."

"Fine, princess. It is considered cut."

"Do you have *any* idea—"

But just then, the antiquated loudspeaker interrupted her, crackling to life and reverberating throughout the cavernous rotunda. "THE The HUDSON Hudson RIVER River LINE Line IS is EXPERIENCING experiencing DELAYS delays…"

"Gwendolyn, cookie. I cannot hear you." But he could tell that she couldn't hear him, either. Which was fine. Let her begin the endless tirade headed his way, which wouldn't blow off even a fraction of the steam she had bottled up especially for him.

"…nothing more than the disgusting street criminal you are…"

He knew it.

"If it wasn't for *me* and what I did for *you*, you would still be…"

He held the phone away from his ear to give the echoing announcement time to pass before he would try interrupting again.

"TRACK track FIRE fire EXPECT expect EXTENSIVE extensive DELAYS delays..."

He turned back to the phone.

"Gwen. This is ridiculous. I cannot hear..."

And then he stopped to listen. Because suddenly he *could* hear. The *same* announcement, with the *same* echoes, through the *same* receiver in which Gwendolyn was blathering at him, *at the same time.*

"That bitch," he whispered. She was there, right now, somewhere in the station. Probably looking right at him.

He did a slow 360, searching around the landmark brass commuter clock, scoping the smattering of phones on the second floor. Nothing. He turned back, repeating the exercise, landscape constantly changing through the heavy flow of humanity until, finally, he saw her. At the phone bank across the atrium, on the upper level in front of her favorite coffee shop. Zivi laughed out loud. As usual, her arms were gesticulating wildly, carrying on in her own special style of over-the-top histrionics.

"Perfect." She was so consumed with her vitriol that she wasn't paying attention to him at all.

He returned the phone to its cradle. Made his way up the steps, across the balcony and over to where she continued her tirade, still oblivious to the fact that the line had gone dead.

He stood behind her, remembering.

The way her auburn hair would fall into his face. The way her powerful leg muscles held him in their ironclad grip. The way the angular cuts of her biceps had hugged him in chiseled perfection. Her beautiful face. But most of all, it was her intellect. He could talk to her about almost anything. She was sexy, unpredictable dynamite. Always seconds away from exploding. Not long ago, they had a perfect arrangement, fulfilling the other's unspoken needs. But she had too many rules. No public contact. No connections. And most of all, never, *ever* be seen together. Eventually, the relationship imploded from the weight of its own complications. And now, here they were, reduced to stalking each other in the caverns of Grand Central Terminal.

He savored the last moments before all hell broke loose.

Finally, he reached out and ran his fingertips across her shoulder. She spun, ready to punch whoever it was that had the audacity to touch her. And then she saw it was him.

He smelled the caramel infusion of her double skinny mocha *con leche* as it left her perfectly manicured hand and rode the damp, humid cushion of air before crashing at their feet.

Her mouth hung open, the receiver dangling in the air.

"You are slipping, cutie," he said. "I thought you had the whole poker-face thing down much better than that."

"You son-of-a-bitch," she managed to choke out.

"Sshhh, Gwen. Sshhh."

"Don't you *ever* sshhh me!" she sputtered.

"Take it easy."

But she was already swinging.

"I hate you. I *HATE* you!"

The theme of the day, he thought, and tried to block her punches, catch the flailing haymakers that seemed to be coming at him from all directions. A long time ago she had taken a few Systema classes with him, but she was too running-centric to modify her rigid workout schedule.

"I cannot believe ... how much you remember ... If only you kept going ... you could have been ... really good." He tried to distract her, as he struggled to contain her blows.

"Don't talk to me. *I hate you.*"

Finally, he just reached out, put his arms around her, and

reeled her in tight. She was panting so hard that Zivi thought she might hyperventilate.

"Sssshhh," he whispered again and this time she listened.

She stopped struggling and tilted her head back to look at him. He met her gaze. Stared into her eyes, which he knew always changed color in the sunlight. He felt her heart fluttering against his pounding chest. Slowly, he lowered his head. As naturally as breathing, their lips brushed once, brushed again, then came together. Passion and desire, once forcibly smothered, reignited in the space of a second. Zivi eased his tongue into her mouth. Was seduced by the titillating tang of her damp perspiration. He closed his eyes and he was home.

As for Gwendolyn, she simply went limp in his arms and then seemed to hang on for dear life.

"Just tell me one thing," he whispered in her ear. "She is my baby, yes?"

Zivi held his breath. He felt the muscles of Gwen's back go rigid as he counted seven long seconds ticking by.

"*Of course she's your baby, you idiot*," Gwendolyn pushed him away. "How many fuck buddies do you think I have time for?"

"*I knew it!*" Zivi threw his fist in the air in a victory punch. Of course, he always knew it. She always told him there was never anyone else. He never would have done it if he didn't think it was so. And the day after he got Nell home, he did a home paternity test. But that was only 99.999% accurate. He needed to hear Gwen's confirmation to close that .001% gap. And now he finally knew. For sure.

"Fuck you." She sounded exhausted.

"Sure did miss your mouth, tiger." He grinned. "For such a highly educated hoity-toity legal person you have quite the, how do you say it, potty mouth, yes?" He was fully embracing that tuff-guy-Bosnian-drug-dealer accent Gwendolyn found so sexy.

"How *dare* you. Where do *you* come off judging *me*? *I'm* the one who should be judging *you*."

He smirked. Sometimes riling her up was too damn easy. Hardly even a challenge.

Gwen closed the gap between them, conscious of being overheard. "Why did you do it?" she whispered angrily. "To fuck with me? To hurt me?"

"Of course not. I never want to hurt you. You know that."

"Then why?"

"I did it because I had to."

"Just so you know, I was really, *really* scared. At first, I didn't even realize—"

"No, tiger." He put his hands on her shoulders and looked her in the face. She had forgotten how intensely dark his eyes were. "I didn't want you to be scared. I gave you the sign. From the back of the truck. You saw it, yes?"

Gwendolyn stiffened. "Did you even bother to think who *else* may have seen your inane little sign? Try *four other witnesses*, Zivi. And they said, each and every one of them said to the police, that it looked like you were using some sort of secret sign language or something."

"Oh, come on."

"It took me days to convince the cops that it was just some kind of spastic fit from a lunatic kidnapper. That there was no way it was a message anyone in their right mind could understand. Then they decided it must be some street gang initiation thing and that this was going to be the beginning of some great baby kidnapping outbreak." She frowned. "Those detectives, they're not all idiots. Why would you do that? Why would you risk it?"

"You know, in all the time we were together, you never listened to me." There was an edge to his voice. "I just *said* to you. I act out of con-sid-er-a-tion. So-you-would-know-it-is-

Zivi." He glared at her. "I did not want you to actually have to worry about her."

"Oh, *pu-lease*."

He lowered his voice. "Look, I could not exactly jump out of bushes and yell, '*Surprise! It is me! I am here to grab my baby!*' This thing must look real, to work. You would yell my name, or you would not have resisted enough, or something happens to ruin the whole thing before it even happens."

"Yeah. I would have hated to ruin your brilliant plan before it had a chance to get off the ground," she sneered. "And if the whole thing was a big act, why did your guy have to beat the shit out of me?"

"Sorry about that. He was not supposed to hurt you. All I told him was keep it real. He is one of my best soldiers. I trust him with my life. Actually..." He looked at her sideways. "I may have said you are type to fight back. And the thing was, we must do it quick, quick, quick. I told him to nip all problems in the bud. I guess he got carried away, eh? I am very sorry about that. But you are okay now, yes?"

Gwendolyn thought about all the reasons she was still furious at him.

"Gwen?"

"What is it?"

"I am wondering. What did you tell them?"

"I told *them*, the cops, that is, that your stupid, hideous, Bosnian, gang-scarred, pock-marked, bleeding skull-and-cross tattooed, partially shaven, broken nosed, chipped tooth, pierced tongue, reeking of garlic and cumin motherfucking soldier put a cheap Duane Reade stocking over his head so I couldn't ID him."

"*Nyet.*" He didn't seem to appreciate that, once again, she had hindered a police investigation on his behalf. "No. What did you tell everyone about being pregnant?"

"Nothing."

He bristled. "What does this mean, '*nothing*?'"

"I said nothing. That it was some guy I broke up with and didn't want on the birth certificate."

"And they left it at that? They do not press you for a name?"

"Well, there was no reason to press, until you grabbed the damn baby. Then I had to come up with something fast. I said I had a million bleary-eyed, drunken one-night stands."

"And they buy this? You, *a drunk*? And wait." He raised his voice. "You—you change the story?" And now he was nearly shouting. "Why the fuck could you not tell them you are goddammed slut the first time around?"

She was completely taken aback by his reaction, but even more alarmed by all the people who were now turning to stare at the enraged hulking man with long wild hair looming menacingly over the much smaller woman.

And *shit*.

There was always the slim chance that the buffoon Gary DelVeccio, who had been trailing her during her run and watching when she got into the cab, might be lurking in the station somewhere. She had insisted the cabbie speed, even paid him extra to blow through the red lights and take a convoluted route. Still, it was within the realm of possibility that she hadn't actually shaken him.

Gwendolyn understood she was completely exhausted, a hair's breadth away from a nervous breakdown and maybe, just maybe, her razor-sharp common sense had gone blunt on her. But she missed Zivi completely, had been literally *aching* to see him. Just to look at him again, even from afar, from across the atrium, would have been sufficient. And those detectives were proving none too swift. So, she had taken a chance. She had done something wild and risked it. Her life was spiraling out of control anyway. She never dreamed Zivi would close the distance and be standing before her. And now it was too late to do anything about it.

"Shut up. What the hell is the matter with you?" she whispered at him, then smiled at the gawking idiots walking by. "Okay. I changed the story. But what was I supposed to say, with the detectives chomping for a name?" Sometimes he was so fucking *facile*. "Oh, yes, everybody. This disgusting, big fat belly? It's nothing, really. Just the result of a huge illicit affair I had with my *drug dealer client*. You know the one. The one I *perjured myself for* and *risked my law license* to get off from his *third consecutive felony wrap*? Exactly. That's the one. *The one who said he loved me.*"

"*HEY!* Back up. I never, *ever* say I love you." She was pleased to see the veins in his neck dance. "Damn it!" He poked his finger inches from her face. "We both know that for fact."

Again, people slowed to stare, to overhear bits and pieces of a far juicier conversation than their own. At least she didn't see DelVeccio's face among them.

"Oh, for Christ's sake. Calm down. Let's go outside and walk or something. Keep moving. Someone's liable to overhear us if we keep standing here."

"Heaven forbid." He was livid. "It is *you* who could never be seen in public with *me*, yes? Now suddenly you want to walk in middle of Manhattan? Fine. *I* certainly do not give a shit."

"I'll leave at Vanderbilt, you leave on 42nd," she instructed. "I'll meet you at the south-east corner of Madison and 39th. Don't dawdle."

He stormed down the grand staircase and across the main concourse before disappearing into the crowd. They met up at the appointed corner and marched silently down Madison

Avenue. Every ten or fifteen steps she craned her neck around—sometimes casually, other times abruptly—to see if the boneheaded cop might inadvertently reveal himself. Eventually, she was convinced they were alone in the sea of strangers.

"A million drunken one-night stands, eh?"

"You should be thanking me. I sacrificed my reputation in exchange for them begging off the name-game. Show some gratitude."

"Do not lecture me."

They continued their trek.

"But once you gave birth, why didn't they swab her for DNA? Run a computer and come up with match?" As they walked the need to make himself sexy dissipated, and his Bosnian accent slipped away.

"I refused to consent. Said I didn't need to know which one-nighter fathered my child. I wanted to raise her as a single mother. Case closed." Gwendolyn sighed. "Relax. Obviously, the last thing I want is for them to ID you and link us."

Another four or five blocks passed. This time, Gwendolyn broke the silence.

"Now I have one for you."

"What?"

"How did you know I was pregnant?"

"One day you love me and can't live without me, next day you never want to see me again? Something was up. I had to make sure you were all right."

"You spied on me?" She was simultaneously appalled and flattered.

"You better believe it." Now he smiled as they walked. "Every morning, exactly seven fifteen, you run up the hill by the Great Lawn." He clucked his tongue. "You looked good, though. Didn't show until the seventh month. But I knew right away. Just a couple of weeks and you lost that spring in your step.

Every couple of days I would go watch. Just to keep tabs on my baby, you know?"

"That's funny. I thought I was just getting run-down. I didn't know until I went to the gyno at twelve weeks. I missed two periods, but I didn't put it together. Because they're so irregular."

He slipped his hand over hers, causing nerve endings to tingle. "You are completely out of touch with yourself. I know you, *knew* you, better than you know you. I made it my business. Your body. It was my business."

She leaned up against him as they walked.

"Plus, I knew it was something very serious for you to break it off so suddenly. Given how much you were addicted to me. Or parts of me."

"No." She swallowed hard. "I loved all of you."

He scowled. "Loved me and were embarrassed by me."

"Yeah, but ... but when you told me you were starting to see someone else..." Gwendolyn turned away.

"I thought that was what you wanted!" Gwen heard his frustration and knew it was true. At the time, it *was* what she'd wanted him to do.

But when he did it, she hated it.

He squeezed her hand then brought it up to his lips and kissed it. Suddenly, she had a sore throat.

"But nothing changed between us, did it, tiger?" he asked. "Everything was still just peachy, no?" The little maxim they used to mean their relationship was exactly as they wanted it. "We never stop seeing each other because of her, right?"

Gwendolyn tried not to blink, looked up at the sky, so the water filling her eyes could dry up before it slid down her face.

"You said it yourself. I am your client. If anyone knew about us, suspected the things you did, you would be disbarred. End up in jail."

"I always hated that that's how it had to be."

"I could never be a part of your life," he said, and she knew it was true.

They continued on, lost in their own heads.

"What I don't understand," he finally said, "is why you decided to go through with it. With your career and schedule and running and health clubs and everything else you have going on."

"I don't know. God knows, I tried. I tried and I tried and I tried." She frowned. "But it was your baby. *Our* baby. Every day, when I looked at my disgusting fat belly and how it was growing bigger and bigger and I was so repulsed by its size, I knew you were with me. It gave me the strength to go on. I thought of it like some sort of spiritual umbilical cord—"

"Stop," he interrupted. "Right now, you are making me sick. It is *me*, not some gullible jury you are preaching to. And I don't accept any of this crap. You expect me to believe the fairytale that there was a little bit of me inside of you and that's what kept you going?" He smirked. "*Nyet*. You do not have capacity for that kind of depth of feeling. You shut down and shut out long before you could ever even approach needing another human being to complete your emotional needs. Not ten minutes ago I was nothing more than a 'fuck buddy.' So let us not kid ourselves. Let's bring this conversation back to *some* semblance of reality."

"I lied."

"You lied?" He stumbled backward, feigning heart failure. "And you admit to it? My only question is, which part? Which part of which lie are you ready to own up to?"

"The fuck buddy part." She swallowed. "You always meant way more to me than that."

"Oh, no! Not you too." Zivi slung his arm across her shoulders. "Please don't get all misty on me, tiger. It is not like you. If there is one thing I could always count on, it was my ice princess and her unswerving commitment to emotional detachment."

"What does that mean?"

"Nothing. Trust me, darlin'." He squeezed her shoulders. "Just don't go undermining my whole Gwendolyn Black belief system by crying at me right now. My plate is already full in that department."

She was quite certain she didn't want to know what that meant.

Soon, the warehouses and sample-sale houses of the garment district, the benignly upscale buildings around Madison Square Park and the breathtaking illusion of the Flatiron Building, were behind them. They took Fifth Avenue to West 8th and traversed the streets of Greenwich Village, passing college students, twenty-something punks and a sampling of trendy middle-aged hipsters.

"God, I'm hungry," she said, and her stomach growled. "I don't even remember the last time I ate."

"As I remember, when you last ate does not necessarily have anything to do with whether or not you're hungry."

"Yeah. Well, I still have issues."

"Come on," he blurted out with the boyish coquettishness that made him even cuter and even sexier, if that was even possible, than he already was. "I take you to dinner. I mean, since we have busted the 'never be seen in public together' mantra to smithereens, what the hell, eh?"

She let him lead. It didn't matter where he was taking her. Just being with him was enough. She had forgotten that he was her pillar of objective intelligence and common sense, her strength, her danger, her gorgeous eye-candy, her incredible sex. She had forgotten the reasons she depended on him and how much she missed him. She used to cling to the notion that she would lose everything if she was ever seen with him. Suddenly, it seemed, none of that mattered. She reached for his hand and snuggled in close to his body.

"Easy, now," he said. "Let's not go too wild."

She didn't much care what he was saying. Her mind was set. She was going to get him back. He just didn't know it yet.

He walked her past the Cherry Lane Theater and prayed that the Chinese joint tucked into the ground floor space of an adjoining brownstone was still in business. It was his favorite place to take a break back in his former life when he used to run product in the area. As he remembered it, the food was good, the room was dark, and the proprietors minded their own business.

Zivi led her into the dimly lit restaurant. The air was warm and fragrant with garlic, ginger and a mystery of simmering exotic spices. Just as he had hoped, it was far too early for the neighborhood to be eating dinner; except for one of the two choice tables near the front windows, the place was empty. A tiny ancient woman with her hair wound up in a bun adorned with intricately inlaid chopsticks emerged from behind the black velvet curtains at the far side of the dining room. She smiled.

"Table for two?"

"In the back, please," said Zivi.

She brought them iced green tea and two voluminous menus, filled with traditional Chinese-American fare as well as pages of unusual authentic dishes virtually unheard of outside of Chinatown. As they silently studied the vast range of choices, Zivi was acutely aware that sitting together in a public space was a dramatic first. Eventually, the old woman materialized again. Zivi looked questioningly at Gwendolyn.

"I guess I'll have the steamed vegetables, sauce on the side. Brown rice."

He rolled his eyes. Same as her takeout orders. He opted for an unpronounceable seafood dish.

Gwendolyn stood. "I'm going to find the ladies' room."

He raised his eyebrows.

"Don't worry. I couldn't even if I wanted to. I haven't eaten in over four hours." Then she disappeared behind the big black velvet curtain.

Zivi snatched the phone from his pocket. He owed Giselle numerous explanations, none of which he had time for at the moment, but the least he could do was tell her that everything was all right, to grab something to eat without him, and that he would be home soon. And, oh, yes. That he loved her. He loved her more than ever and was thinking about her.

The phone continued ringing until her voicemail picked up. He frowned. That was odd. They always carried their phones. It was essential that they be able to speak to each other all the time, at any time. There was no telling what some insane, deranged, psychopathic lunatic might do to her. Just as he was starting to get the bad feeling, unable to come up with a single explanation for why she did not pick up, the big black curtain swished open. He slipped the phone back into his pocket.

CHAPTER TWENTY-THREE

DELVECCIO AND MCMILLAN

"You will never fucking believe what's going on here."

Brian McMillan proffered a guess. "My life expectancy decreases each time I talk to you?"

"She's on a payphone, *a payphone*, on the second level in the atrium, when this guy comes up from behind."

McMillan clapped his hands. "I knew it! They set her up so the runner can make contact."

"That's what I thought, too."

"But?"

"But he taps her on the shoulder, she's shocked, her coffee goes flying ... and she starts trying to beat the shit outta this guy."

"Jesus Christ." McMillan leaned against the desk. "Did anyone do anything?"

"No," said DelVeccio, "because things got real weird, real fast."

"*Because?*"

"Because," DelVeccio paused, "the next second, the two of them are sucking face like they've been doing it for years."

"Fuck." The air deflated from McMillan's chest. "Then it wasn't about a ransom."

"I highly doubt it."

"Then what?"

"They argued a bit, left separately, then met up again."

"And now?" asked McMillan.

"I'm about three quarters of a block back."

The conversation paused to allow a fire engine to wail its way past.

"Brian?"

"Yeah?"

"They're holding hands."

"Ooh. She has a boyfriend after all. Or maybe—*hey*. Maybe it's the *father*."

"The lucky one in that long line of drunken one-nighters?"

McMillan slapped his desk. "Exactly."

"Six-one, two-ten, left bicep tat, could be gang. Long wild hair. Frankly, doesn't look like the safe kind of total stranger I would imagine our lily-white going home from a bar with."

"You got no fucking idea what type she'd go home from a bar with. I'm on it."

CHAPTER TWENTY-FOUR

ZIVI AND GWENDOLYN

Like the cleaned-up drug addict convinced he can handle one snort of cocaine, the former alcoholic certain one social drink won't hurt, or the recovered smoker whose one borrowed puff doesn't count, Zivi's craving was no less insidious. It was adrenalin. The adrenalin rush that surged through his nervous system as he packaged up all his hopes and dreams and needlessly tiptoed on a tightrope suspended high above a bottomless pit of needless risk, a rocky abyss waiting to shatter his precious bundle into a million tiny pieces. If he went too long without it, he found himself craving the high, looking for challenges that would surely endanger whatever was currently good in his life.

Running his fingers over white powder bricks worth tens of thousands, *hundreds* of thousands of dollars, proximity to preposterously powerful weapons—these were the things that made his heart sing. He personally would never, ever use the junk or shoot the guns, having too often witnessed the damage they inflicted. But the poor souls whose lives were held captive by a small glassine envelope of chemicals? They would get their fix from somewhere, anywhere. If not from him, it would definitely be from the next guy. He wasn't proud of it, but it paid the bills. And at times, they had been substantial.

Zivi broke his life into two simple halves. Business—and everything else. The law provided that irresistible danger, the constant threat to his profession. As for the poisonous attraction, which jeopardized the 'everything else' part? That was obvious. It was Gwendolyn Black. He knew he was a fool. Gwen—powerful, unpredictable, uncontrollable, jealous and vengeful—could bring a swift end to his entire existence in a matter of moments.

He watched her, silhouetted against the black curtain. She had changed out of her running shirt into a pastel sweater set that obscured the hard, aggressive angles of the body underneath. As she sauntered back to him, he hardly had enough time to think through all the decisions he now had to make.

Gwendolyn walked to his side of the table and kissed him. She wanted it to be an aggressive move. As she gently pulled at his lower lip with her teeth, Gwen wanted to see if he was up to the challenge, if he was willing to kiss her back. He tugged deliciously at her tongue. Then he slipped his fingers through her hair and held her ear next to his mouth.

"I saw them leave," he whispered, referring to the other customers, who had departed while she was in the restroom.

Gwendolyn looked at him quizzically, as if she had no idea what he was talking about. She would have to tread lightly; he was not as easily fooled, nor could he be as easily manipulated, as other men she'd bedded.

They sat in silence. He put his hand over hers, traced her veins with his big calloused fingers. Gwen watched her expensive manicure disappear under his leathered workman's palm and wondered how her craving for this person, who was completely off-limits in every way, could be so total and consuming. He caught her gaze and they stayed that way, eyes locked, until the Chinese woman had delivered their food and retreated backstage.

He picked up a pair of chopsticks, peeled back the paper wrapper, and held them across the table to her.

"You just don't get it," he said between bites, shoveling it in as if he hadn't seen a decent meal in months. "The food in this place is great. I am sure they don't make authentic Chinese like this in your *super cool* neighborhood." He smiled that stupid, ignorant, irresistible, gorgeous little boy grin and leaned over the table toward her.

"Don't be shy. Splash some of that spectacular 'sauce on side' right on top of ever so boring tofu and veggies."

She watched, mortified, as he sloshed more than half of the grease-laden sauce on top of her naked low-cal vegetables. She cringed, watching helplessly as he mixed it all up, contaminating the entire plate of perfectly good food.

"I am sure it will be the best you've ever had. And now *I* am going to eat my meal just as if *I* was normal person. Watch how it is done. Then you can copy me and pretend like *you* are normal person too."

He turned back to his dwindling pile of food. She could not bring herself to eat; being back in his presence made her too nervous. For the first time that she could remember, she was happy. Until that moment, she hadn't realized how much she had missed him, and this time she knew it was more than just his body. Unlike those other men who were put off or intimidated, he was never afraid to challenge her, to laugh at her, to insult her. He had stroked her in ways she would never allow another human being to touch her; he had made love to her in ways she had never before imagined.

She remembered back to all the times they had lay in bed

together for hours, discussing the most important and mundane issues with equal fire. He was her intellectual soulmate and she tried very hard to remember why it had been so important for her to let him go. The answer was there somewhere in her head, elusively flitting about, but she was in no mood to focus in and catch it.

And now they had a child together. How *convenient*. He'd always spoken of being a simple family man at heart. Now, it wouldn't be too difficult to convince him that it was all right there—beside him. She dug in and thoroughly enjoyed the best Chinese food she'd ever had.

"I'm glad you ate."

"You were right. It was delicious." She placed her hand on the table so that her fingers brushed his. "No surprise. You're usually right."

Zivi lifted one eyebrow. "Stop trying so hard. It doesn't become you."

She blushed.

He opened his mouth to speak and then thought better of it. He had to be sure to approach it in the right way. It was important that they discussed it calmly, not with her flying off the handle like some kind of lunatic. She nodded a slight nod of encouragement and gave his fingers a light squeeze.

"Gwen?"

"Yes?"

"Gwendolyn." He struggled with how to start. It would be best if he could do it simply.

"It's okay." She patted his hand. "Whatever it is. You can say it."

"I want to talk about the baby."

"The baby?" She seemed stunned. She drew her arms back and crossed them around her waist. "The baby."

"Yeah."

"Oh. I thought you might want to talk about us."

"No. Not us. The baby. I want to talk about baby." He did his best to sound firm, without being aggressive or threatening.

"I can do that." She cleared her throat and sat up stiffly. "What about the baby?"

"I want her."

"You? Okay, I guess," she said, and Zivi could tell her mind was scrambling. "We'll share her." She nodded. "We'll raise her together."

"No. You don't understand. I *want* her. For my own. Just me. No strings attached."

"What?" She stared in disbelief. "Are you joking?" The smile on her face was obviously fake. She was rattled. "You're a thug. A frigging drug dealer for God's sake."

"Gone straight."

"No." She shook her head emphatically. "No *way*. She needs a mother figure. I'm her mother. She needs me to be her mother."

"Let's be real and talk calmly and rationally. And let's be honest." He took a deep breath. "The fact is, you are about the worst example of a mother figure I can think of."

"What the hell are you talking about? How could you possibly know what kind of a mother figure I am?" she whisper-yelled. "You've never even *seen* me with her. Where do you come off—?"

"I do not *need* to see you with her," he whisper-yelled back, "to see what kind of a mother figure you are." He squeezed his lips thin. "I can tell everything by the way you have been acting for the past three months," he said, incensed. "If you are such a great mother, why the hell didn't you ever pick up phone? Why did it take until today? You knew it was me who took her from day one. You could have picked up phone. You could have said, '*Give me back my kid, you prick.*' You could even have turned me in! But you didn't. Why not?"

She opened her mouth to answer, but he wouldn't let her speak. "I will *tell* you why not. Because you didn't want her back. *That's* why not." His voice cracked. "Because you *did not want her back*." He shook his head; he still couldn't quite believe the enormity of it. "You were *glad* I took her." He stared at her, trying to read some kind of emotion behind those steely eyes. "You did not even pick up the phone to see how she was doing. Let's be honest. The whole motherhood thing. It is just not you."

He had to press his thumb and forefinger into his eye sockets before he could continue.

"You haven't even asked me how she is, how she's doing." He looked around the restaurant and then back at her. "All this time we've been together. Walking all the way from Grand Central. Eating an entire dinner. You never even asked how she's doing."

He could not believe he had to spell it out for her.

"Please. I'm begging you." Zivi leaned his arms heavily across the table. "Just for appearance's sake. Just *ask* me. Ask me how she is. Ask me how my little girl, how my beautiful baby girl, is doing."

"How's she doing?"

"She is amazing. She is great. She is smart. She is healthy. She is beautiful. She is awesome." His voice was quivering.

"Cut the drama," she snapped. "Of *course* I give a shit. It's just that I knew you would take care of her." She shrugged. "So, I wasn't really worried. That's why I never called. And I didn't want to get you in trouble. I didn't want them to be able to connect you—"

"Save it. We left no prints. We changed vehicles three times. There was no way of connecting me and you, and you knew it."

Zivi sat back and crossed his arms.

"I think you were plain relieved I took her. I think you were glad to be rid of her and that is why you never called." There was no denying it. It was *obvious*. "All that was left for you to do was to come up with plausible version of why she was gone that didn't include me."

He smirked.

"She must have been the needy little monster you were always afraid of. Something that couldn't care less about your ridiculous work schedule, your endless exercising, your inane binges and seventeen trips to the bathroom to puke your guts up. Poor you."

Gwendolyn cleared her throat. "Let's just put aside what I may or may not have been thinking when you arranged for my baby to be violently snatched from me." Her voice was composed. "Let's focus on what we do now, moving forward. What do we do next?"

He tried to protest, but she did not stop. The question, apparently, was rhetorical.

"First, for the purposes of this discussion, I'm willing to take it at face value, to accept your word for it, that you actually have, as you said, 'gone straight.'" She sat rigidly upright. "Let's assume that you actually have managed to find some kind of," she made air quotes with her fingers, "honest, legal way of making a living. I'm willing to concede that point for now."

"I'm not interested in what you're willing—"

"It seems to me that the baby, especially because she's a girl, will be in need of a strong maternal figure." He opened his mouth, but she held up her hand and kept going. "Now, again, it seems to me that since *I am* her mother, and you *are* her father, that together we should be able to—"

"She already has a strong mother figure."

"What?"

"I *said*, it is not an issue. She has strong mother figure when she's with me."

"What are you talking about?"

"I am in a relationship," he said, matter-of-factly. "That is how."

"*What?*"

"You heard me. I said, I am in a relationship."

"Oh, come on. You can't be serious." Gwendolyn scowled. "With whom?"

"Nobody you know."

"Who is it?"

"None of your goddamned business. She stays out of this."

A nasty smile crept across her face. "It's that skinny little bimbo you brought to court, who constantly stares at you with those ridiculous puppy dog eyes." She flipped her hand dismissively. "That's nothing more than a fling and you know it. That's never going to last. It's purely physical."

He smirked at the irony of her last statement.

"So, you're not tired of her yet?" Gwendolyn asked, feigning exhaustion. "What's her name again? Some animal. Oh, right. Gazelle."

"*Gis*-elle."

"*What*ever."

"Listen. I'm not in the mood for your games and I guarantee you, I have no sense of humor about any of this right now."

"I am not playing games. I'm trying to look at this thing objectively. I understand you said you want the baby. I got that. But with respect to a long-term maternal figure, I know that right now you may *think* that you're into *what's-her-name*, but honestly," she gave a patronizing chuckle, "soon she'll be out the door. In the meantime, while you're waiting her out, this bimbo can't possibly be a good role model for our baby. I'm a lawyer. *I'm* someone the kid can look up to. *I'm* her real mother and—"

"Listen to me, Gwen. *What's-her-name* is an incredible mother. The baby stays with us."

"No, YOU listen to ME." Her eyes were wild. "She's *my* kid." She stabbed herself in the chest with her thumb. "I'm the mother and the kid stays with *me!*"

"Are you forgetting something?" He stabbed his finger at her. "She is *my* kid too. *I* am the kid's father and I say that she stays with *me*."

"Oh, *please*." She rolled her eyes. "Even if some judge takes kindly to you, any rights went right out the door when you, as the non-custodial parent, *kidnapped* her. Why don't you get that selective memory of yours working a little better?"

"Selective memory? How about fact you knew where the baby was all along, could have picked up a phone and asked for her back, but you never did?" For a moment he lost his breath, gulped at the air greedily. "Instead, you let whole world feel sorry for you, poor grieving mother on TV and in the newspapers, when inside you were secretly rejoicing.

"I'm willing to take my chances against your long record any day. Ergo, It's YOU who had better listen to ME. I want that baby. Me. For my own. All mine. *No strings attached.*"

Zivi sat back, folded his arms and calculated. Evaluated his options. He had not planned to bring out the full arsenal, but he could see that he had no other choice. At another time, in another place, he could have loved Gwendolyn. Just not now and just not here. Not this time around. Already, he felt the deepest remorse for what he was about to do. He did not want to hurt her any more than she had already been hurt in her life. He knew that he was one of the only people who realized the hostility and anger were just an act, a coping mechanism helping her to function. But if she was going to fight with him for the baby then he had no other choice. He needed to keep his child.

He took a deep, weary breath. Because he already knew. Things were about to get hideously ugly.

CHAPTER TWENTY-FIVE

"Okay," he said, a bit too loudly. "You want your kid so bad? Let us decide here and now what we are going to do about this."

He was making her nervous. She shifted her weight from one thigh to the other.

"I have her and I ain't givin' her up. Possession being nine tenths and all, yes? So, if you really want her, you are going to have to come get her. You are going to have to turn me in. Because there is no way I am giving her up without a fight."

Oh, this is stupid, she thought, relieved. She had given him too much credit, expected more from him than this.

"Now wait, I know what you are thinking. But my mama didn't raise no fool. I know that if you turn me in for kidnapping, I go down for another felony rap. And I know enough to realize that without my name on the birth certificate, kidnapping my own flesh and blood away from her wholly inadequate parent, even for her own good, is a genuine first-class felony."

Gwendolyn drummed her fingers on the table.

"And that fucker Judge Warner already laid it out," he continued, "which you, as my lawyer, know better than anyone.

So, this is it for me. He already said, one more time and he will see to it that I spend the rest of my years behind bars. I am no idiot, darling. You got me. There is no way I am going to beat this rap. I'm down for the count with this one.

"But there's a big problem here. I don't *want* to go to prison ever again. So I'm going to do every last single solitary thing I can to get my time reduced. Because I got a woman uptown I'm crazy about. And I don't want to live the rest of my life without her." He cupped his hands over the left side of his chest. "That would just break my little ol' heart. Just give me a minute to think."

"Zivi—"

"Help me out here. What can I do to curry good will with the judge? What is the only thing I have left for trading? What could I barter to get time knocked off the prison sentence staring down at me? Think, tiger, think. What could that be?"

And then she knew. Her jaw dropped and she gave herself away.

"Yes, cupcake." He was smiling. "The only thing I have left to bargain is information. Hot, juicy, secret, *damning* information. Just think of it," he said. But she didn't want to.

"Let's go through it together. If you turn me in, I turn you in, too. I will be glad to take you down with me, sugar. With those two hard priors, I have nothing to lose and everything to gain by copping a plea with some damn serious evidence of tampering and good old-fashioned perjury."

Goddamn it. He was acting as if he was just coming up with this stuff now. But Gwendolyn knew better. She knew he had been thinking of this for a good long time. Probably rehearsing it ever since he figured out she was pregnant.

"I'll practice it right here, right now," he said, "if you don't mind." He held up his left hand. "Whole truth and nothing but." Then he cleared his throat. "Judge Warner, Your Honor, two years ago I was facing my third felony drug conviction."

Gwendolyn remembered as if it were yesterday. The cops had busted him alone in a room with a large brick of heroin. The DA's case was ironclad. Open and shut. No room to wiggle. Even for her. But it was Zivi. *Her* Zivi. In a cage for the rest of his life. She was a tenacious mastermind, determined to get her way. Somehow, she would finagle a way to gain access. Then, it would just be a matter of time.

"And then, a miracle! My wonderful legal-aid attorney told me, *unequivocally*, that she made all the critical evidence in my case disappear! *Poof!* Like *magic!*"

With no case to prosecute, Zivi had waltzed out of that courtroom.

"Absolutely right, Your Honor," he said, nodding to the imaginary judge. "Evidence does not just up and disappear ... Sounds like she did what, Your Honor? ... Tampering with evidence?"

Gwen was one of many swept up in the official inquiry. She, along with everyone else, was deposed. All signed affidavits swearing they had no knowledge of what happened to the evidence. To this day, the investigation remained open.

"Disbarment, Your Honor?" His mouth dropped open in mock surprise. "*How* much jail time? ... Wow. That seems harsh ... *Perjury?* Mandatory jail time when it is in conjunction with a felony offense, Your Honor? Oh, my."

Gwen felt sick. She wanted to run to the bathroom and vomit. But her legs had become logs and were glued to the chair. As one of the city's most prominent criminal defense attorneys, assigned more than her share of the toughest cases, she had nowhere to go but up. Yet, she had risked it all for him...

"That is the million-dollar question, is it not, Your Honor? I'm not *sure* why. The only thing I can think of is, well, I don't know if I can say this, Your Honor ... Under oath? I am under oath, Your Honor? Yes, of course I understand what that means. Okay, then. The reason, I believe, that she did what she did, is that we've been fucking..."

Gwendolyn groaned.

"...fucking each other's brains out for years now, Your Honor ... Oh, I am sorry, Your Honor. I did not mean to offend the court ... It's just that I am so used to hearing my lawyer refer to our relationship in that way." He glared at her. "I hear it so much that I didn't realize that type of language was offensive, Your Honor."

"You made your point. It's enough."

She was his court appointed lawyer at the time of his first arrest. Fucking a client. My *God*. What the hell had she been thinking? And still. To this day. To this minute. She *ached* in his presence.

"Mention it to the presiding judge? I do not believe she did, Your Honor ... Inform the prosecutor? I do not believe she mentioned it to the prosecutor... not to the jury either, Your Honor ... *Official misconduct?* Oh, my."

"Stop," she croaked. "Please."

"Ah, good question, Your Honor. We are not. She broke it off with me ... *When?* Why, right after she discovered she was pregnant with my child."

Gwen felt the nausea, the peristaltic waves going the wrong way up her esophagus.

"Why yes, it *is* the same baby that I kidnapped ... Of *course* she knew I kidnapped the baby, Your Honor. She saw me with her own eyes. That was me waving..." Zivi pretended to gasp. "Lying to an investigating officer? ... Misleading and hindering an investigation? ... Abetting after the fact?"

Gwen felt herself deflating; her heart, her spirit, her physical body, all seemed to be pressing in on her.

"Pretty good, eh, cookie?" he asked, without intonation. "How much time will a plea bargain like that take off my sentence?"

"What does it matter?" she whispered. "When they discover what happened to the heroin they'll recharge you with possession. It was dismissed without prejudice, remember?"

"Bummer. I was afraid of that. I guess I am going to be spending a whole mess o' time with all my buddies in the slammer." He shrugged. "I can handle it. After all, those are my brothers. My *braćo*. But what about you, Gwen? What are *you* going to do in the joint?"

She looked at him, exhausted.

"You know, there is price for playing God with people's lives. You didn't want me to go to jail, so you arranged it so I wouldn't. But I'm wondering about the flip side. How many characters are there, the ones you thought were downright despicable? How many cases did you tweak the other way, I wonder, burying some exculpatory evidence or not fully pursuing an alibi, just so you could send some scumbag to jail because you decided they deserved it, but who you really could have gotten to walk? I can think of at least six you told me of over the years. How many others are there? How many other cons are chilling out, waiting, just thinking about what they would do once they got you cornered in the bathroom or library or, heaven forbid, the *exercise yard*?" He shook his head sadly. "That would be a shame. You in prison, afraid to use the exercise yard."

"You finished?"

"Just one more thing. See, I love my little baby girl very, very much." He leaned in. "It's important I figure out exactly who will be watching over her while both her parents are rotting away in the Big House. And you love her too, yes, Gwendolyn, honey? You want to figure out who will gain custody of the baby you love so dearly, the one you are such good mother to."

She knew it was about to go over the top, border on sadistic. Yet she sat there, expressionless, waiting to take her poison.

"Who is she to live with? You and me? *Nope.* Up the river. *My* family? Nah. No one there worth a hill o' beans who can look after a baby. So, let us consider your side. Your mother? Nah. Mental breakdown then drank herself to death. Too bad. Your brother? He's still around, no? But a user and abuser, as I recall. Total drug addict. Who is left? Give me a minute. Oh, right!" He snapped his fingers. "Your *stepfather!*"

A pathetic, inarticulate gurgling noise rose up out of Gwendolyn's throat. Her stepfather. Next in line to be legal guardian of her child.

Zivi stared at her.

"Wait a minute," he said. "Is something the matter with having stepfather look after your precious little girl?"

She focused on the floor, firewater in her eyes.

"You cannot fool me," Zivi was saying, tapping the side of his head. "There is something about this stepfather, yes?"

He slapped his forehead.

"Of course. How insensitive of me. How could I forget? Your stepfather, he *likes* little girls! I am *sure* he would love custody of a female child."

Gwendolyn shook her head slowly. If it came down to that, she would surely contest it. But those kinds of inquiries require the recounting of details. Such specific details that were far too excruciating to articulate then and, having never been properly defused, were no less devastating now.

"Next step: paternity hearing," he said, as if reading her mind. "I am sure you will finally summon the courage, for the sake of your little girl. True, you would be a convicted perjurer at that point. Not much credibility left ... Well, I guess there *is* a chance for Grampa after all." He leaned back and shrugged. "Something to think about, I suppose."

She wiped her eyes on a dirty napkin.

"So, let's take each other down. Then we will know just how much you really care for your own flesh and blood."

The involuntary heaves took hold of Gwendolyn's body. She began to gag. In another minute, the dinner would be back up, all over the table.

"*Oh shit,*" Zivi whispered.

He jumped up and grabbed for something, anything, for her to puke into.

"You can do it. Relax, tiger. Relax and take some deep breaths with me."

They breathed deeply together. He rubbed her back until the nausea passed.

"You know, you are a lot like a baby yourself," he said, as he sat back down. "You don't know how to eat and you spit up a lot."

Then he took her hand.

"I'm sorry. I didn't want to do that to you. But you must understand. I cannot have you even hinting at bringing in the cops. You must know that I'm serious. No going to the cops, okay?"

"Okay," she mumbled.

Her eyes closed as she tried to recover from the emotional and physical pummeling.

"I need to splash some cold water on my face." She stood on unsteady legs.

He nodded. "I'll get the check."

CHAPTER TWENTY-SIX

Somehow, she managed to stand tall and walk steadily through to the other side of the curtain. When her knees buckled and she almost collapsed, she had to remind herself not to grab on to the heavy black velvet sheath for support, or she would have brought the whole thing down with her. She stumbled into the bathroom. It was a single person facility and she quickly locked the door behind her.

Gwendolyn leaned heavily against the sink and stared down into its cheap pink porcelain finish. The weight of the world once again settled itself upon her back. She was too exhausted for this much deceit, this much denial. She was not as strong as she once was. Her life was breaking her. She was tapped out. Everything inside was heavy. Weary and heavy with misery. *So very, very sad.* Her bones. Her blood. Her muscles. Her brain. Profoundly sad.

She forced herself to look into her dull green eyes in the mirror. They were pretty, once. She knew that. Zivi used to tell her that all the time. *Smashing.* That's what he used to say. But now, as she stared at herself in this dirty smelly bathroom, they looked flat. Empty. She thought about what she had just done.

Eaten all those calories. While doing it she had enjoyed it. But she knew it wasn't the food that made her happy. It was him. *He* had made her food taste good. She always told him that he was not good enough for her. An embarrassment. A burden. But she could see now, that was a lie. *He* was not the problem. It was *her*. He was not unworthy. It was her. He was not the problem. She was the problem. It was she who did not deserve him.

You are dirty. You are disgusting. You are worthless.

Gwendolyn closed her eyes. Now she had to give it back. She needed to be empty. Her mind did not deserve the comfort; her body did not deserve the nourishment. She inhaled the fumes of the rundown, disgusting, cheap pink bathroom. She breathed in with her deep, strong runner's breaths, as deeply as she could until her lungs ached, until they felt like they would burst. The smell was filthy. Like a thousand shits, a thousand pisses, a thousand years of camphor and mothball scented air fresheners. Her eyes watered as she stumbled to the toilet and shoved her finger down her throat. This time she did not even need to use her magic powder.

When she was done, she did her best to clean herself up. To pull herself together. Because she had to go back out there and grab on to her life preserver. With all her might. Before he got away. She had been adrift for the past year. She could not do it anymore. She needed him back. She could see that now. She was too weak. She needed him back, or her nightmares would become real. And then she would surely drown.

As Gwendolyn swished back through the curtain, Zivi's cell phone disappeared under the right side of the table, another call to Giselle unanswered. His left hand reached out, caught Gwen's forearm and pulled her face down so he could kiss her.

She seemed pleased. "What was that for?"

"Just checking. And I'm not so sure you passed."

"I'm sick," she said, sinking back into her seat.

"I know."

"All right, Sigmund. What else you got?"

He looked deep into her eyes. He wanted to explain her addiction, why her bingeing, purging and over the top exercising were obsessive compulsive crutches to get her through her day. He wanted to tell her that it was all a defense mechanism she used to submerge any thoughts of her stepfather, conscious or unconscious, when they started to rise to the surface. How at those times, she had found a way to refocus, to get lost in the whole bulimia process—the picking out of the food, the eating, the vomiting—until there was no room left to think of anything else.

He wanted to tell her that on so many levels, she blamed herself for the horror that had happened to her during her childhood. How, when anyone as fat phobic as she was went around stuffing their face, it was an act of violence and disrespect against their own body. He wanted to make her see that the very act of forced vomiting was self-mutilation, inflicting a sadistic punishment on her own physical being.

Instead, he smiled sadly and said, "Not tonight, tiger. It is getting late and I have to get back."

As he started to slide his chair back from the table she wormed her shoeless foot up into his crotch.

"I can't," he sighed.

"Sure you can." Her eyes narrowed and the corners of her mouth flared upward ever so slightly. "Just for a little while."

She kept her foot there, gradually pushing it up and down, up and down, slowly wiggling each toe back and forth, until he couldn't help but react.

"See?" she said, smugly. "You know you want it."

There was a lot riding on his next move. If he pissed her off, he knew she wasn't above doing something irrational, just to keep him at her mercy. On the other hand, he was willing to bet she was too smart for that. He hadn't been bluffing when he said he would go to the DA. That made the stakes equally high for her. He closed his eyes and decided that the odds were in his favor. Tenderly, he took hold of her foot and let it fall gently back to the floor.

"Thanks, tiger," he said as delicately as he could. "But I just can't."

When they finally walked back outside the air was scented with patches of grass, sidewalk trees, and flower boxes bursting with blooms. As they meandered along the sidewalks, she shivered slightly. He saw it out of the corner of his eye, draped his arm around her and rubbed her shoulders as they slowly headed back north.

"You never told me why you finally decided to call," he said.

"I wasn't ever going to call. But then today, I went for a good long run and finally got to some new crap you obviously downloaded on my phone."

He threw his head back and laughed. She wanted to own him.

"I forgot about that," he said.

She dug in her bag and pulled out a bottle of water. Four or five pieces of paper fluttered to the sidewalk. He picked them up.

"Jesus Christ. Look at this stuff. Is this all for you?" He held the prescriptions Moss had written for her earlier that day. "When were you planning on filling all this?"

"Oh, I don't know." The very sight of them annoyed her. "I don't know if I'm ever filling them or not."

"You *are* filling them." He sounded like the Zivi she used to know, the one who cared about her. "Right now. Right here. While I watch you do it."

He gave the scripts to the pharmacist in the twenty-four-hour Duane Reade at the corner of Seventh and Christopher. They wandered around the store as they waited.

"You can't even take care of yourself," he scolded. "How in the world could you ever consider taking care of a baby?"

"Well, obviously I'm not." She was emotionally flat, exhausted.

They walked around some more, quietly checking out the heating pads, the cold remedies, the pain relievers. Before she realized it, they had made their way into the baby aisle. He reached out for a tub of Desitin, but that was simply too much for her; she grabbed his hand before he could pick it up and dragged him back to the pharmacist's counter.

He told them it would be a few more minutes.

"You're killing me," he complained, but without conviction. "I really have to go. When you called, I ran out and didn't tell her where I was going. I don't know what I am going to say when I get home."

Gwen sighed. She had known about Giselle from the beginning. That didn't make it any easier.

"So, you love her?" she asked, focusing on some Band-Aids.

"Yeah, I do."

"Tell me about it," she said, turning the box over in her hand. Her stomach was in knots. "I need to hear."

"Gwen?"

"Yeah?"

"I'm going to marry her."

"Ah."

"Can you understand? I am being totally honest right now. What we had? It was not love. It was lust. And that's not bad. Don't get me wrong. It was good." He smiled. "We had good strong lust going for good long time. But love. It is different. You wait. Someday, you will find someone to love. Then you'll know. Then you'll see."

She put back the Band-Aids. Fingered the anti-bacterial creams. She was empty inside. She had nothing. Nothing worth anything in her life.

"Listen." He waited for her to look at him. "I want to be sure you understand why I did what I did. I thought it would be the best thing for everyone. You told me you never wanted to have children. You said you couldn't bear it after everything you went through. And I thought you were telling truth. Plus, you wanted me out of your life. It was getting to be too much. It was getting too complicated."

'Yeah, but I was an idiot,' she wanted to shout. *'Why didn't you make me figure out a way to do it?'*

"And once you had her, well, I knew I could take care of her. But there was no possible way I could get her. Obviously, I couldn't adopt her."

Oh. She was sinking in sadness. *It really was all about the baby.*

"It would raise a million questions we just couldn't answer. The truth would have come out about our affair and that would have ruined you. So, I did it my way instead. In the end, we all got what we wanted, yes?"

"She'll be a good mother?" Gwen asked, trying to sound interested.

"The best. I always was honest with you about there being someone else," he said. "But you never listened."

"I never wanted to know."

He took her hand and squeezed it.

She sighed. "Want to know something funny?" Gwendolyn smiled, but there was no joy in her heart. "The tattoo. I always pretended the 'G' was for me."

"I know you did, tiger. I'm sorry about that."

The pharmacist signaled that the meds were ready.

"You know," she said, as she gave her credit card to the cashier, "you're the only person in the whole world who knows everything there is to know about me."

"Don't you still see your shrink?"

"Yeah. But I don't *tell* her anything."

"Why not?" He looked at her sideways.

"Because it's none of her business."

He frowned at her.

"Because it's too hard," she said. "That's why."

Several minutes later, outside, the car she called glided to the curb.

"Please come home with me," she begged. "One last time. Just wait five minutes. Then take a taxi. Here," she said, holding out the Duane Reade bag. "Say you're delivering these. She'll never know. We can even talk about the baby if you want. It'll make it easier for me to make my final decision."

He shook his head, opened the back door of the car and guided her inside. Then he bent over and kissed her through the open window.

"I can't do that anymore, Gwen. I am trying to tell you. I am already gone."

She pulled herself away and abruptly sat back in her seat. She considered spitting in his face, or at least slapping him, but somehow managed to contain herself.

"I have some things to think about." She could no longer look at him.

"Yes. I guess you do," he said.

As the car moved away, her jaw muscles clenched tightly

around themselves until her teeth ached. She had always fought on his behalf. Now they were on opposite sides. If he thought that he could just waltz away from this unscathed then he had badly underestimated her. He had no idea what he was up against.

She would make him pay, if it was the last thing she ever did. She would make his life miserable. She would bring the whole legal system down on his motherfucking head if that's what it took. She didn't know how, and she didn't know when, but eventually he would get what he deserved. Of this she was completely certain.

He was almost out of money, but that was okay. As he walked slowly to the train station there were a million wonderful things to think about. But foremost, he had to explain it all to Giselle, to make her understand just how wonderful all those million things were. Unlike Gwen, he had never told Giselle there was another woman. Only by admitting to the affair could he explain the incredibly fabulous news that Nell was truly his own biological, flesh and blood daughter.

It was a good thing he had a long trip home. He needed all the time he could get to calculate the odds. To evaluate his options.

CHAPTER TWENTY-SEVEN

DELVECCIO AND MCMILLAN

"Gary. You there?" Brian McMillan asked.

"I'm here."

"I ran a check of her clients and I think I got an ID on the boy toy. Name's Petar Zhivinovsky. Impressive rap sheet. Distribution, mostly. Suspicion of weapons here and there. If he's the guy, there's a direct connection. She's been his court appointed attorney for years. Just emailed you his mug."

DelVeccio glanced at his phone. Zivi's image scowled back at him from the small screen. "That's a positive," he said.

"Goes by the name of Zivi. But he's probably a long shot on the kidnapping."

"Why?"

"Just got off with his parole officer. He says this Zhivinovsky is trying to go clean. Reports in weekly, never misses an appointment, has a job as a super up in the one-seventies. The PO's been over there, says the place is well run and the tenants all seem to like the guy."

"Shit."

"Yeah."

"What about arguments? Retribution? Bad blood?" DelVeccio rubbed his eye sockets. "*Anything?*"

"The PO says not a chance. The only reason this fucker is out on the street is through some sort of technicality that Gwendolyn Black finagled. The guy was facing real heavy time—thirty to life. If anything, the PO thinks this character owes Black his life."

"*Damn* it. What about the spit exchange?"

"The PO said forget it. They were just being friendly."

"Absolutely not." DelVeccio wasn't buying it for a second. "It was more than that."

"Listen, Gary. The PO says Zhivinovsky likes Black, respects her as a lawyer."

DelVeccio thought about that kiss in Grand Central, the two of them grinding their knees, their hips, up into each other, just about at the limit of what this ultra-liberal city accepts as a public display of affection. He wished he had a video of their little exhibition, because he knew no one would believe him. Hell. He was even beginning to doubt it himself. And yet the image that he remembered continued to taunt him, quivering seductively across his mind's eye.

"Well, what the fuck am I supposed to believe, Brian?" he snapped. "I got nothing, here. I'm willing to believe anything."

"But what you're saying. It doesn't make any sense."

"I *know* it doesn't make any sense! I'm just trying to come up with something. Anything."

"Here's another piece of the puzzle for you. This Zivi guy and his gal pal had their own baby a month or so ago—"

"Are you shitting me!? That's it! That's our kidnapped baby!"

"*Gary*! The PO said he knows every detail of this Zivi's girlfriend's pregnancy, practically from the minute the kid was conceived. For nine months, that was all the guy talked about."

"Hold on. Here they come. They're leaving the restaurant together. They're holding hands. They're *holding hands*."

"Listen. I never thought I'd say this to you. Especially in this case. But sometimes, things are just things. Nothing more, nothing less. The scumbag was facing a major-league sentence. She got him off. They're friends. They had dinner. Listen. I don't mean to burst your bubble. But let this one ride. It's not the right one, yet. But it'll come. I promise. Just be patient. Listen to me, man. Sometimes a spade ... Gar ... sometimes it's just a spade."

"Not this time. I even have *you* convinced. This one's a bitch—no—worse than a bitch. This one doesn't have one friend in the whole entire world. I bet everyone this one ever met has a reason to hate her. This one doesn't go out to dinner with other people for fun. And meanwhile, there *is* no one else. This Zivi guy is the only person she's had contact with. He's a bad dude. I don't believe they were shooting the breeze in there. Some kind of business went down. It had to."

"You need a break."

"You need some common sense."

"Call me when she gets home."

"And before this is over—"

"In the morning, I'll take over the tail myself."

"I'm gonna prove to you I'm right."

CHAPTER TWENTY-EIGHT

ZIVI AND GISELLE

Boxes bearing logos from restaurant supply mozzarella and tomato sauce were cast about. Baby Ethan lay sprawled out, fast asleep on a blanket and Nell, tucked into her bassinet, slept peacefully in the other room. There wasn't much talking, just an occasional gentle question from Sabrina or Martin regarding the ownership of one item or another, and monosyllabic grunts from Giselle in response. For whatever urgent reasons Giselle had, she would not share her thoughts, she had insisted on packing up all of her belongings that very night. A look had passed between Sabrina and Martin, a tacit agreement that Giselle should not be left alone.

The stillness was abruptly shattered when the service elevator thundered to a halt in the vestibule outside the apartment. The rusty, worn-out gears shrieked in agony as the elevator door was flung open. One by one, keys attacked and dropped each of the five deadbolts on the apartment door. A moment later, Zivi stood in the doorway, speechless. Sabrina and Martin looked at their half-filled boxes. Giselle simply looked away.

"What's going on?" he asked, as calmly as he could.

He carefully placed his keys on the table. Bent down to kiss Giselle, but she leaned out of reach. He lowered himself to the sofa and waited for an explanation.

The silence resonated in his ears.

"*Beba?*" he said, his patience challenged. "It's four thirty in the morning. You wanna tell me what is going on?"

She turned her head the other way so that he could no longer even see her in profile.

"*Where the hell you been all night?*" demanded Sabrina.

"Helping a sick friend," he answered, his gaze never leaving the back of Giselle's head.

"Yeah, right." Sabrina chortled with knowing superiority. "Then why didn't you call and tell her?"

Zivi looked around, then retrieved Giselle's phone from under the overturned lamp, where it had landed hours earlier. He tried to turn it on, but it sat lifeless in his hands, the battery dead. He pulled his own phone from his pocket and flipped it into Sabrina's lap.

"Twenty-nine unanswered calls to Giselle," read Sabrina. "*Shit.*"

Martin cleared his throat and strode over to Zivi. Tilted his head, gesturing for him to follow. The absurdity of the situation, Zivi being summoned around his own home by this moron, was almost too much to bear. Nevertheless, he followed Martin the few steps across the room.

"Look, man," Martin stage whispered. "Shit went down tonight when we met your woman at Papa Vinny's."

"*So?*"

"So," Martin said in his torturously slow drawl, "I guess you could say Gissy swallowed something, or I guess she didn't really swallow it so good. What I'm trying to say is that, well, she starts choking."

"*What?*"

"Yeah. And, well Sabrina here," he turned to Sabrina and smiled, "she saved your Gissy's life."

Zivi had trouble processing what the simpleton was saying.

"And yeah," Martin was still talking. "Then she started freaking out and said she had to move."

"Yeah, we plan on moving," Zivi's voice was measured, "but not at four thirty in the frigging morning."

"Me, Zivi. *Not* you," Giselle said flatly. "Not *we*, me. I'm moving out. I'm leaving you. It's over between us."

"*What?*" he sputtered, barely pushing the word from his tightened chest. "What the *hell* is going on here with you people?" The panic that their deepest, darkest secret might slip out in front of these idiots was almost too much to bear. "Giselle, you're *not* leaving me. You're not going anywhere. And what the hell is he talking about, you choking?"

Giselle turned her face away again.

He crouched down next to her and forced his voice to sound relaxed and casual. Like this was a conversation they had all the time.

"Gissy, honey, I'm asking you. What is this about choking?"

He searched the room, desperate for clarity. But she was not giving anything up.

Once again, Martin gave Zivi the 'chin wave' and steered him back toward the wall.

"She's been acting nuts and talking nonsense since we got back here," Martin whispered. "Babies in jail and babies dying and on and on. All *kinds* of crazy crap."

"*Giselle?*" Zivi's voice cracked. *We're almost there, beba.* He tried with all his might to will the words into her head telepathically. *Please God, don't lose it now.* "What happened? Are you all right, sweetie?"

"Oh, no," broke in Sabrina. "She's not all right *at all*, are ya, girlfriend?"

Zivi had forgotten Sabrina even existed.

He dug his fingers into the back of the sofa.

"We all go to dinner, she's late, and then what happens?"

"How the hell am I supposed to know?" Zivi snapped.

Sabrina glared at him. "I'll *tell* you. She takes one bite into her 'za and before you know it, it gets caught in her throat. But I mean, *really* caught. Like, she can't breathe or nothing. So, I'm trying to figure out what to do, and then I think, '*Shit!* I just took that CPR course over at the Y.'" She frowned. "And Lord help me if my girl isn't already turning blue, and she's fainting and everything, just like they said in the class if a person don't get air. Slipping under the table and what not. So then, of course, I just squeezed her that way they showed us, and I'll be damned if that little old bite of 'za came up just like they said it would."

Sabrina sat back and smiled.

Zivi was speechless.

"Oh, yeah. Except then she started saying she needed to move out, so I said she could move in with my mama and me. So, now we're gonna take her back with us, and some of her important stuff, and tomorrow we'll come back and—"

"*GODDAMMIT!*" Zivi slapped the table. He had reached his breaking point. "Giselle is not going anywhere. She's staying right the hell here with me. She's not moving in with *anybody*. This is where she lives. This is where she stays, damn it."

"I dunno, bro," said Martin. "She seemed pretty upset."

"Look, Martin," Zivi said with as much false earnestness as he could muster. "Just let me ... just let me ask her a few questions myself, all right?" He turned to Giselle. "*Beba*, are you okay? Just tell me what happened. *Please.*"

She angled her body away from him.

"Oh, all right," Martin burst out. "I'll tell you what really happened. She had that baby feeding off her titty's what happened. And at the same time, she's trying to feed herself. So of course she choked. Who wouldn't?"

"Oh, shut up," snapped Sabrina. "That's not what happened. You men, you all have the exact same ignorant one-track frigging mind. She was trying to eat when that story came on the TV and she got all upset and choked."

Zivi held his breath. "What story?" He knew it. He had waited too long to tell her.

"What the hell do you think could upset her like that and make her choke? The story about that poor little baby girl snatched away from her mama in the park. What other story do you think would set a person off like that? I swear. What'd you live under a rock?"

Martin laughed.

"Oh, right," Zivi whispered. "*That* story."

"*That* story," Giselle echoed back at him.

"You know what?" Zivi bolted around the room, collecting Sabrina, Martin and their kid's belongings. "Hey! You guys were great. But now that I know what happened, I can handle it from here. Giselle's gonna be fine." He grabbed Sabrina's arm and roughly yanked her onto her feet. "She just needs to get some rest. So, thanks again for coming and it's very, very late, and she is kidding about whole moving out thing. Sometimes she makes crazy jokes, but she's never serious. She's never leaving me. So, thanks again. *Really*." He was throwing things into their stroller. "Don't forget anything. You don't want to come all the way back here because you forgot something ... So, yes, that's it then ... We will be seeing you around real soon."

Sabrina looked at Giselle doubtfully. Giselle nodded slightly.

"Yeah. Well, I guess it's late." Sabrina yawned. "You sure you're gonna be okay if we leave?"

Giselle nodded again. "I'll come by your place tomorrow,"

Giselle told her. "I guess it really is too late to move my stuff tonight."

"That'll be fine, sister. You'll be all right here all alone?" Sabrina eyed the lamp and table lying on the floor. Rubbed her arm where Zivi had wrenched it when he jerked her up. Then she looked at Giselle. "He's not gonna hit you, is he? I took that Batterer Intervention Program last spring. This isn't some kind of pattern, right?" She tried to examine Giselle's face. "You're not covering anything with makeup, are you?"

Zivi held himself back; he held his mouth from cursing the halfwit's head off and held his foot from escorting her out the door that very second. Giselle actually smiled.

"Yeah, I'm sure," she said. "I'm fine. Thanks again. I'll call you in the morning about my stuff."

Sabrina collected her baby and Giselle gave the other woman a hug. Zivi, practically pushing them, tried desperately to expedite their departure. Once outside the apartment, Sabrina turned back to Zivi before he could slam the door.

"*O. M. Gee*," she sang at him with unfettered glee. "You're in trouble now. Some deep motherfucking trouble."

Then it was Martin's turn. He reached out and shook Zivi's hand.

"Good luck, bro. You're gonna need it."

Zivi nodded. Tried not to punch their lights out. Closed the door behind them and dropped the five deadbolts. Latched the chain. Rested his weary bones against the door and listened as they made their way into the elevator.

It will all be fine in the end, he assured himself. It's getting there that's gonna suck.

"*You took your lawyer's baby!*" The words flew from her before she could stop them. "What is *wrong* with you? Are you out of your *mind?*"

"No. No." He was trying to say something, but the last things she wanted were pathetic explanations and excuses.

"I. Saw. It. On. TV. With my own eyes. *Do not* tell me 'No!' Now I know why you didn't fix that television when it supposedly broke. You broke it so I wouldn't find out. Well, I *did* find out. How long did you think you were going to keep this from me?"

"Giselle—"

"Don't talk to me!" she screeched. "Don't even try. Because I don't want to hear it. I hate you. I *hate* you. You know what I have to do now? I have to give Nell back to her. Now that I know who her real mother is, I have to give her back." She crumpled against the couch and slowly shook her head. "I knew it from the beginning. Nell is not our baby. What's the *matter* with me? We can't keep her. We never could. I always knew that. I should have taken her straight to the police right when you brought her home." Tears were running down her face.

"No, *beba*. Just lis—"

"*No!*" She was trembling with rage. "You let me live in a fantasy world. And you almost got me believing everything was going to be all right. *Damn it!* I am *such* an idiot!"

"Gi—"

"Now, because of you, I'm going to lose *two* babies. *Not one. Two.* How could you do this? And what about Nell? What about this poor innocent baby? You ripped this poor child away from her *mother*. How could you take her from her mother? How could you do that to a baby? And, oh my God." Giselle gasped and put her hand up to her mouth. "What about the lawyer? I saw her on TV. You took her baby. She was hysterical! She's going *crazy* trying to find her baby. And all this time—"

"No. She's not. Listen to me. I did it bec—"

She put her hands over her ears so she wouldn't have to hear any more of his twisted, lame, pathetic lies and excuses.

"I DID IT," he shouted, "BECAUSE NELL IS MY DAUGHTER." He took a deep breath. "Giselle, Nell is my real, true, biological daughter."

Her hands fell back down, limply, into her lap.

"*What?*"

"Nell is my daughter. I am her father."

"Don't be ridiculous," she scowled. "You're a bigger idiot than I thought."

"*Beba*, listen. I am telling you the truth."

"Please stop," she begged him. "Just stop. Stop treating me like a moron. I can't take it anymore. I want you to go away."

"I swear. Nell is really my baby. Hon? Listen to me. Together, we can make this into great news. Nell is really and truly mine. I mean *ours*. Not mine, *ours*. No one will be able to touch her. She'll be ours forever, free and clear."

"Are you hallucinating? You kidnapped her, Zivi. You stole her. She is *not* your baby. She is *not* my baby. She's that lawyer's baby. It's over. We have to give her back. Period. End of story."

"Listen to me." He sat next to her and held his hands on her shoulders. "I met her tonight." Giselle shoved him away. "Gwen Black, I mean. That's who called me before. And she told me that Nell really was my baby."

"I don't believe you."

"I didn't want to say anything to you till I was one hundred percent sure. I did a paternity test, but there was still the slightest, *slightest* chance of an error. But then she called me. And she told me it's true."

"Now the situation is even worse than before. Now," she stifled a sob, "when I give her back to that woman, I will be giving away your own flesh and blood. So don't tell me how 'good' everything is. Don't say anything else to me about it, or about anything else, ever again. I am done with you. You have lied to me and now you have cheated on me. You broke me. I'm broken. I'm leaving and I'm never going to see you again."

And with that, she pulled herself together enough to get up and walk shakily into the bathroom. Then, for the first time since they had moved into the apartment, she kicked the mattress aside and slammed the bathroom door.

CHAPTER TWENTY-NINE

Zivi followed Giselle into the bedroom. As he waited, he gazed down into the bassinet. He could barely recognize this magnificent baby as the same scrawny infant who had come into their lives three months ago. An infinitesimal amount of time, yet he could no longer imagine life without her. He watched her entire torso tremble up and down with each rhythmic breath. He noticed for the first time that her lips moved while she slept, almost as if she was trying to speak. Gossamer, milk infused bubbles of saliva danced around the corners of her mouth with each exhale. The delicate, paper-thin skin of her eyelids fluttered. He reached out and ran his fingers over her tiny toes—toes that were an exact miniature, though much more delicate and beautiful version, of his own.

Of course, he had suspected it all along, *knew* it, really. Gwen had told him there was no one else, or he would have never, *ever*, have taken her away. But now he knew for sure. Nothing had changed, but everything was different. Could he love Nell any more now than he did before? No, but something had definitely shifted. Maybe it was that now he could believe she was really going to stay. His love was more relaxed, more unburdened. And the part of him that had been holding back, just in case, in case it all ended badly, well that part was now freed up to love her too. So, maybe he *did* love this child more now than he did before.

Zivi considered it for a second. What did it all mean? It meant that he would give his own life for this child in a heartbeat. Without a second thought and without a moment's remorse. It meant that his whole life was now dedicated to ensuring she got only the best that he could give. That he would protect her from everything that he could, no matter what it was —no matter how big, no matter how small, no matter the odds, no matter the cost to himself.

When Giselle opened the bathroom door, Zivi was waiting. She slunk past him because his very existence disgusted her. She slid under the covers, turned away and closed her eyes.

"I have one final thing to say to you," she said into the wall, "while you're trying to convince me that I should be happy that you slept with her."

"I'm saying that Nell is our baby and that's why you should be—"

"*Stop interrupting me!* Just *listen!* You always carried on about your big plans to be better than your father. Well, I have some bad news. You are *exactly* like your father. How many other babies do you have with other women? And *don't* answer it, Zivi, it's rhetorical. Because from now on, I don't care."

Then came the muted sound of cotton rubbing against skin, as he pulled his shirt over his head and his pants fell to the floor.

She stiffened. "Don't you *dare* think of getting into this bed with me. You have abused that privilege for the last time. Tomorrow I'm gone. Then, you can sleep *wherever* and with *whomever* you want. Although, obviously, you've been doing that all along."

"You may not want to hear this, but I'm telling you anyway."

Her back was to him, her eyes were closed, and she was stuck. Until she fell asleep, she would have no choice but to listen.

"I slept with her, yes," he said. "But I never cheated on you."

She wanted to scream for him to shut up, but her need to cut off all contact, all interaction with him, was even greater. So she lay there, facing the wall, tears soaking the pillow, trying with every fiber of her body not to sob out loud.

"I swear. I never cheated on you."

She heard him pacing the floor along the foot of the bed.

He was nervous and the pacing helped him concentrate.

Starting at the end was out of the question. It was too complicated to explain that from the minute Madison died the plan was in the works, even though, at the time, he didn't yet realize it. So instead, he started at the beginning. He took Giselle back to the time before they met, to the time of his first arrest.

"It started the first time I was arrested. At the arraignment. Gwendolyn was my court appointed attorney. And she and I, well, we had chemistry. For each other, I mean." Zivi knew that he had to be completely honest.

"So I figured that, well, hooking up would only help her enthusiasm for my situation. So, yes." He swallowed. "I slept with her. And she got me off."

He explained it all to Giselle, as gently as he could. What began as a self-serving fling soon segued into something more. It turned out Gwendolyn was brilliant. And funny. He found himself looking forward to their time together. But as much as he enjoyed her, she *really* dug him. For her, Zivi was the real deal. A genuine drug dealer. The ultimate in forbidden fruit. The antithesis of what she was supposed to be attracted to. An affair with him was snubbing everything she supposedly embodied. A big *fuck you* to the Man.

"She kept calling. I kept answering."

Zivi told Giselle about the Farguss Avenue sweep. How she got him a great deal, sent upstate for just a few months. None of the other defendants pled out as quickly, or for as short a sentence, as he did.

He decided to ride the wave for as long and as far as he could. Every time she buzzed, he answered. Every time she said 'now,' he was there. Things flowed smoothly until, in an instant, they did not. Gwen spooked. Suddenly, it was all too much. Too intense. She was falling in love with him, which was not the way it was supposed to go. She broke it off. They could never see each other again.

"That's when I came into the bar and met you." His voice cracked. "And you know how that went. Lightning striking. I was crazy in love with you from very first minute."

All they wanted was to make each other happy. Every single day. Everything they did. He quickly came to appreciate what an accomplished artist she was. All he wanted was to provide for her so she could stay home and pursue her passion.

It was for both of them, equally. The fancy apartment. The car. They loved it all. But everything has a price. Zivi had to spend more and more time in the business. To get a bigger cut, Gavric insisted that Zivi arrange to move more product into the US from his Balkan Route connection. Take chances. Cut corners.

That was about the time Gwendolyn started calling Zivi again. It got him thinking back to advanced quantum economics and the 'positive inverse probability theorem.' He saved Giselle the gory details, but obviously, the more specific one can be with respect to the known knowns and the known unknowns, the more predictive the theorem will be. It gives the odds, so to speak. Of course, it's the *unknown* unknowns that'll kill you every time.

Zivi had calculated. To maintain their lifestyle, he needed to stay in the business a while longer. There was no legit job he knew that could satisfy their needs. He couldn't quit until they had enough money for his grad school tuition plus enough socked away to maintain the finer things they were used to. Making matters worse, based on the assumptions, there was an approximately eighty-five percent likelihood he would get pinched again before achieving their goals. *Eighty-five percent.*

He did what he could to shift the odds. He increased security at the office. Delegated most of the crazier shit Gavric wanted him to do. He ruminated over what else would lower the chances of a lengthy prison vacation. The first and best thing was to retain a good lawyer.

"So, purely a statistical decision, based on odds and applying theorem, well, she already proved herself a valuable asset in the past." He held his breath. "So, I returned her calls."

He had used Giselle's fear of long-term commitment to help rationalize what he was doing. But unlike with Giselle, Zivi had told Gwendolyn from the outset. Told her he now had someone serious, someone he was wild about. Gwendolyn seemed happy about this development. It was better that way, she said.

Then there was a second conviction. And even though seven months wasn't long considering the bigger picture, surviving their time apart was the hardest thing either of them had ever done. Giselle's visits were the only thing that kept them alive. Both existed in their own private hell, calculating the hours, the minutes, the seconds until they could be together again.

When he was finally released, Zivi still believed he had a few years left with the Balkan Route Motha Fuckas before he could financially afford to walk away. He was certain that by exploiting his relationship with Gwendolyn he had successfully dodged representation from some trampled-down-by-the-system, couldn't-give-a-fucking-shit defense counsel. Repeat drug offenders in New York faced an additional thirty years tacked on to their sentence. And that Judge Warner had sworn, if Zivi ever appeared in his courtroom again, he would sentence him to the max. Therefore, he couldn't afford the risk of breaking things off with Gwendolyn.

He turned back to Giselle. "You're wondering how I can say 'I love you,' ten times a day while I'm sleeping with her. I'll tell you. Because it was *business*. Gwen was business. Insurance. An insurance policy that meant I had a lawyer who would go over the top for me if the situation presented itself. Which it was eighty-five percent likely to do. Because, well ... living that large lifestyle. Goddamn, it's addicting."

And then it really did happen. But this was no little felony they got him on. Someone in Gavric's operation, Gavric himself if Osmani was to be believed, set Zivi up. Set him up so he'd be out of commission for a long time. They found him in a room with two Ks of smack and thirty large. An open and shut case. He was facing life. Going to die in prison.

But now Zivi told Giselle what really happened. That Gwendolyn made all the evidence, all two kilos of it, disappear. And then she swore out an affidavit saying she didn't know what happened to any of it. But she did know. She knew *exactly* what happened to every last gram, and where it all went. She never told him how, she never told him where, but she did it. She risked everything. *Everything*. Her future, her freedom, her career, to save his ass.

He sighed.

"And then, *beba*, I swear. As soon as you got pregnant, I retired from the business and it was over between me and her. I no longer required her legal services. Let the insurance policy lapse, so to speak. That was it. Finished. Until she called. Until she called earlier. Before. When we..."

He scraped the stubble on his cheeks.

"So, my economics quantum theorem worked. More than worked. We won. Because I'm out. I'm a free man. And now, just like we agreed, I'm totally clean, out of the business for good. Listen to me. We didn't just *win*, we won the mother lode. Because now we have Nell. We have a baby that is really and truly my biological daughter. She is all ours now."

Giselle half gasped, half sobbed. He tried to touch her shoulder. She recoiled violently.

"I had to see Gwen tonight. To make sure everything is understood about us keeping Nell."

He implored Giselle not to let the academy award performance she saw on TV fool her. Gwen was an actress. The best there was. The best legal aid lawyer, best plea bargainer, in the city. After all, that's what being the lawyer for a bunch of thugs is about. Hysterically sobbing because some stranger took her beloved baby? Don't, he warned, fall for her bullshit. Zivi insisted that she knew it was him. Knew it was him from that morning in the park. He explained how he had made extra sure she knew it was him, just so she *wouldn't* worry. Gwen *had* to act all distraught and panicky for the press and the police. Otherwise, they'd suspect that she knew something. That she was hiding something. She even asked him tonight. She asked him if he liked her TV performances. That's what she called them. '*Performances.*'

Zivi knew he had to dig deeper. He had to admit that, in order to get Gwen to want to do anything and everything for him, to get her so wound up that she would risk it all just to get him off the hook, well, it took a lot of work. As in, a whole lot of time. As in, he probably knew Gwen better than anybody else knew her. He knew a lot of private things. Like the fact she has a crazy problem with throwing up. That she vomits something like seven, eight times a day. He explained how she drank a horrendous, vile concoction of baking soda in warm water to make herself barf.

"She made me taste it." He shuddered. "It's sick what she does to herself."

Then he told Giselle about how Gwen exercises like her life depends on it. Every morning, 6:45am—rain, shine, hot, cold, snow, sleet, hail—she's out there in Central Park, running the big loop. "She has obsessive compulsive eating and exercising disorders," he concluded. "Insane hang-ups, ones that wouldn't be curtailed just because of a baby to take care of."

Once Zivi realized Gwen was pregnant, he told Giselle he watched. And he waited. Months later she was still at it; not jogging, exactly, but engaged in a big pregnant-belly power waddle. Then suddenly, nothing. He was riveted. How long would it take? Not long, it turned out. Two weeks. *Two weeks* before she was jogging with his baby. What the hell was she doing with a tiny baby, running up the hill by West 90th street at 7:15 every morning? It was an outrage. But there was nothing he could possibly do. Until Madison. Until they lost Madison. Did some vague concept come whispering in his ear as soon as Madison died, or did the obvious inevitability smash into him like an A train barreling down the tracks? Even at that moment, having spun his thoughts over and over and over like a Rubik's Cube, he couldn't say.

It took another two weeks. Two more weeks to recruit the

most loyal soldiers he knew he could trust with his life, to put the plan in motion. As Giselle sunk deeper and deeper down, he became more and more certain of his decision. Nell was four weeks old and, it turned out, a small baby. No one would know she wasn't a two-week-old. Even *she* was perfectly poised to play her part.

He paused now, considering if there was anything left between him and Gwen. He decided there was not and revealed Gwen's most private and unspeakable secret. That, when she was a child, her stepfather had molested her. For years. It was horrifying and grisly, and gruesome and abhorrent, and every other revolting word one could think of.

He was telling this to Giselle so she would understand that, to this day, Gwen could not fully give herself to another person. Even if it *was* Nell. Gwen was so cold and emotionally detached, Zivi doubted she could ever really love another human being. Her life was all about her. She was afraid of opening up, even a little bit, to anyone, because she was too afraid of being hurt.

"*Beba*, listen to me. She could never love our little baby girl the way a baby needs to be loved."

He had pleaded the most important case of his life and now he threw himself on Giselle's mercy. She was the only judge who mattered.

"There it is. And I guess, what I am asking you ... I am *begging* you, really, is to stay with me. To stay with me and Nelly. To be a family. A real family. I need you. *She* needs you. I ... I don't know what I would do ... I would just *die* if you..."

Looking at Giselle, two feet away but completely out of reach, was too painful to bear. Her breathing was slow and rhythmic, her ribcage gently rising and falling with each breath. At some point during his rambling explanation, she had fallen asleep.

"*Shit.*"

He stumbled into the living room and collapsed on the couch, completely miserable. He could see by the meagre soft glow filtering in through the kitchen window that the sun was beginning to rise. He thought he had covered all the bases. After all, hadn't he disconnected the television cables? Hadn't he gone through the settings on her phone, deleted the relevant apps and blocked all news content with words like 'kidnapped' and 'stolen?' And yet, it was a simple TV interview, replayed three months after the fact. How could he ever have guessed that Gwen would beat him to the punch? Zivi, you schmuck, he scolded, as his consciousness slipped away. You really should have known.

Giselle had feigned sleep because she had heard enough. She could not stand to hear another word. But now she had a lot to think about. Zivi had cheated on her. *Despair.* But because of it, Nell was his biological child. *Elation.* For the first time in three months, she could actually relax because the cops were *not* going to break down their door at any second. *Elation.* They could maybe, actually, possibly, keep Nell. *Elation, elation.*

But whatever Zivi said, the birth mother wanted her baby back. Giselle had seen it with her own eyes. The crying, the hysteria, the panic. Giselle knew what it felt like to lose a child. What she had seen was not acting. It *couldn't* have been. *No one* was that good. Nell was not theirs to keep.

There was only one thing she could possibly do.

CHAPTER THIRTY

GWENDOLYN AND GISELLE

She was so tired, sitting on that park bench with Nell next to her in the stroller, that she started to nod off and almost missed her. The runner was coming up over the last of the three hills on West Drive near 90th Street. Because she had been sitting for such a long time, straining her eyes to study each jogger as they went by, it was hard for her to be sure that this particular bouncing russet brown head was really the one she was looking for. The hair was pulled back into a frizzy ponytail. Giselle did not recognize her at first, because in court Gwendolyn always wore her hair down. But then there was no mistaking the bulging calf muscles, the angle of the cheekbones and the ramrod straight posture.

The power of Giselle's convictions drained from her body. Before she lost her nerve completely, she forced herself to stand up off the park bench and call out the other woman's name.

She took a deep breath. *"GWENDOLYN BLACK!"*

The woman hesitated.

Oh. My. God.

The ponytailed head looked around. Giselle could tell by her expression that she was clearly annoyed at the interruption, yet curious enough to stop. The dark eyes darted around, like a hawk searching for prey. Then, they zeroed in on Giselle. For an uncomfortably long moment they stood, apart from the rest of the world, staring at each other.

Finally, Gwendolyn crossed the street, stepped up onto the curb, planted her fists on her hips and glared. Condescension oozed.

"Who the hell are you?" she snapped.

"I'm Giselle. I'm Zivi's ... I'm Giselle Vaughn."

"*So?*"

Giselle was flabbergasted. A warm prickly blush crawled across her face. Zivi was right. This one was a jerk.

"What the hell are *you* doing here?" Gwendolyn pressed.

"I have something that belongs to you." Giselle had found a tree, way out beyond the right side of Gwendolyn's head, to focus her eyes on. "You're her mother. I came to give her back. Because ... well, I mean ... how you must feel. I know how you must ... what it's like to...."

"What in *God's* name are you doing here? Last night, he threw down the fucking gauntlet. He said he wanted to keep her *no strings attached.*"

Giselle dropped back to her seat, mortified.

"Why the hell did he send you?"

Despite herself, Giselle's gaze shifted back to Gwendolyn's face. Could they actually be having a conversation? Why hadn't the jerk just grabbed the baby and run away?

"He-he doesn't know I'm here," Giselle stammered. "Look, Gwen." *Oh, my God.* "I mean Gwendolyn. I'm sorry. I just found out—last night. That it was you, I mean. Otherwise, I would have come sooner. Really. I—"

"I'm not getting it. Why-are-you-here? Yesterday he insisted, *insisted*, that you two wanted to keep her."

"We do. Of course we do. Want to keep her." Giselle was

struggling on every level. "But then ... last night. I saw you on TV. It was the first time I ever, the first time I heard, about how it happened. Zivi, he messed with all my devices and the TV, so I didn't know. I mean ... I saw how distraught you were, and then I finally realized that I couldn't ... how horrible it must ... and ... but ... Well, she's your baby. *You're* her real mother. I ... I had to come. To do the right thing. And all."

How could it be, Giselle wondered, that she was sitting here trying to come up with a plausible explanation as to why she was giving up the child she loved? And then she heard Zivi's words floating through her brain, reminding her that Gwendolyn was an ice-cold lunatic. Last night, she'd thought he was exaggerating. This morning, she knew he may have understated his case.

"Let me get this straight," Gwendolyn said. "Now you suddenly decide to show up here and give her back to me because *it's the right thing to do?*" She sneered. "How fucking biblical. Why don't you just cut her in half? Then everyone can go home happy."

And just like that, something inside Giselle's head clicked. She woke up from the somnambulant semi-consciousness that had enveloped her since Madison's death. She was finally able to break free of the layer upon layer of ethereal, grief laden cobwebs that had blanketed her brain, obscuring her vision and deadening her thoughts. She had a new, fresher emotion to contend with.

It was fury.

Of course, she had recognized her immediately. It was that Gazelle, or whatever person Zivi was so hot for. Gwen was pleased to see that Giselle's eyes were blood red and nearly swollen shut, obviously the result of some real heavy duty crying. Yeah, Giselle, you look like shit, she thought. That made Gwen happy. She already had the upper hand and they hadn't even started.

"Listen," said Giselle, with a surprising edge to her voice. "I don't need your sarcasm."

Oh, thought Gwen. *Sassy.*

"You really want to know why I showed up now? Because I just found out about you. By accident. I'm sure he had no intention of telling me anything about you and your little *relationship.*"

Gwen smiled. This might get interesting.

"He didn't tell me anything. Not about you, not about where he got the baby. Nothing. And he still wouldn't have, not yet anyway, if I hadn't finally seen the whole thing on TV. He never let on for one second that he knew the real mother. And that he is the real father. *My God.* Let me tell you, he knew exactly what he was doing."

This notion intrigued Gwen, but she forced her expression to remain indifferent.

Giselle whispered. "It's all so obvious. Don't you see?"

Gwen closed her eyes, lifted her eyebrows and shrugged, as if to say she didn't care one whit about Zivi or his motives. But that was a lie. She cared deeply about every little thing he did, said, or thought.

"He was biding his time," Giselle was saying. "Because he knew that otherwise, I would do what I'm doing now—giving her back." Giselle paused. "He thought about every detail, so that I wouldn't find out about you. He wanted me to become totally attached, totally committed, totally *dependent* on this baby before he told me anything about her background."

Gwen had no idea about what the hell Giselle was talking

about, so she allowed a slight eyebrow arch, meant to encourage her to continue.

"He knew that once I was so emotionally attached, I couldn't possibly give her back. *Yes*." Giselle nodded slowly. "That's when he planned to tell me. And the fact that he slept with you? As long as he had stopped, he knew I'd get over it. All that would be important was the fact that he is her biological father. It would seal the deal. There would be no way I could possibly give her up. I would *never* give up his child.

"Guess what? It almost worked. Right now, I love your daughter exactly as much as I could possibly love her if she were my own flesh and blood. But that doesn't matter. I don't matter. Only she matters. That's why I'm giving her back to you. Because if I don't do it now, I'll never be able to do it."

Gwendolyn stood, forcing impassivity.

"So, I don't need attitude from you. If it would make you happy, just start screaming and have me arrested and thrown in jail. That's fine. I deserve it. But you don't know what I'm going through. You have no right to judge me."

Gwendolyn, feigning boredom, looked away. It was just in time to see that buffoon Gary DelVeccio sneaking behind a tree, his face bright red. This little tête-à-tête must have given him time to come huffing and puffing round the mountain. She and Little Miss Cutie pie would have to keep their voices down.

"Hey! Look at me!" Giselle shouted and Gwen brought a finger up to her lips. "This baby? This baby right here?" Giselle said more quietly. "Her father is the man who told me he loved me, who told me he couldn't live without me, the man I was supposed to spend the rest of my life with. Now, all of a sudden, not only do I find out that he was sleeping around behind my back for *years*, but that this baby is actually his baby from that affair. But I still love him. Despite everything, I love him."

Gwendolyn smirked, although she too knew the pain of being hurt by Zivi.

"And now, for some stupid reason, I'm here with his baby and I'm *giving her away*. Even though he loves this child more than he loves me, wants to keep her and raise her, and be a father to her, I'm handing her off to you. I'm giving away his very own flesh and blood, because I know how you feel, and because *it's the right thing to do*.

"What do you think he's going to do when I tell him what I did today? I'll probably never see him again. Giving you back your baby means I lose everything. I lose the baby I love. And the only man I ever loved. The man who is *everything* to me: the reason I get up in the morning, the one who makes every day worth living. The one who used to be my whole future."

The little artery pulsated wildly in Giselle's neck. Gwen guessed that meant Giselle had good circulation; she could be an excellent runner.

Tears welled up in Giselle's eyes. "I'm throwing everything away to do the right thing for this baby. So *don't* you give me your sarcasm."

Gwendolyn smiled. "Glad you understand. This'll save us a *lot* of ugliness down the road. I'm the biological mother. I win. Case closed. But you're not just going to hand her over to me right here, are you? Not now, after all these people have seen us here together? And just so you know, there's an undercover detective tangled up in the bushes over there, allegedly keeping an eye on me. I suppose it's just in case you or your boyfriend approach me with your demands."

Giselle leapt up. "*Where?*"

"What the hell's the matter with you?" Gwendolyn practically pushed Giselle back onto the bench. "Shut up and calm down, and he won't have any reason to come over here."

Giselle was trembling.

"Would you *relax?*" Gwendolyn hissed.

Giselle took a tremulous breath. "Okay," she said. "This is it then. I'm going to just walk away." She swallowed. "Right now. I'm going to do it. Calmly walk away and leave her here with you." She sat, immobilized, hand clenched firmly around the handle of the stroller.

"Hmm. You really want to do that, Miss Co-conspirator?" Gwendolyn tilted her head toward DelVeccio. "How many people, including that detective, have seen you here and will know you left her behind? Free legal advice. I hear life behind bars gets old really fast."

The color drained from Giselle's face.

Gwen loved convincing a jury, even if it was just a jury of one little twit who no longer looked quite so crappy.

"And regardless, I can't just show up with some baby. The first thing the detectives are going to do is check her DNA to be sure she's mine. Of course, in addition to *my* DNA, *Zivi's* DNA will show up. His DNA is already on file, being that he's a convicted felon. It won't be long until you'll be connected to him, and then both of you will be connected to the kidnapping anyway."

Gwendolyn took another step forward and tried to catch Giselle's gaze, but Giselle kept her eyes downcast under their swollen lids.

"*Damn* it," Gwen mumbled. Her mind was racing to the cross-examination, five steps ahead of what her mouth was saying. Trial attorney cardinal rule number one: never ask a question to which you do not know the answer. "Like I said, that kid is a repository of *my* DNA as well. Between my doorman, my neighbors and some stray unaccounted-for witnesses, they're bound to dig up some idiot who's seen me and Zivi together. There's no doubt."

Gwen silently contemplated the annoying, unexpected

implications. "With all the friends I've made over the years in the prosecutor's office, once they establish a romantic link between him and me, they'll be knocking each other over to reinvestigate the missing smack in his last case. And guess what?" Gwen looked accusingly at Giselle. "Fucking your client creates a true to life, big-ass motive for evidence tampering. The DA will *definitely* start a formal inquiry. Then I'm sure Zivi will cop a deal, somehow connecting me to all that missing heroin, and *voila*. I'll have my own room, right down the hall from you."

She slumped down on the other end of the bench. "No public give-back. We'll do it privately. That's all. But any way we do it, I'm up a baby and you two are down a baby. I'm going to have to help you guys come up with a damn good explanation as to what happened to your kid. Otherwise, there's always going to be that tremendous risk someone might connect the dots and figure out that the two babies are one and the same."

Giselle sat very still. "What are you saying?"

"Do I have to spell it out for you?" Gwendolyn snapped. "It has to be done in a way that the whole *truth* thing will never come out. Otherwise, *I* would end up in jail. And that's not going to happen."

A slight grin tipped the corners of Giselle's lips.

"Don't get all excited. There is a safe way for me to get my baby back. I just haven't figured it out yet. That's all."

She watched, with empty satisfaction, as Giselle's face once again fell into despair.

Nell's cries brought Giselle back from the dark places her mind was taking her to. She pulled the stroller closer. Hazel green eyes stared back, and the corners of the precious mouth reversed themselves into a toothless grin. Giselle now knew what she wanted. Zivi was right. The choice could not be more straightforward. Either Gwendolyn got her baby back, they all implicated each other and everyone ended up in jail, or Zivi kept his baby and they all walked away happy. At least, she and Zivi did. And that was all that mattered. Gwendolyn Black was nothing more than an obstacle. All Giselle needed was a little more time to figure something out, to get Gwendolyn to agree that was exactly what she wanted, too. Giselle reached into the stroller and picked up the baby.

"So that's her?" asked Gwen. "I would never even recognize her."

Giselle leaned back and placed Nell across her lap. A wave of nausea rose through her gut. At three and a half months old, Nell weighed a solid ten pounds and all of it was resting squarely on Giselle's bladder, which hadn't been emptied for the many hours she had been sitting and waiting. Giselle shifted the baby and adjusted her own position.

"You sick?" asked Gwen.

"No," said Giselle, "I have to pee."

Nell kicked impatiently. By the time Giselle unbuttoned the third button of her shirt and slipped her nipple into Nell's mouth, the baby's eyes were already half closed in blissful anticipation of what was to come.

Gwendolyn gasped. "What the hell are you doing?"

"What do you mean?" Giselle asked, not really caring about the answer.

"I *meeaan*, what the *hell* are you doing?" Gwendolyn sputtered, saliva spraying from her mouth. "You can't do that! She's not *really* your baby, you know. No matter what he may have told you. You can't do that!"

Giselle felt her composure slip away.

"Oh, come on," Gwendolyn sounded impatient. "It's not like this is news."

Giselle opened her mouth, then closed it. She took a deep breath and looked directly at Gwendolyn. "You mean he didn't tell you?" Her voice was softer than she would have liked, but at least it didn't tremble.

"Tell me what?"

"That I ... That we..."

Now it was Gwen's turn for surprise. "Oh, my God," she murmured. "Don't tell me. He got *you* pregnant, too?"

Giselle looked away.

"My God." Gwen shook her head. "He's *exactly* like his father."

Giselle's mouth slipped open.

"Relax." Gwen discounted Giselle's angst with a flip of her wrist. "I'm his lawyer, remember? I have to know shit like that about him. It's my job." Then she folded her arms across her chest. "Well?" she asked. "Where is it?"

"What?"

"What do you mean, *what*? His other baby."

"You're serious? He really didn't tell you?"

"No," said Gwendolyn, "he really didn't tell me. Did he tell you about this one?" She pointed her chin at Nell.

Giselle paused. "Our baby died," she said.

"Isn't *that* just great." Gwen threw her hands into the air. "My child is being held captive by two baby killers."

Giselle gasped. "How *dare* you."

"You just told me your baby died! What the hell am I supposed to think? That you two are pillars of responsibility?"

"Zivi and I planned to have our baby." Giselle spoke her words slowly and deliberately. "We waited until we could afford it through earning a legal living. I never missed an OB visit. Everything was fine until the very end. Now correct me if I'm wrong, but was it not you who got knocked up by accident? Is it not you who is the irresponsible parent?"

"Touché," Gwendolyn said, with a slight tilt of her head. "So, what happened? With your baby."

"Why do you want to know?"

Gwendolyn shrugged. "I just do."

Giselle considered it. Nobody had ever asked her what happened to Madison, because nobody knew there ever had been a Madison. Except Zivi. And Giselle hadn't told *him* everything. It would have been too painful. And there was no point. Once he had seen the room, he knew. So, the words had been stuffed down, smothering her.

"It's a long story," said Giselle.

"I'm late for work anyway."

Giselle dabbed the milk from Nell's chin, then eased her to her other breast.

She explained that they had stopped using protection a little more than a year ago. By September, the test was positive and his drug dealing days were over. "Zivi knew a guy. He used to control all of Washington Heights. Went by the name Big TaTa. That's Bosnian for Big Daddy."

"Big TaTa?"

Giselle nodded.

"I think I remember him," said Gwen. "I heard he disappeared right when they were closing in." What she really meant was, *Oh, yeah. I know all about Big TaTa. Helped him out of a big jam, too.*

Giselle continued. "That's right. All the bosses were well connected with the cops. Big TaTa knew exactly what was coming and when. He put all his money in real estate and walked away. He had an elaborate business plan ready to go. Bought vacant apartment buildings from the city. One by one, he renovated them. Then he rented them out for a ton of money."

Zivi ran into TaTa and told him he was leaving the business, too. TaTa had a proposition. Zivi and Giselle could live in the basement apartment of one of his buildings that had yet to be rehabbed. Free rent, if Zivi would be the super.

They hadn't realized how rundown the place was until their first night there, but it was a small price to pay. For the first time, Giselle stopped worrying about whether tonight was the night the DEA would finally kick in the door.

Everything in their lives had finally fallen into place. Giselle would go downtown and spend a few hours painting at her studio while Zivi went upstairs to work. They had dinner together every night and breakfast the next morning. Like normal people.

"No more drug dealer hours," Giselle explained.

"Because I was out of the picture."

"I guess that's right." Giselle sighed. "Being pregnant, even in that disgusting apartment, was the best time of my life. I saw the doctor, I painted, I waited. They always told me the baby was healthy. Strong heartbeat. All of that."

Then came the Tuesday, thirty-three weeks and two days in. Giselle was nauseous at breakfast. Zivi wanted her to stay home, spend the day in bed. But she didn't want to. She wanted to finish something at her studio. He told her again to stay home, she told him again to quit worrying. He went upstairs to work. She wouldn't hear from him for hours; he knew not to call while she was painting because she didn't like breaking her concentration to answer the phone.

She was about to leave for the studio when the first pain hit. Her knees buckled. It took her legs right out from under her. She had been having sciatica for weeks, but never like this. If she hadn't grabbed a chair, she would have fallen on her face. But something happened. She wrenched her body and fell to her knees. Placental abruption, but she wouldn't know that till days later when she looked it up.

Giselle's water had broken. Her shorts were drenched, her legs warm and sticky. She had to get help. Every time she tried to put weight on her legs, the pain was unbearable. She couldn't walk. But this was a life or death situation. She managed to crawl to her phone and found herself back in the kitchen. But as much as she tried, as much as she struggled with every last fiber of strength, she could not stand, much less twist herself up over the sink and hold the phone to the window for reception. One, two, ten, fifteen calls to Zivi didn't go through. Not to 911. Not to 0. Nothing.

She dragged herself to the bedroom and somehow managed to get herself onto the mattress. Giselle had to change so she would be clean and ready to go the hospital when Zivi got home. But then the contractions slammed into her. Not the ones she'd read about in her books. There was no easy, slow, gentle build-up. These were: KABOOM! Your guts are now being ripped from your body. She started screaming. But of course, no one could hear her in the basement apartment. She could barely breathe. Her back felt broken. She couldn't walk. Couldn't move. She was trapped.

She waited to pass out, certain that no one could endure pain so severe and yet still be conscious. Something was very, very wrong. Was she dying?

Why do expectant mothers practice breathing? Because otherwise, they don't do it. It took all her energy to take one breath. But breathing left her with no strength to move. No strength to shout. Giselle lay there, alone, in harrowing pain. Immobilized by fear. She *had to be* dying.

How much time elapsed? How long did she lie, paralyzed in terror? Impossible to know. There came a point when an invisible claw reached up into her body and began pulling the organs right out of her abdomen. The baby was moving down and out.

It couldn't be happening. Not to her. It could not be happening. And then the next round hit. Really, really strong contractions, as if her whole body was being crushed downward and inside out. Suddenly, there was barely any time between them and she knew instinctively that it was time to start pushing, but she didn't want to because Zivi wasn't there and she was all alone and she wasn't in the hospital and she knew she couldn't do it all by herself. It was all totally, totally, totally wrong. It wasn't supposed to happen that way.

She pushed, but nothing happened. Nothing moved. She was being ripped open, and her hip bones were cracking, and she was utterly too weak to keep going.

"But then I reached down and I felt her. I felt her head starting to come out of me. And I was so excited. I pushed until I just couldn't push anymore."

What happened next? Maybe Giselle really did faint. But at some point she reached down and the baby's whole head was out. Giselle could feel her nose and her mouth and her ears. It was incredible. She tried to psych some strength back into herself, but she had so little left, and nothing was happening. Until, suddenly, the shoulders popped out and then the rest of the baby slid onto the bed.

Giselle lay there so happy, so relieved, but so tired. So weak. Every muscle was totally spent. She shook from head to toe with complete exhaustion.

The placenta slipped out and she knew it was over. All she could do was stare at the ceiling and think how surprised and proud Zivi would be when he got home. She wanted to smile, but even her facial muscles were too exhausted to move. She closed her eyes and tried hard to relax. But something was wrong. Chills raced across her skin, but she couldn't figure out why.

"And then I knew." She closed her eyes now and replayed

the scene, as fresh in her mind as if it had all happened that morning.

The baby wasn't crying. Giselle had tried to sit up to see her, but she didn't have the strength. She dug her heels into the mattress and inched her body over. She reached out and managed to hook the baby's arm, pulling her in until she could hold her. That's when she saw her face. She looked down at that tiny face for the first time. It took her breath away. It was perfect. But at the same time, it was *all wrong*. It was mottled in so many different shades of blue. All different hues. Her tiny little cheeks were cerulean. Her eyelids were steely, steely gray. The lips were almost white. A cold, white slate. And her skin. So thin. Almost translucent. Giselle was afraid she would tear it just by touching it.

"I tried to get the umbilical cord off." Giselle's lips trembled. "I tried to untie it from around her tiny little neck. But I couldn't."

By then, she knew it didn't matter; it was already too late. The baby wasn't moving. "She never moved. Never took one breath."

Giselle had rocked her. Rocked her and rocked her and kissed each and every one of her fragile fingers and toes even though she knew her baby was dead. Then there was nothing left to do but die right along with her. So that's what she did. She died. She rocked the precious little body, while she felt her life slipping away so she could be with her baby.

"I don't know when Zivi came home. I didn't hear him come in."

He saw the disarray in the living room and he barreled into the bedroom, screaming Giselle's name. And when he saw her there, in the bed, in that horrible bloody mess, he started to panic. Giselle told him that she was okay, but then she turned the baby so Zivi could see her face.

He took the baby and held his lips against the cold, lifeless forehead for a long time. Then he steamed up the shower and led Giselle to the bathroom. He washed her with lavender and goat's milk soap. She had stopped using it because it was too expensive and she didn't want to use it up. But it was her favorite. He washed her whole body, again and again, until she was clean. He rolled up the dirty sheets and he remade the bed and then he disappeared. And when he came back, he didn't have Madison anymore. Giselle never saw their baby again.

Then he crawled into bed and put his arms around her while she slept. She slept, and he held her, and watched her all night long to be sure she was okay. And when Giselle awoke, he said it was all his fault, that he had failed her and she told him 'no,' that it was her own fault. It was a stalemate, each blaming themselves.

"Look. I ... I'm sorry," said Gwendolyn. She may have even sounded sincere. "I had no idea."

"It's okay." Giselle tried to smile. "I guess I just needed to tell someone. I'm just sorry it had to be you. I mean, I'm not sorry I *told* you, I'm just sorry if it was inappropriate of me. That's all. That's what I meant."

"No." Gwen shook her head slowly. "I hear things like that all the time. Much worse, even. I mean, not much worse for *you*, but I hear about bad things happening to people all the time."

Giselle laid the baby out in the stroller and quickly changed her diaper. She sat back down, just for a moment, to catch her breath.

"But what about you?" Gwen asked. "Did you go to the doctor, to make sure you were all right?"

"No. I made him swear he wouldn't take me to the hospital. I knew he did something with her body and they wouldn't let us go until they found out what. I would never turn him in to the police like that. Anyway, all I wanted to do was die. That disgusting apartment seemed as good a place as any."

Giselle didn't realize it at the time, but refusing to go to the hospital was the wildcard that had enabled Zivi to set his plan in motion. If she had allowed him to take her, they never could have gotten Nell.

"No, no." Gwendolyn shook her head. "You should have gone anyway. Women can bleed out after a bad delivery. Some people still die in childbirth, even today, and even in this country. It's not unheard of. Anyway, it just would have been illegal disposal of human remains. I could have gotten him off easily for that one. Especially under those circumstances."

"Yeah, no." Giselle swallowed. "That night. When he disappeared. He took her to a funeral home. She was cremated the next day."

Giselle didn't tell Gwendolyn that it wasn't a traditional funeral home. It was the kind that does favors for the Big TaTas of the world. Because last night, Zivi had explained how on the night Giselle gave birth, he was already seething. Sickened by the thought that Gwen had taken his baby out with her jogging at two weeks old. *Outrageous*. But there was nothing he could do. Until their precious Madison was dead. Then Zivi had an inkling. He dismissed it as ridiculous, but nonetheless, his gut dictated he bring Madison's remains somewhere they would be handled discreetly. No questions asked.

"What about now?" Gwendolyn asked. "You must have gone back to the doctor by now."

"Yeah," Giselle answered. "Two weeks after we lost our baby, he took yours. That's when I went back. I never even missed an appointment. I was fine."

"Good."

"Listen," said Giselle, getting painfully to her feet. "I have to go. I have to find a bathroom. I really, *really* have to pee. In the meantime, I'll try and figure out how to—"

"And I really, *really* have to shower," interrupted Gwendolyn. "Come. My apartment is right up the block."

Giselle tried to say *no*, but before she knew what was happening, Gwendolyn had grabbed hold of the stroller and was already pushing it up the hill and out of the park.

CHAPTER THIRTY-ONE

DELVECCIO AND MCMILLAN

"Brian?"

"Yeah?"

"Get ready." DelVeccio could barely contain his excitement. "She finished her run, meets up with some lady with a kid in the park, they have words, Black grabs the woman's kid and now they're all hightailing it outta here."

"I know."

"Whaddya mean, you know?"

"Wanna know what else?" McMillan loved surprising his brother-in-law with shiny details.

"What?"

"That's not just 'some lady' she had words with." McMillan paused for effect. "That's Zhivinovsky's girlfriend and *their* baby."

DelVeccio's jaw dropped. "You mean it's not Black's baby? Shit. Where the *fuck* are you?"

"Up the hill in the playground, watching you watch them."

"Be right there." DelVeccio limped up the street, his hamstrings cramping. "What the hell're you doing here, anyway?" he asked, once he joined McMillan.

"I didn't go home last night. I knew I wasn't gonna be able to sleep. Spoke to Zhivinovsky's PO again. Pushed him on the kiss. He still thinks his boy is clean."

"Fuck."

"However, in deference to your suspicions, I spent the night in front of Zhivinovsky's apartment. But when the female left this morning, I decided to trail her instead, and got Barkley to follow the male. And now, here I am. Back at the doorstep of Ms. Gwendolyn Black. So. What do you think now?"

"I don't know *what* I'm thinking anymore." DelVeccio's frustration was palpable. "Every time I come up with a plausible explanation, it gets blown to smithereens. Like the fact that Hillman just called to say that he spoke to this Giselle's doc. She gave birth to a healthy daughter. Home birth. You know these artsy types. Besides. I just watched her breastfeed that kid. Seems unlikely that the baby in the stroller is anything other than Zhivinovsky and Giselle's kid."

McMillan arched an eyebrow. "Unlikely?"

"All right. *Friggin'* unlikely. That better?"

"Much."

"Thoughts?" DelVeccio asked McMillan.

McMillan rolled ideas around his brain for a while before answering. "My theory is that these people are all about the same age, living in Manhattan. Gwendolyn gets pregnant at the same time as Giselle. They're already friendly because Gwendolyn saved Zhivinovsky's ass. They may not *socialize*, but they are friendly. Zhivinovsky calls Gwen to console her in her time of need, or she calls him to have someone to talk to because the poor bitch has no one else. Either way. It doesn't matter. What counts is they have dinner together. He doesn't come home till late. Giselle gets jealous. Delusional enough to think there could be something between her boyfriend and the lawyer. The next morning, which is today, she confronts

Gwendolyn. Gwendolyn says, 'You've blown a circuit, you've gone crazy, how could you possibly think anything could happen between me and Zhivinovsky?' They go upstairs to make nice, have a cup of coffee, a scone. Whatever. Then they come down, Gwendolyn goes to work and Giselle goes home. You wait and see. Nothing will come of it. End of story."

DelVeccio frowned.

"Okay. How 'bout this." McMillan tried again. "Two women and one baby are upstairs. The only thing we know is, based on the few lovely moments we've spent in the presence of Gwendolyn Black, no one in their right mind would ever ask that woman to babysit. So, we wait. If Giselle comes down with her baby, everyone calls it a day and goes home. If, on the other hand the girlfriend of former drug dealer Zivi leaves *without* her kid, meaning she leaves a poor innocent baby in the custody of that yeti up there, then something ain't kosher. If that's the case, we gotta at least move in and ask some questions. Deal?"

DelVeccio sighed. "Deal."

CHAPTER THIRTY-TWO

GWENDOLYN AND GISELLE

Gwendolyn pushed the stroller up the hill and onto the sidewalk outside Central Park. The traffic light at the corner was green, but she did not cross the street. Instead, she turned to look at Giselle, who seemed to be having difficulty standing straight and was stumbling up the sidewalk. Only when the light turned yellow did Gwendolyn hurry to the other side. She stepped up onto the sidewalk and smiled. For at least the next three minutes, Giselle would be stuck on the wrong side of a heavily trafficked Central Park West and Gwendolyn would have full physical custody of the baby.

By now, the compassion Gwen had felt while she'd listened to the horrific tale of Giselle's deceased newborn, sincere while it lasted, had evaporated as surely as the sweat on her forehead. After all, hadn't she experienced more than her own share of pain and heartache? And *she* had survived, hadn't she? The pity party was replaced with smug pleasure as she imagined Giselle panicking, separated from Zivi's child, unable to get across the street, pee streaming down her legs. She even considered slipping out of sight into the service entrance of her building, but decided against it. That was too over the top, even for her.

With a twinge of trepidation, Gwendolyn allowed herself to look down into the stroller. For the first time in over three long months, she studied the child. She felt a slight release of facial muscles as she realized that the baby had been lulled back into a groggy twilight sleep by a full belly, the heat and the humidity. She noted with satisfaction that the child was still gorgeous. In fact, the baby looked even more like her father than she had before. Right down to the spindly, knobbly toes sticking out from underneath the light summer blanket Giselle had so fussily draped over her.

Gwendolyn tilted up the stroller, so she could more critically evaluate her daughter. The sudden shift caused the baby's body to shudder in a startle reflex and she opened her big hazel eyes. Gwen froze. Held her breath. Please don't wake up. Please don't wake up. Thankfully, the baby simply licked her lips and once again dozed off.

But it was all the reminding Gwen needed. Her heart pounded, her head throbbed and she gasped for breath. The frightening, claustrophobic memories of being a full-time mother for all of thirteen days came flooding back. She now remembered how panicked she had felt each time the baby awoke and demanded a piece of the one commodity Gwen didn't have enough of, even for herself. Time.

Gwendolyn realized it was all true, what she had been less than half-heartedly denying to herself and what Zivi had clobbered her over the head with the night before. She was many things, some of them good and some of them bad, but mother material was not among them. With the admission came relief. Once a problem was acknowledged, there was always a solution. She took a deep breath and regained her composure.

"No big deal," she told the sleeping baby. "I'll just hire two nannies to take care of you."

Gwen waited for Giselle to shuffle her way over. She

pretended not to notice when Giselle tried to reach into the stroller and readjust the blanket. Instead, Gwen pushed the uncovered baby inside the air-conditioned building before Giselle had a chance.

Giselle knew Gwendolyn's building. She had studied it in school. The lobby was a classically magnificent architectural space designed by the much-heralded New York City architect Emery Roth, completed in 1931. The design incorporated every aspect of the Art Deco grandeur of that gilded age. As she passed under the famous stainless-steel archway, and through the elaborate leaded glass doors, Giselle tried to absorb the beauty of the spectacular gold leaf moldings and wall murals, vintage period furniture and intricate marble floor motifs, but she had to use the bathroom so badly that she was practically fainting from the pressure. It was hard to focus. What she did notice was that both the doorman and the concierge barely glanced at Gwendolyn, giving her terse, perfunctory nods. Giselle felt embarrassed and self-conscious as the two men let their eyes linger on her own face longer than she would have liked. They offered her warm, ingratiating smiles. But then again, maybe they were just being sympathetic once they realized whose home she was visiting.

The elderly elevator operator opened the beautifully paneled elevator door and followed the two women and the stroller into the deep mahogany paneled and arch-mirrored compartment. He closed the solid door and then slid the accordion gate into place. At least, he thought he did. Because when he turned the handle to start their upward climb, the elevator cab rose no more than six inches before lurching to an excruciatingly abrupt and bouncy halt. It was about all Giselle could stand as she felt her bladder muscles begin to give way. She braced herself into the corner of the dark wainscoted walls, secured a white knuckled grip onto the polished brass handrail, and prayed for just another three minutes of internal muscular integrity.

The elevator began its quiet hum upward. When Gwen's phone vibrated to life, Giselle helplessly felt another two millimeters of muscle spring free of what was precariously close to a lost effort. The phone had been going off intermittently during their entire encounter, but Gwen remained oblivious to the persistent buzzing, with no apparent intention of responding.

The elevator operator slowed the cab as they approached the twelfth floor. Giselle closed her eyes and braced for impact, knowing full well she was but one precipitous lurch away from a mortifying situation. Thankfully, he demonstrated the highest level of elevator-operating prowess and slowed the mechanism to a gradual stop. Nevertheless, the gentle rocking as he unhooked the accordion gate and opened the solid door felt like sea swells. Giselle went weak in the knees and focused on the tiny white spots dancing inside her eyelids. When she dared to look around, Gwendolyn was already well down the hallway with the stroller. It was all Giselle could do to croak 'thank you' to the old man and painfully stumble along after them.

By the time Giselle made her way down the ridiculously long hallway, Gwendolyn was opening her apartment door. The two women entered the narrow entry shoulder to shoulder. Giselle involuntarily put a hand on Gwendolyn's arm to steady herself. Gwendolyn stiffened.

"You okay?"

"In a minute. Need the bathroom," Giselle gasped.

"It's right here. Just give me a second to straighten up."

"No." Giselle could feel that it was almost too late. "It's fine."

"It would be better—"

"No. You don't understand. I've been sitting in the park since the crack of dawn. I can't wait."

Then Giselle barreled past Gwendolyn, into the bathroom, and slammed the door in her face. It was just in the nick of time.

Gwendolyn pushed the stroller over to the far side of the room and onto the parquet floor so that the wheels would not dirty her smart, pastel colored rug. Next, she went into the kitchen, filled the teapot with water and put it on the stove to heat.

As she watched the blue flame lick the bottom of the pot, Gwendolyn tried to unravel why she did not hate Giselle. Giselle stood between her and Zivi. That made Giselle the enemy. She thought about Giselle lying alone, giving birth to a dead baby. Maybe *that* was it. Maybe it was the curiosity effect; Giselle had survived a devastating experience all alone and was none the worse for it. That certainly was admirable. This other woman intrigued her, and these days, she wasn't often intrigued. Mostly, she was bored.

Or maybe it was simply because Gwendolyn needed Giselle to give her a few tips on raising that child.

Or maybe it was simply a touch of guilt. About the whole bathroom thing. Maybe she should have been more forceful and not facilitated the spectacle that was undoubtedly unfolding, at that very moment, behind the closed door.

Giselle shut her eyes and tried to relax. It took a few seconds. Her muscles were so tightly clenched she had trouble letting go. But finally, slowly, she was able to find relief. Sitting there, she thought how insane it was for her to be in Gwendolyn Black's apartment, using her bathroom. Then she thought about Zivi, tried to imagine his expression when she told him where she had peed today. She even laughed out loud. *Quietly* out loud. She was not about to share anything about Zivi with Gwendolyn, not even some silly, passing thought. Sometime during the past hour, Giselle had reconciled his affair by accepting that in life's great cosmic order, his impropriety had brought her Nell. She believed things always worked out in the end. It was the getting there that often proved serpentine and unpredictable.

These thoughts were still swirling through her head when she turned around and flushed the toilet. That's when she saw them. Three beautiful photographs, tastefully mounted inside three obscenely expensive red and black genuine antique Chinese cloisonné enamel and gold frames, sitting on a shelf just above the back of the commode. They housed three selfies: one of Zivi and Gwendolyn laughing together, one of them holding hands, the last of them kissing. But the pictures hardly even mattered. It was the frames that had her riveted. Two years ago, when money flowed freely, Giselle had spent countless hours in some of the most exclusive and ridiculously over-priced NoLiTa antique shops picking those very frames for Zivi's birthday. That's how she knew they were obscenely expensive. He had told her that he loved them and said he had a perfect place for them in his office. She had never seen them since. When they downsized their lifestyle and moved to Wickum Avenue, she had forgotten all about those fancy picture frames. And now, here they were. Displayed on a shelf above Gwendolyn Black's toilet. That *prick*.

As she washed her hands, Giselle glanced at herself in the medicine cabinet mirror. She looked terrible. Eyes swollen, bloodshot and ringed with dark circles. She had no excuse for acting on her next impulse, she had never done it before, but she simply could not resist. Giselle pulled the mirror back a crack and peeked inside. It overflowed with all the typical junk—face creams, eye makeup removers, tampons and hair products. But Giselle didn't notice any of it. Instead, her eyes were drawn straight to the bottom shelf. *His* bottle of patchouli oil. *His* shaving cream. *His* brand of razor. She grabbed the sides of the sink so that she would not fall.

Giselle snuck out of the bathroom. She still wanted to run home to Zivi, although no longer to hug and kiss him. She prayed that she would be able to collect her baby and slip back out of the lair unnoticed. But alas, it was not to be. Like most one-bedroom apartments, even this fancy one on Central Park West, it was not especially big. And Gwendolyn had stationed herself in the middle of the living room, exactly between Giselle and the stroller, which was now parked under a large picture window.

"That can wait," Gwendolyn said into the phone. "Reschedule the DA meeting for next week. Then I'll present it to the court next motion day."

As Giselle tried to glide by as inconspicuously as possible, which of course was impossible, Gwendolyn smiled tightly and put a 'just one second' finger up in the air. Giselle checked that Nell was still securely buckled into the stroller. Her business here was done. She was leaving and no 'just one minute' finger was going to stop her.

"Marla, gotta go."

Giselle pushed the dusty front wheels of the stroller onto the tacky rug with the washed-out colors.

"Don't want to hear it. *You* handle it. See you Monday." She ended the call and was about to speak when Giselle cut her off.

"Listen, Gwendolyn. I said everything I came to say. I'll be in touch." Giselle remembered Gwendolyn's decree: after everyone agreed to a satisfactory excuse why she and Zivi no longer had a baby, they would have to relinquish Nell somewhere private. Giselle knew she had to distract Gwendolyn so she could leave with Nell. Instead of some petty argument about antiquated picture frames or hurt feelings over toiletries, it was critical she and Zivi regroup and come up with some kind of revised strategy.

"No." Gwendolyn put her hand on top of the stroller. "Don't go. I just told them I wasn't coming in to work today. I've never done that before." There was a firmness about the tone that conveyed an order, not a request. "Let's talk. I'm making tea. What kind do you like?"

"You know," Giselle said, bracing for the ambush, "given everything, I'm thinking that's not such a great idea, you know what I mean? I should go." She tried to inch her way closer to the door.

"No, stay." Gwendolyn's voice had softened, no longer ordering, but not quite asking either. "Please. I really have no one to talk to. Everybody at work hates me. Three times a week I pay someone to listen to me. How pathetic is that? Zivi was ... like ... my only friend." She paused. "And now he's gone. He wants no part of me anymore. He only wants you. Please?"

Zivi had insisted that Gwendolyn was an award-winning actress. Yet, at that moment, Giselle thought her completely sincere.

"Just for a little while?" Gwendolyn persisted. "I'd like to get to know you a little. We could even talk about the baby. If you want."

Giselle felt a flicker of hope.

"Look," said Gwendolyn. "I need you to tell me about how

to take care of this kid."

And then, as fast as it had ignited, the ember was snuffed out.

"It's just one cup of tea." Gwen smiled and gave Giselle a helpless look.

Truth was, Giselle needed more time to figure out how to get Nell out of there. And she was parched. A cup of tea sounded reasonable. Perhaps it would help her think. "All right," she conceded.

Gwendolyn rubbed her hands together.

"Excellent."

Giselle waited alone in the living room feeling awkward, while Gwen went to the kitchen to collect two large mugs of hot water, and a basket holding several boxes of teas. She put everything down on the coffee table, then held one particular box up for Giselle to see.

"This one is actually kind of good," she said, dipping a bag into her own mug.

After the picture frame incident, Giselle had decided that nothing about the day would surprise her. She was wrong. To her utter disbelief, Gwendolyn was holding a box of Giselle's favorite decaffeinated blueberry nutmeg spice chai. The one that was nearly impossible to find. The one that was only sold in two places she was aware of: a tiny, below street level, hippie health food store near her studio on the Lower East Side, and online from a website based in Marrakech. Giselle rummaged around the basket for a suitable alternative.

"Zivi turned me on to this tea," Gwendolyn was saying, staring at Giselle intently. "He told me it would help me kick my coffee habit. He thinks I drink too much caffeine." She pushed the box at Giselle. "Try it," she said. "You'll like it."

Giselle rooted through the alternatives, arbitrarily selecting a nondescript purple box.

"Sweetener?" Gwendolyn dumped two packets of Splenda into her own mug.

Giselle shuddered and looked away.

Several uncomfortable minutes passed.

"Turned out to be a nice day," said Gwendolyn.

Giselle nodded. Studied the fabric on the chair.

"Summer running is a whole other ball game," Gwendolyn said, as if bestowing something that could, in a million lifetimes, ever be even remotely relevant information. "You burn a lot more calories for the same amount of mileage."

A stray twig had escaped from the teabag in Giselle's mug. She abandoned the drink to the coffee table.

"Because the heat makes it so much harder."

"I guess," Giselle mumbled.

They fell back into the awkward silence.

"Too bad about Zivi." Gwendolyn smiled.

Giselle lifted her eyebrows.

"About me and Zivi, I mean." She shrugged. "I'm going to miss him."

Giselle shifted in her chair. The air was forming a phantom rope, knotting itself about her neck.

"He sure is a great fuck," Gwendolyn said, shaking her head sadly.

What did she say?

"*What* did you say?" Giselle croaked.

"I said you're lucky," Gwendolyn repeated, more slowly and deliberately this time. "Zivi is a great fuck. Probably the best I ever had."

A gasp escaped from Giselle. "The best? *Really?* Even better than your father?"

Giselle's hand flew up over her mouth. She could not believe what had just come out of it. The room was suddenly electric.

CHAPTER THIRTY-THREE

Gwendolyn was the first to recover.

"I think I'll go with a rape scenario," she said with chilling calmness. "Yes. A rape scenario is perfect. That will explain away Zivi's DNA."

"But he *didn't* rape you." Giselle's heart was hammering. "You *wanted* to have sex with him."

"So what? I'll say I didn't. And that he did it anyway."

"But we'll deny it. You're lying," Giselle insisted. "You know you're lying! I'll *tell* them!"

"Ha!" Gwendolyn gave a very loud, very false laugh. "Who in their right mind is going to believe the two of you?" Her eyes had turned to slits and she stood up. "You? You'll say anything to keep your boyfriend out of the slammer. And who's going to believe you over me, anyway? *Excuse me*," she said, her voice shrill, "but I think I have a *little* more credibility than some art school dropout."

"But ... but Zivi," Giselle sputtered. "Zivi was there. He'll just tell them the truth. He'll say what really happened."

"No one is going to believe Zivi. The jerk is facing *life*. Do you even have the capacity to understand what that means? No one with half a brain would ever believe him. Even for a second."

Suddenly, Giselle was very cold.

Gwendolyn scoffed. "Do I have to spell it out for you? I am the *mother. The mother always wins.* Neither of you have a prayer of getting away with this. For God's sake, you kidnapped my baby. There's a detective hiding outside in the trees right now. You might as well just give up."

Gwendolyn was right. *The mother always wins. She should just give up.* Giselle took a cleansing breath.

No. There had to be a way around this. A way to get to the truth.

"People have seen you two together!" she shouted. "Zivi told me the thing with you two went on for years. There had to be other people who saw. People who would come forward and testify about the two of you—"

"You are so ignorant, *Giselle*." Gwendolyn was raging now, her face an angry scarlet. "Do you actually think that I would have let anybody see us together? How stupid do you think I am? For all those years, I made him use the *servants'* entrance. We never went out in public together. *Never.* I forbade it. And now? If anyone says they ever saw us together, anyone in the building, anyone in the street, anyone *anywhere*, I'll say he was stalking me!"

Giselle stumbled backward.

Nell started to cry.

"That's right," Gwendolyn bellowed. "He was stalking me. And then he raped me. Violently. Do you understand? And then I didn't report it because he said he would get his goddamned *članovi bandi* to *kill* me! That's right. I kept my mouth shut because I was petrified for my life!"

Giselle was frightened.

Gwendolyn was panting.

Nell was screaming.

"I'll tell them about the heroin," Giselle yelled, grabbing at her very last straw. "I'll tell them how you did something with it for Zivi. So he could get out."

"*What?*" Gwendolyn roared. Her mouth was tight and quivering. "You don't know anything about that heroin. *Zivi* doesn't know anything about that heroin. I never told him anything about that heroin."

"Oh, yes he does!" Giselle shouted back. "He told me you made it disappear."

Gwendolyn grabbed the back of a chair. The tips of her fingers dug into the padding. Her knuckles turned white. "Are you kidding me?" she hissed. "No one knows what happened to that evidence. A million people were in and out of that evidence room before anything was discovered. It'll be his word against mine."

Gwendolyn stopped, put her hands up to her ears and grimaced, as if the noise in the apartment was driving her mad.

"But—" Giselle was trying so hard, desperate to come up with something. Anything.

"Some sadistic drug dealer," Gwendolyn interrupted, "is going to testify against *me*, the woman he raped, accusing me of evidence tampering? Some drug dealer with a mysterious grudge against his former lawyer? A convicted felon with zero, and I repeat, ZERO, credibility. And he's going to come forward with some ridiculous story against me that he completely fabricated? *Are you for real?*"

Giselle immediately came to the shocking revelation that the only way out of this, the only way to leave with her baby, would be to have a fist fight with Gwendolyn. She had never had a fist fight before. Never even thrown a punch. And Zivi had told her how much Gwendolyn worked out. Giselle knew she wouldn't stand a chance. She was stuck. Finished. She didn't know what to do. She had come to the end. She wanted to cry.

And then Nell was screaming like she had never screamed before. Loud, strong shrieks that were ear-shattering, teeth-rattling, chalk-on-the-blackboard, deafening wails. And every once in a while, the cry caught, as if on a protruding nail. Giselle knew that eventually, Nell was going to blow. That sooner or later, one of those arrested cries would end in a massive eruption. And Nell would throw up. And since she was so desperately upset, the heaves so pathetically deep and arresting, the vomit would bring up bile. And baby vomit filled with bile really, really, really stinks. Those were the things that Giselle knew. The only things, at that moment, that she could be sure of.

She thought about what Zivi would do if he were in her shoes. And right then, on the fly, she came up with a plan to keep the baby.

Gwendolyn was breathing hard, panting, dizzy. She put her hand to her head and squeezed her eyes shut. What in the hell is going on? she wondered. A panic attack? A dizzy spell? Or is it all a nasty hallucination?

"Gwen?" The woman must have been saying something, but it was so hard to hear over that damned screaming baby.

"Gwendolyn?"

Gwen could hardly make it out.

"Your baby is crying!" shouted the woman.

Oh, right. This is that Giselle person.

"She's hungry," Giselle said, pretending to eat, so Gwen could understand the pantomime over the racket bursting from the stroller.

"She needs to be fed, right away. And burped," Giselle was yelling. "She needs a diaper change. She's starting to get a diaper rash. You need to check. If she is, use the Desenex. If not, Balmex is okay. I'll leave you the diaper bag until tomorrow. Then you need to buy your own."

Diaper rash?

"If you put her down on her stomach, you have to stay with her the whole time. She can't keep her head lifted up for all that long. She could suffocate."

Suffocate?

"But don't leave her on her back for too long either. They say that their heads can flatten out in the back."

Flatten?

"But she really doesn't like to be put down, anyway. You'll see. She really likes to be held. All the time."

Gwen stared at Giselle's face, trying to make sense of the words. *Wow.* Her teeth and mouth really are pretty.

"And of course, she needs tons of oral, visual and tactile stimulation. Constant attention, really. It's essential at this age. For brain development."

And she's *so thin*, thought Gwen. Really nice and thin for someone who just had a baby.

"...a change of clothes and tons of love and attention. Never too much attention. Do you understand? Gwendolyn. Look at me. Do you understand what I'm telling you?"

Gwen looked at Giselle. Giselle's eyes were big and round and wet, and it looked like she might burst out crying. But she didn't. Instead, she said, "I'm going home now."

And then she turned and disappeared out the door.

Gwendolyn closed her eyes. She allowed all the images swimming in her head and all the assaults on her senses to come together, to collect themselves into a semi-cohesive picture in her mind. She realized there was a reason—some reason—that the Giselle person shouldn't be going downstairs by herself—leaving empty-handed, without the kid. Gwendolyn just couldn't close in on it right then. But she let the thought go because it was taking too much effort, too much brain power, to hold on to. How had it come to this? Stuck with a shrieking, reeking baby she never really wanted. But it was too late for questions.

Because now she had to keep it. She would never, ever admit she had made a mistake. *Never*.

She looked in the general direction of the stroller. Maybe she should try to pick it up. She walked over and looked down. It was covered in a yellowish orange vomit that smelled so putrid, Gwen herself became nauseous just being near it. The idea of smacking it, of smacking it and yelling at it to *shut-the-hell-up* crossed her mind. But intellectually, she knew that would never work. Besides, she really didn't want to hurt it, she just wanted to make it shut up. It was buckled in, so it was not about to go anywhere. Maybe it would just cry itself back to sleep. Yes. That was probably right.

But the *noise*. Who in their right mind could tolerate such a racket?

She needed quiet. Quiet to think, to shower, to finish the crossword puzzle, to eat lunch. She suddenly realized that she was starving.

What was she supposed to do? Could she really go about feeding herself, caring for herself, with such hysteria no more than a few feet away?

She almost called for the nanny, but there *was* no nanny anymore.

At times like this, there was only one thing that could ease her over the hump. Is there still that unopened bag of Oreos in the cabinet above the stove? There's ice cream in the back of the freezer. But it's probably covered in freezer burn. It's probably spoiled.

So what?

Gwendolyn knew that this time, she would have to eat every last crumb that existed in that kitchen. Then she would force herself to throw it all back up. Violently. Until her insides bled. And then she would have to go out, buy more food, and do it again. And who knows. Maybe today she would even have to do it a third time—again, after that. Because today was turning out to be a very bad day.

When Giselle reached for the door, she did not think she had the strength. The only thing she was aware of was Nell's desperate cries for help. For that is what they were. Cries for help. Desperate pleas not to be abandoned. It was the only way the helpless child had to communicate.

If she went back, Giselle knew what she would see. She would see the child's bulging eyes filled with fear, see her crimson, desperate face contorted in panic, and her trembling, outstretched arms begging to be picked up. So, Giselle did not go back. She knew that she could not afford the luxury of one last look. Because then she never would have been able to leave. The time when she almost lost it, when she almost caved, was when she heard the crying buckle. That's when she knew Nell had thrown up. Had thrown up acidic, corrosive stomach fluids that were sure to eat away at the baby's fragile skin. Giselle had listened to be sure Nell was still breathing, to be sure the child had not choked on her own vomit. And then she took those last few steps out the door without even turning around.

She did not know why, but she *needed* to make it look easy.

She did not want to betray the struggle as she took those last five steps out the doors. Giselle did not want Gwendolyn to know that her arms and legs were Jell-O and she could barely maintain her balance. She did not want Gwendolyn to see that the white lights flashing before her eyes were blinding her. That her hand had to maintain contact with the wall so she could keep her balance.

For some unfathomable reason, it was important that Gwendolyn saw none of these things; that Gwendolyn did not know how weak Giselle was; that the pain in her chest was debilitating; that her heart had been shredded, left to bleed out, taking with it what little life there was left to take. Giselle closed her eyes and pulled the door to Gwendolyn's apartment closed behind her.

But once she was alone, her composure crumbled. Tears collected, thick and salty, in the back of her throat. She stumbled down the long hallway, farther and farther from her baby.

It was an eternity before she reached the elevator. Giselle stared at the buttons for several seconds, deciding what to do. She thought about what lay ahead. How she would have to go home and tell Zivi. Explain that she had *tried* to be like him, had tried to evaluate the situation and play the odds. How she'd thought Gwendolyn would have realized she could not care for the baby. How Giselle assumed Gwendolyn would have folded. But instead, Gwen had called her bluff. She had let Giselle leave, empty-handed. Giselle had bet it all. Nell was the ante. And she had lost. It was gone. All gone. Giselle remembered how Zivi told her not to do this. Had told her in no uncertain terms not to come and see Gwendolyn. But she did it anyway. She had not listened to him. Now, she had lost two babies. And Zivi, too.

She leaned hard on the button marked 'down.' She punched at the call button again. And again. And again.

The man flung the accordion gate open and then opened the solid elevator door. Giselle could see that he was annoyed. She wanted to apologize, but her face was paralyzed. His expression softened and he nodded. *She breaks us all*, he seemed to say.

Giselle hesitated but would not let herself look back. She stepped carefully into the elevator. The elevator operator closed the solid door, then began to draw the accordion gate into place.

CHAPTER THIRTY-FOUR

ZIVI

At first, he didn't remember why he was waking up on the living room couch, nostrils ripe with the sour smell of leather upholstery, saliva bonding his face to the tanned animal hide. He must have passed out. Nothing else could account for the brain-splitting headache and unfocused grogginess.

Slowly, painfully, he turned to face the bedroom. He felt like an old man. His body was ravaged from too many years on the Systema mat, too many years in a dangerous profession; his psyche was suffering from holding too many secrets, too many lies. When this was all over, they would start a new chapter. That is what he would tell her.

He steadied himself with a shaky hand and quietly padded to the bedroom. He would just slip under the covers next to her. Who knows, she might have already forgiven him and he could even get lucky.

But the sheets and blankets lay crumpled on her side of the bed. He stopped and stared, confused by what he was seeing.

"Giselle?"

He stepped tentatively into the room.

"*Beba?*"

He took two giant steps and glanced into the bassinette. It was empty. He leapt over the corner of the mattress and looked into the bathroom. *Empty.*

"*Giselle!*"

Half-relieved, half-annoyed, he hurried to the kitchen, the only other room in the apartment, the only other place they could be. Now he was ready to scold her for this not-funny game she was playing, because it was giving him agita. But they weren't there either. The throbbing in his head was now echoed by the pounding in his chest.

Of course, the answer to the riddle was right in front of him. The door. The chain was not hooked. He knew he had hooked it last night when big blabbermouth and little wimp-man left. Well, probably. Almost sure. The elevator wasn't there, meaning the last passenger had gone up, not come down. He took the stairs three at a time to the lobby, then bolted back down, slamming the door behind him.

He rifled through his pants pockets, came up with his cell phone, and dialed her number. Shrill music split the air. He bounded back to the living room to find her phone exactly where it had been plugged in the night before. He grabbed Giselle's phone and scrolled through her contacts. He stared at the list blankly. For the life of him, he couldn't remember Sabrina's name.

The phone was trembling. It took him a moment to realize it was because the hands holding it, his hands, were shaking. Finally, he realized she had entered 'Sab Well' for Sabrina Wellington.

Tensely shuffling back and forth in front of the sink, waiting for 'Sab Well' to pick up her *goddamned* phone, telephone hand stiffly suspended up in front of the locked window, he smashed his little toe into the corner of the cabinet. He doubled over, yowling in misery. Now he was *really* pissed off at that massively annoying bitch.

"'Lo?" Sabrina's disembodied voice came wafting sleepily through the phone.

"Put her on," Zivi snapped.

"Who, Giselle? What makes you think she's here?"

"Because last night," Zivi stammered. "She said ... I thought you two said..."

"Yeah, well, she's not here."

"Yeah, well, then where in the hell is she?" he demanded.

"How am *I* supposed to know?" Sabrina yawned. "Anyway, she knows how to take care of herself. And she was mighty pissed at you last night, boy. She probably left you. *Ha!* Yes—"

Zivi ended the call.

If Giselle wasn't with Sabrina, he had no further use for her. Although, she did say one thing that was reasonably legit. Giselle knew how to take care of herself. Even though Zivi didn't care to admit it. Ever since she had given birth to their child while she was trapped down here all alone, the only thing he had wanted to do was to take care of her. Because it was all his fault. There were no limits to the reasons Zivi had come up with for totally and completely failing his woman on that singularly most important day. So, the fact that she actually could take care of herself was a little annoying to him at that moment.

Giselle had just gone out for an early morning walk. She would be home any minute. Soon, they would be laughing at how silly he was, thinking she was so fragile, that she was in some kind of trouble.

But something wasn't right. He didn't know where Giselle and Nell were, and that was unacceptable. He had to go and find them.

Zivi knew that going from the Upper West Side to the Lower East Side was a long trek under the best conditions but now, sitting at the edge of his seat on the southbound train, waiting to reclaim his life from the brink of disaster, it felt like an eternity.

He stared out the window as the blurred stations flew past. In the old days it would never have occurred to him to set so much as a toe in the subway. Back then he rode around town in his blacked-out Lexus, double parking like he owned the street, his posse never more than one step behind, ensuring that he did. Sometimes, when he thought back, it all seemed like ancient history.

He could no longer even remember why he had stopped in there that night. Probably because the woman he was with liked the kitsch: the neon palm trees on either side of the door, the velvet rope, the fact that it had no name. In any event, she had insisted on going into the trendy Rivington Street bar, and he had agreed to it just to shut her up and because if she was happy, he would get laid. If he could, all these years later, he would thank her. But now, her face was hazy and he could not remember her name.

Zivi recalled how he had made room for himself at the end of the bar, as he always did, staking out his territory and surveying the scene. It was only later, when he turned around to order his friend a second drink, that he saw *her* working the other end. He remembered losing his breath. For the first time since he was a schoolboy, Zivi—the brash, handsome, wealthy, fearless man—felt like he was, once again, a schoolboy. Tongue-tied and blindly head-over-heels in love at first sight. He could not take his eyes off her. Eventually, his date got the hint and disappeared. At 4am the bar had closed. She came over to wipe the counter and take away an empty glass. Somehow, he managed to sweet talk her all the way out to the sidewalk. He offered to drive her home, but she refused. Told him she did not know him well enough to get into a car with him. So she walked and he drove alongside her the seven blocks to her studio apartment on East 6th.

The next night he was back and this time, although she still would not let him drive her home, she did let him take her out for coffee. By then, he was hers. He slept in her apartment every night for the next seven weeks before he found the courage to bring her uptown to his place. He was embarrassed by the opulence, the space, the lack of furnishings, the 2,000 square foot terrace. A year before, she had a falling out with her controlling, philandering father—rejected his values, his wealth, his Short Hills McMansion—and chose instead to work nights as a bartender to put herself through the Fine Arts Program at Parson's. It took Zivi many months before he could convince her to let him pay for her education, and only then on the condition that she would repay him, a debt he never intended on collecting. After a few semesters and an outpouring of faculty encouragement, she took a hiatus to paint full time. That was fine with him. Anything she wanted was fine with him. Eventually she succumbed, agreeing to make the unofficial official, and moved into his penthouse, keeping her tiny rent stabilized apartment as her painting studio. From that moment on, he had always known exactly where she was. Until now. Until *this*.

By the time Zivi emerged from the train station back uptown at 168th and Broadway, the midday sun was glaring down unmercifully. The sight of food trucks lined up at the corner made Zivi realize he hadn't eaten all day. He was starving, didn't feel like eating, but ordered a falafel anyway. One bite in and an idea that was so obvious, so glorious, yet at the same time so completely mortifying, landed in his head.

"Thanks, mate," he said, paid the vendor, and then bolted down the street.

CHAPTER THIRTY-FIVE

GWENDOLYN AND GISELLE

The accordion gate had slid halfway closed when the outer elevator door was whipped open. At first, all Giselle saw was the expensive French manicure. There was a twinge of embarrassment as she thought of her own nails, so often in the past stained with stubborn pigments of oil paint, but now, more often than not, tinted white from thick diaper creams that adhered defiantly to her skin.

"Can you come back for five minutes? I know. I understand that you must have a million more important things to do."

No. Nothing more important.

"I could really use your help with something."

Nothing better. Nothing better at all.

"The thing is, it's just that, she's kind of dirty."

Giselle stopped breathing.

"Filthy, really. And I'm just not exactly sure..."

The elevator man turned slowly, looking for direction.

"Just for a minute," said Gwendolyn, again.

The gray fuzzy eyebrows on the old man's face rose in question. He worked for Gwendolyn but would take instruction from Giselle.

For her plan to work, she had to say 'no.' Now was the time. The only time. Before Gwendolyn had the chance to hire legions of help. The only time Gwendolyn would face the reality that she was incapable of managing a child. Saying *no* was the only way for Giselle to somehow conjure up a victory.

There was nothing to be gained by returning to Gwendolyn's apartment. Nothing but the momentary, fleeting comfort of her child.

Once inside, Giselle found Nell was covered in acidic, fluorescent orange, corrosive bile that was already damaging fragile skin, already causing it to erupt in a salmon-colored rash. The baby looked at Giselle, stopped crying for a second, then arched her back, threw out her arms and began screaming even louder than before. Not knowing whether to laugh or cry, Giselle did both. She lifted the baby to her body and held her there, as tightly as she dared, until Nell was able to calm herself. She picked up the diaper bag, with its change of clothes, washcloths, soap, balm and lotion, and headed to the bathroom. Giselle filled the sink with warm water, stripped the child of her clothes, and bathed her.

When Nell was washed and dressed, Giselle draped a towel over herself, for now her own clothes had become smeared with regurgitation. For the last time, she held Nell close. Gwendolyn appeared in the doorway, holding out a neatly folded pile. She lifted it closer so Giselle could reach it with her free hand. It was a stack of clean women's clothes.

Giselle looked at the clothes and then back at Gwendolyn. Gwendolyn nodded and Giselle knew that her time was up. She handed the baby over. Nell reached her arms out to the stranger and smiled. Gwendolyn had even brought a washcloth. So,

Giselle got undressed. Once again, she ran the warm water. She took Nell's baby soap and lathered the washcloth. Then she stood there, exposed, looking at herself in the mirror, and tried to feel nothing.

"It was my stepfather," said Gwendolyn.

"Excuse me?" Giselle whispered.

"It was my stepfather," Gwendolyn repeated. "Not my father."

Giselle squeezed the excess water from the washcloth.

"My dad died when I was nine years old. He was hit by a taxi. We were all standing there when it happened: my mother, my brother, and me."

Giselle methodically washed the stickiness from her arms as Gwendolyn let her story unfurl.

Her father had been a public defender, just like Gwen. But in those days the benefits weren't great and he had miscalculated by not carrying a life insurance policy.

Gwendolyn shrugged. "I guess he didn't plan on dropping dead."

While her father was alive, Gwendolyn's mother took advantage of her law firm's flextime option. In exchange for a lower salary, she left the office mid-afternoon to be home when her children were dismissed from school. But as a single parent, her mother soon struggled financially. With two kids to support, she was forced to return to the office full time.

Giselle rinsed out the washcloth, placed it on the side of the sink, and dried herself off. She picked up the clean shirt.

"Not long afterward, she met a man. He had lots of money. He came on like a whirlwind. Swept her off her feet. Did my mother really love him?" Gwen shrugged. "But marrying him enabled her to resume her flextime hours arrangement."

Giselle slipped on the clean shirt. Gwendolyn felt bad that

she had not given her a better one. It looked good on Giselle anyway.

Even back then, the flextime option was all smoke and mirrors for a lawyer intent on making partner. Eventually, to be taken seriously, her mother had to put in the long hours at the office. She asked her new husband to help with the children while she stayed late at work. He owned his own business and he made his own schedule. He could be home when the kids got back from school. But instead of watching them, he locked his bedroom door and spent hours on the computer.

"My mother found out later it was child porn. She never told a soul outside the family. Because after we found out, I begged her not to."

Gwendolyn stepped into the bathroom, picked up a hairbrush and handed it to Giselle. Then she moved back out to the doorway.

Finally, Gwendolyn exhumed the memory that was supposed to be dead and buried. "The first time happened one day after school. He was right there, waiting for me." She swallowed. "His face was blank. Not that he ever smiled or laughed, but that afternoon he seemed different. Calm. Flat. Detached."

Gwendolyn hugged the baby closer to her breast.

"I was scared, although I didn't know why. He was my father now, right? Even so, I had an overwhelming urge to run, to get out of there. I never actually thought he would hurt me. I told myself there was no reason to be afraid."

Giselle felt cold in the warm bathroom.

"But he wasn't really my father."

Gwendolyn felt weak. The baby was heavy. She went into the room, put the toilet lid down and sat.

"My brother was at soccer practice. My mother was at work.

He grabbed hold of my wrist. I tried to pull away. But he wouldn't let go."

The baby was too heavy. Gwendolyn had to switch her to the other arm.

Gwen felt nothing, and she knew she would feel nothing, as she released her story into the air. It had been decades now, decades of suppression. Like a muscle caught in a spasm, she was confident her emotions would remain exactly where they should be. In check. Beyond reach.

He told Gwendolyn that this is what happens between fathers and daughters, and that it was very special and very private. That no one could ever know. And he squeezed her wrist until it was on fire. He said that it would break her mother's heart to find out what they were about to do. That if she knew, she would be jealous. She would blame Gwen. She would hate her daughter forever.

He told Gwendolyn that if anyone found out he would know that she was the one who ratted. That they would take her away, put her in a terrible foster family. That her mother would be declared unfit. She would go to jail and Gwendolyn would never see her again.

He told Gwendolyn that if anyone found out he would hurt her very badly. He would take away all their money. Then he said no one would ever believe her anyway, a stupid little girl against a big smart businessman.

He told Gwendolyn, what the hell. If she told anyone it would be easier to kill them all, Gwen, her mother and her brother, too.

Gwendolyn stared blankly. "Yeah," she said, far away from her own words. "He covered all the bases. And I believed every word."

She had to force herself to continue.

"He pulled me. Dragged me by the wrist into my

bedroom. Made me sit on the bed. I was scared to death. I remember saying, 'Please, no.' But his hands were already reaching out."

Gwen paused.

"I tried not to look at him, but he was standing right over me. Naked from the waist down. I was horrified. I had never seen anything like that before. Never even *imagined* it."

She slowly blinked. Remembered.

"I turned away and started to cry. I begged him. *No. Please, no.*"

Something wet and sticky pulled at Gwendolyn's hair.

'You're a slob,' he'd said. *'A fucking pig.'* Gwen was shocked to hear him curse. It was extremely upsetting. It frightened her. He told her she was about to get what she deserved. *'You are dirty. You are disgusting. You are worthless.'*

He'd picked up her new zebra print sweater with the fur collar from the floor. It was her favorite new sweater for the new school year. He flung it on the bed. All she could think was what was he going to do to her new sweater. Her new favorite sweater. Then he pushed Gwendolyn down. On top of that beautiful sweater.

A small wet hand gently patted Gwen's face.

"And then he raped me."

Gwen looked down at her free hand. Ever so slightly, the hand was trembling.

"My God, it hurt. But I was too scared to cry out. Scared that he would kill us all."

She sighed.

"I still have that sweater," she said. "Can you imagine? A treasure trove of DNA, and I still don't know what to do with it ... I never told a soul about the sweater ... until Zivi..."

She shivered.

"And now you."

Gwen felt her mouth quivering but would not allow the weakness or give in to the emotion.

When he got home, her brother stopped and stared into her room. After a pause he said, '*Did he touch you?*' Gwen thought about it. '*No*,' she said. '*He didn't touch me.*' Then she asked him. '*Did he touch you?*' '*No*,' he said. '*No. He didn't touch me either.*'

The wet hands poked Gwen's ear.

"He did it for years. Two or three times a week for years."

She developed coping mechanisms. Whenever she came home and he was there, she taught herself to go numb. Mentally and physically. She went to a private place in her mind where he couldn't touch her. Then, when he was on top of her, she would make herself feel nothing. She focused on a crack in the ceiling. Imagined it was a path and she was running on it. She was free and running away. Sometimes it worked. She would lie still, waiting for it all to be over, but in her mind her arms and legs were pumping and her heart was pounding.

Gwen slipped her free hand underneath her thigh. To hide its trembling.

He began to comment about her body. Ridiculed her every day. '*You're grotesque*,' he'd say, '*You need meat on your bones.*' That's when I became desperate to keep myself skeletal, because he said he didn't like that. Any time I thought I was starting to get breasts or hips I would stop eating. If I got so hungry that I had to eat, I would throw it all up. But that was hard. Once, I even fainted in school. They didn't know about eating disorders back then. So they sent me home. To him. To more of the same. But they did teach me one useful thing. The health teacher was talking about poison control. Told us how to use baking soda to induce vomiting. That made things easier. After that, at least I could eat."

Gwen was getting dizzy. But she kept it in check.

"Wednesday, June 8th. The day before my math final. He was waiting when I got home. He was in the middle of the second time when my mother came home. Opened the door. Walked in on us."

Giselle made a soft gasp. The baby jumped up and down in Gwen's lap.

Her mother had yelled, *Gwendolyn!* She said it over and over again. Because she knew it was Gwen. But she hadn't yet realized it was him. Thought it was some guy Gwen had brought home from school. But then, with her mother standing there, for the first time in all those years, Gwen had the nerve to push the bastard off.

Finally, Gwen cradled the baby's legs to stop them from hurting her. To stop the pain.

Her mother screamed for him to get the hell out. Slowly, he got up. Casually collected his clothes. And then he was gone. Her mother was shaking and crying and asking her if she was okay and saying over and over how sorry she was and hugging Gwen and kissing her, and asking herself how could she let this happen to her little girl. She wanted to take Gwen to the doctor, but Gwen knew what would happen if anyone found out, so she panicked and insisted that no one could ever know. It wasn't the first time. It was the millionth time. Gwen promised she was okay. She didn't want a doctor. Her mother told Gwen not to move while she stepped out. Gwen heard yelling. Then her mother started a shower. By the time Gwendolyn came out, he was gone. The next day, all his stuff disappeared. They never saw him again. As if he never even existed.

"But—" Giselle tried to ask a question. Gwen cut her off. She was not ready to relinquish control of the conversation. She couldn't. Because she was finally ready. And if she didn't do it now, she knew that she never would.

For a long time, she had thought about going to the police.

Her mother begged her to. But Gwen was too afraid. She still believed that if she told anyone he would come back and kill them. After all, Gwen was dirty, she was unworthy, she was worthless. She had gotten what she deserved. Her mother was so consumed with guilt that she did whatever Gwen wanted. Even back then, Gwen could be persuasive. It was easy to convince her mother that the best thing was to act like it never happened, to not relive the pain over and over with the cops and the lawyers. "He's gone," she'd said. "What's the point?"

Gwen sighed. The next part was the worst.

Her mother never stopped blaming herself for letting it happen. From the minute she found out, she never looked the same again. Her eyes. They became lifeless. And her smile. Gwen couldn't remember her ever smiling again. Every day, she would ask. 'Do you think he started another family and was doing the whole thing all over again to another little girl?' Eventually, the guilt drove her crazy. She started drinking. Couldn't hold down a job. Couldn't make decisions. She stopped going out. Stayed in the apartment. She never left. That's the thing about the city. You can get anything you want delivered.

By now, the tremors had slipped up beyond Gwendolyn's hand and her whole arm was shaking.

But Gwen knew the truth. The truth was that it was all her fault. If she had just been able to hang on. If she had just been able to keep it a secret until she moved out for college. Then she could have gotten away from him. Everything would have been different. Her mother would never have found out. She never would have had a breakdown. Everything would have been fine.

The shaking was in her stomach now, under her ribcage and in her breasts. When she spoke, it sounded like she was shivering.

When Gwen became a lawyer, she explained why she

worked all the time. She never wanted to be her mother, dependent on someone for money. It made her sick to be around her mother. She had become so fragile and vulnerable. Gwen couldn't stand her weakness. In the end, she rarely saw her. Then one day, the building called. The locks had been changed and there was a terrible odor. They needed her permission to drill the deadbolt.

Gwen could feel the sob coming now, slowly rising in her chest. A sob, long and deep. "*She was all alone, curled up in my bed when they found her.*"

And now, weakness washed over her and she could feel herself slipping to the floor.

Giselle knelt beside her, hands brushing along the length of Gwen's trembling body, bracing Gwen's own arms around the baby. Giselle, supporting them all. Only Gwen would not have it. Not any longer. Her days of denial, her days of jealous spite, had exacted their toll. Honestly recounting her story suddenly left her appalled and ashamed about what she had become.

"No," she croaked. "No," she repeated, blinded by tears, but seeing things clearly for the first time. "No, no, no, no."

Giselle pulled her hands from Gwen and drew back.

"No," Gwen said again, more gently this time. "What I am saying is that I know I can't care for a baby. I can barely take care of myself. I know that. Zivi knows that. You know that. Hell, anyone who has ever *met* me knows that."

Gwen's tears splashed onto the floor.

"I saw you with her," said Gwen. "You're incredible. And Zivi is much more of a father than I'll ever be a mother. This baby business isn't for me. At least not yet. I'm not ready. And the two of you are."

Gwen wanted to hold the child out to Giselle, but her arms, which on any other day could do countless curls, countless repetitions with twenty-pound dumbbells until her biceps and triceps burned, only releasing themselves to the exquisite pain of total exhaustion, those arms no longer had the strength to complete the gesture.

At that same moment, Gwendolyn's words, admitting she wasn't ready to care for Nell, left Giselle in despair. She was in despair for Gwen, for the violations that had excised the childhood, the youth, the happiness, from an innocent young girl, leaving scars and demons that followed her to this day, culminating in the tortured woman breaking down before her.

But those things were in the past and the past was sealed and could not be altered. There was only the future. The future with its unrealized potential was the only thing that could be molded and nudged. So, Giselle looked to the future.

Therefore, it was not a decision based on right and wrong, noble or ignoble. It was not a selfless decision. On the contrary; it was a completely selfish one. One based on self-preservation. Giselle knew she did not have the fortitude to relive the trauma of this day. To give Gwen the time she would need to recover. And then to say goodbye one more time. Giselle was simply too fragile. She would shatter. She knew this for a fact. And that realization left her only one option.

And so, she was in despair.

Because she knew Nell was not hers and would never be hers. She knew she would have to relinquish the child to her broken birth mother and walk out, once more, alone.

CHAPTER THIRTY-SIX

ZIVI

Back in the apartment, he grabbed Giselle's cell phone from the *biblioteka* coffee table, scrolled down to 'SabWel,' and contorted himself over the sink. It took five and a half rings before the meathead finally picked up.

"She there yet?" he demanded.

"No. She isn't *there yet*."

"Has she called you? Have you spoken to her?"

"No, Romeo, she has not and I have not. However, should she, at some later time during the day—"

Zivi pounded the red 'end' key. How could she have gone out and not taken her cell phone? They had a pact. An agreement. A *rule*. Never be without your phone. They were always supposed to be able to get in touch with each other. How could she risk such danger, and for the second time in just days? Didn't she realize that people today were crazy? Rapists. Murderers. *Terrorists*. Who knew what kind of terrible things could happen when he wasn't around for her?

He opened the phone to see if it held any clues to her whereabouts. He scrolled through everything yet again. Again, there was nothing to help him. He thumbed into her photo gallery. She had 2,057 saved photos. He smiled to himself. That was just like her, to have a ridiculous number of photos squirreled away. On his own phone, he didn't have any. Not one. He pressed 'view.'

He arranged them chronologically, oldest to newest. The first few were of him mugging for the camera when they had first gotten the phones. But then, as he scrolled down, his chest began to tighten. Picture after picture was of him; candid pictures that he never knew existed. Pictures of his face profiled in shadow against the midday sun. Pictures of him cleaning the apartment while she was pregnant and he thought she was sleeping. Pictures of him sleeping. Pictures of him with his head in the building's boiler as he cleaned it. Pictures of him polishing the handles and the spigots in the front of the building. Pictures of him reading the morning paper, choking down her horrible, wonderful, cup of joe. Beautiful pictures of his body parts. Of his calloused hands. Of his big, ugly feet. Of his rough elbow. Of the back of his neck. The back of his knee. And then there were the most recent ones. Pictures of him sneakily reading her pregnancy books. And finally, pictures of him with Nell. Pictures of him kissing Nell. Pictures of him cuddling her. Pictures of him trying to change her diaper. Pictures of him singing in her ear.

Zivi dropped heavily onto the couch. 2,057 photos. Mostly all of him. He shut the phone and gently laid it on the table. He thought about those pictures—how she watched him, waiting for the right second to sneak a speck away just for herself. Not to share; just for herself.

He looked at the camera and tried to envision himself through her eyes. Why did she love him so? Then it dawned on him. He was the one who betrayed *her*, not the other way around. How, when she sat alone, waiting for him to come home so they could build a life together, he had been out deceitfully cultivating the favor of his lawyer. With his body. Like he was a prostitute. The same body which she had magically transformed, with the help of her little phone camera, into an art form.

Then he thought about *her* body. That *her* body was already a piece of art, without the assistance of some cheap camera. About how proprietary he was about her body. About how if anybody ever violated that body, he would kill them. And then he thought about how he would feel if she actively, aggressively and clandestinely, sought out another man to give her body to. Freely. With abandon. While at the same time telling him she loved him, while she was making a home with him, while she was making love to him, while they were trying to have a baby. While she held their child inside of her. He thought about that. He thought about what that would do to him. He thought about how that would make him feel.

But wait.

Hadn't he done it all for her? Didn't she appreciate that the only way they could afford their lavish lifestyle was if he took out an insurance policy guaranteeing the best legal representation they could afford? That he had to pay those premiums—unusually high and unconventional premiums, to be sure—but insurance premiums nonetheless? And they had reaped the benefits he had banked on, and then some. Hell, Gwen didn't simply go out of her way for him, she had literally jeopardized her own future, her own *freedom*, for him.

What had happened? What went wrong? He thought back on all the time they had spent together—the easy and the hard, the good and the bad—until finally it dawned on him. Just being together was enough. They never needed the bling. Sure, it was nice, it was fun, but the pound of flesh it extracted was way too dear.

He knew he would have to do everything he possibly could

to earn back her trust, earn back her love. Because if the situation was reversed, and it was she who had wandered, no matter how noble the ends, it would be difficult for him to return home. He now understood that he had broken her heart, and that knowledge alone was more than enough to break his own.

The first step for putting his plan into motion was asking a favor of his boss, former drug kingpin turned real estate mogul, Big TaTa. Convincing TaTa that Zivi should give Giselle the stove from the vacant apartment instead of jewelry as a peace offering took some doing. At first, Big TaTa insinuated that Zivi didn't know how to control his woman. 'The American concept of equal rights had no place in Bosnian familial hierarchy,' he insisted. *'Trust me, my kuzen,'* the big man said. *'Nothing good comes of giving them too much power.'* But it must have been a joke, because eventually Big TaTa caved.

"Thanks, *brat*," said Zivi. "And don't you worry. Any day now you'll meet some hot piece of ass who is happy with a stove, a dishwasher and a washing machine. And when she is really good to you, you go wild and throw in a vacuum cleaner, too."

"I hope not my *kuzen*," TaTa said, and Zivi thought he heard him shudder. "If that happens you may shoot me. In fact, I insist."

Half an hour later, Zivi was up in 8-B with a can of oven cleaner, rubber gloves and rags. He had done this job a hundred times before when other apartments were between tenants, but this time he was impatient and annoyed with every stain he could not completely remove, every scratch he could not perfectly buff out. Nevertheless, by 3:30 that afternoon, he knew he had done the best job humanly possible and he left to track down the large dolly and the moving straps. He desperately hoped to get the thing into their apartment and hooked up to the gas line before she got home, but he now realized that was not a realistic deadline. Because she would be walking through the door any second now. If she wasn't already home waiting.

Still, he was able to single-handedly maneuver the 300-pound appliance into the elevator, down to the basement level and into their apartment before she returned. As he eased the stove into the kitchen, he considered the long-term implications of his actions. Somehow, by the grace of God, he had managed to go this long without installing an oven into their tiny but otherwise fully renovated kitchen. He had always been able to talk his way out of it, telling her he was getting to it, that it was the next thing to come as soon as he had time. But he never planned on finding said time. Because installing a stove meant she would 'cook.' That's what cooking was, wasn't it? When perfectly good ingredients are mixed together, put into an oven, and through a chemical process caused by the application of a catalyst, in this case heat, those ingredients transform into something entirely different. Technically, that was cooking. The problem was that then, she would expect him to eat it. And he didn't need to lose weight. So yeah, what he was doing was not merely installing a new appliance. It was instituting a life change. But he would do it for love. The afternoon slipped past. The stove was installed.

He went to the bathroom. Looked in the mirror. Was disgusted by what he saw. He was hot and sticky and grouchy and he stunk. He had to shower before she got home. He just needed a moment first. He sat on the floor, back against the couch, legs wedged beside the *biblioteka* table. He considered all the infested corners of the city where she could be lost without him to protect her. Got sucked down into a dark, restless sleep.

CHAPTER THIRTY-SEVEN

GISELLE AND GWENDOLYN

Giselle propped the baby in Gwendolyn's lap the best that she could. She stood up and watched as Gwendolyn's baby smiled up at her, the bright eyes never leaving Giselle's face, as if they were all about to commence a big, happy game of hide-and-seek.

Giselle hoped it was safe to leave Nell with her mother.

Goodbye, my little one.

She assumed she said the words and did not merely think them. As Giselle backed out of the room, her heel smacked into the unyielding stone door saddle. The pain was sharp and crisp and she stumbled. A cold hand grabbed her ankle. She assumed it was a pitiful attempt to help her catch her balance, an automatic act meant to save her from embarrassment. But when Giselle looked down, Gwendolyn's face was ashen and her eyes had a wild fear to them.

"No. You can't go," Gwendolyn choked. "You can't leave me with her. I'm not ready."

Giselle leaned against the door frame, the heft of her decision bearing down on her. "Listen to me," she said.

More than anything else she wanted to be nurturing. Understanding. Giving. It was the only way she knew to be.

She wanted to comfort Gwendolyn, to tell her everything would be okay, that it would all work out in the end. That she, Giselle, would make it happen. But she did not. She could not. Because Giselle was in self-preservation mode. So, she forced herself. For once, she forced herself to help herself and not the other person. But it was hard and she did not like it.

"I can't do it, Gwen," she sighed. "You said it yourself. You are the biological mother. I am not. In fact, I'm nothing to her. And I won't be a babysitting service. I can't take care of her until you're ready to take her back. I won't do it. Giving her up one time is too much in itself." She swallowed hard. "Twice will kill me."

Gwendolyn was silent.

Giselle had no idea where the inner strength germinating somewhere deep inside her chest was coming from. Maybe, she thought, it was born of the lack of anything left to lose.

"You need to start taking responsibility for your actions," she said. "You're the one who got pregnant. You chose to have a baby. Now that baby is here. You have to deal with that."

Giselle stared down at the grown woman acting like a spoiled child. "You have to grow up. You are not the only one anymore. Now, there are two lives involved."

Gwendolyn's pupils were dilated. She seemed to lose focus and her grip on Giselle's ankle tightened. Nevertheless, Giselle stood planted and silent, waiting for Gwendolyn to react, to give an acknowledgment, to find her way back to the moment, to do something. Giselle was only so strong. It was now past time for her to leave.

"You're right," Gwendolyn finally said, but Giselle had to strain to hear. "It's not just about me. It's about what's best for her."

Gwendolyn stared up at the ceiling for such a long time that

Giselle, too, glanced upward, to see if the answers lay in the little gray cracks spidering above their heads.

Gwendolyn turned her head and rubbed the mucus from her nose onto the shoulder of her running top. Finally, she shifted her gaze back to Giselle.

"Tell me something," she said.

Giselle stared back.

"Are you a good mother to this baby?"

The question made Giselle sick. It was insulting and demeaning. It made her heart ache and she wanted nothing more but to turn and disappear out the door. Instead, she stood perfectly still, took three deep breaths and forced herself to stay calm. "I am the only mother this child has ever known." She struggled to speak as atonally as possible. "She is happy. She is healthy. She is clean. She is thriving. Draw your own conclusions."

With one blink, Gwendolyn's pupils transformed.

"Just as I thought," she said, with such conviction that it made Giselle nervous. "I've done my due diligence," Gwen announced, "and now I'm ready to give you my final verdict. A gift," she said. "A non-returnable, un-appealable gift. Something more generous than anything I've ever given anyone in my entire life. I'm giving you the gift of knowledge. And in my little corner of the universe, knowledge is power."

Gwen fixed her gaze firmly on Giselle. The faint smile which had made its way onto her lips slipped away. "I want you to understand," she said carefully, measuring her words, "I am not being melodramatic. I am giving information to you, and only to you. With it, the game is rigged. You hold all the chips. You have all the power. The power over me."

Giselle broke out in a cold sweat.

"The only reason I am doing this," Gwen said, "is because I've finally found someone I can trust. *You.* I trust you. And, as someone told me, because it's the right thing to do. For the baby."

Then Gwen let go of Giselle's leg and turned Nell around so that she could gaze into the baby's face. Giselle glanced at her ankle. The pressure of Gwen's fingernails had left small, magenta half-moon crescents.

"Remember when they clipped him on that last big felony?"

It seemed to Giselle that Gwen was asking the question of the baby and not her. But she answered anyway. "Of course I remember."

"Yeah." Gwen smiled at the baby. "That was a lot of drugs," she cooed. "Two kilos of pure, uncut heroin." She stroked the child's head. "That was going to send your daddy away for a good long time, wasn't it, baby?

"You know what?" Gwen glanced at Giselle before looking back at the baby. "I'm sorry. I knew about you."

For a second, her voice caught.

"He told me about you." She pursed her lips. "But I didn't care. I just wanted to be with him. To hold him. To have him next to me. I always knew he was using me. That he was just pretending to be interested in me. I knew it, but I didn't care. Somehow, because I knew he really didn't care, it was safe to let him in. I was able to open up to him in a way that I was never able to with anyone before. I made myself vulnerable. I guess it was my only currency. The only way I knew to show how much I cared for him." She paused. "I guess you already know that he's a smart guy. Your Zivi. He really knew what he was doing."

A slight, joyless smile clouded Gwen's face.

"And he took his time. He *really* worked me. In the end, he knew all my buttons. How to pick me up. How to throw me back down again. But you have to understand. Even Zivi doing an act, having him next to me playing a part, was better than no

Zivi at all. So, I let him play me. And like I said, he did it just right. I would have done anything for him. And he knew it."

Gwen blushed, but it was Giselle who felt embarrassed. She recognized part of herself in Gwen's story.

"So yeah. Then one day, I finally got the call. Boy," she smirked, "did he ever go out and get himself busted. Obviously, I had to get him out," she said to Nell. "I couldn't stand to see him behind bars, even at Rikers, which security wise, was pretty low-end compared to where he was going to end up."

But she had to bide her time, to do it right, so she wouldn't get caught.

"The evidence was already tested and tagged, stashed away in the big safe room down at One Police Plaza. It's where everything is held until trial. I had to be patient. It was months before the preliminary hearing date. That's when Zivi's evidence was finally brought back to the evidence room in the courthouse. There would be a small window to make it work. I knew I would only have one chance."

Evidence room desk officers loathe letting civilians in back. Especially those high-priced arrogant attorneys from Park Avenue doing their prissy white-collar stuff, the ones who've never been to a crime scene, never seen a warm corpse lying in the filthy street, never been woken up in the middle of the night to watch them play good-cop bad-cop in the foulest back room of the precinct. Those pristine, unsullied millionaires in their 5,000 dollar suits never rub shoulders with the real cogs in the criminal justice system. The guys in the back hate those show-offs. But Gwen. She was real. They saw her working hard for her money. Defending the true dregs the system pretends to care about. She saw those same dorky clerks almost every week. They knew her. They may have hated her, but they knew her. She told the officer she needed to get another visual to prepare for trial. He didn't want to let her back there. But she gave him her best performance. Hinted at all kinds of nasty personal favors she could do for him.

Eventually he caved. Seems he only had eyes for the slut-suit and the fuck me shoes she was wearing. Never even noticed she was lugging her big litigation bag in behind her.

Gwen smiled at the baby. "He should have trusted his instincts." The baby smiled back at her.

Later that same afternoon, she went to the judge and asked for a sixty-day postponement. It was critical he granted it. That way, there'd be a hundred people in and out of the evidence room before anyone noticed anything suspicious. In addition, the closed-circuit cameras blanketing the place were on a thirty-day loop. Beyond thirty days, the tape is wiped. Of course, there still was a risk that someone could view the tape within the thirty-day window. But Gwen was willing to bet they were all precisely as lazy and inept as they seemed.

"Wow. We never knew why the trial got delayed."

"I couldn't tell him. In case he turned on me, or something. I loved him, but that didn't mean I could trust him."

Neither spoke. Giselle sat patiently, waiting. It seemed as if Gwen was once again far away, forgetting Giselle was even there.

She brought her eyes back level with Nell's. Giselle noticed that the colors, the vivid green, hazel, dappled mosaic of their irises, matched exactly.

"Well," Gwen said to the baby. "Seems I was getting myself into a bit of hot water with the judge." She frowned.

Judge Warner was really leaning on Gwen and the DA to cut a deal. Given what the DA had, barring any errors at trial, there would be no basis for appeal. For all practical purposes, Zivi's life was over.

A bitter chill ran down Giselle's spine.

Gwen told the judge it was a case of mistaken identity. That

Zivi had an alibi, that it was just a matter of time before they unearthed the people Zivi was actually with when the whole thing went down. That Zivi was one of the guys who was hanging outside the house, not inside, that he was just standing around on the street which, last time she checked, still isn't a crime.

She laughed out loud.

"I told that judge so much bullshit that even I could barely keep it straight."

Then she became serious again.

"With the stakes as high as they were, with a real life on the line, judges are always lenient in granting extensions based on the possibility of unearthing exculpatory evidence. Even if it seems remote. Otherwise, their perfectly good trials can get overturned on appeal. Trial judges hate that.

"And guess what, baby girl?" Gwen asked Nell. "He bit. Cover-His-Ass-Warner granted a whole two-month extension right then and there, directly from the bench."

Then they just had to sit and wait. Three weeks before the trial, two weeks, *one* week. She wanted to scream at them, '*It's time. Go look at the stash, you idiots! Go back and look. Can't you see it's been tampered with? Can't you see it needs to get retested!?*'

Giselle held her breath. She was almost afraid to ask. "What did you do?"

Gwen sat forward and looked Giselle straight in the eye.

"Baking soda," Gwen said, and she slowly leaned back against the toilet.

Giselle swallowed. "No. *No way.*" She looked at the other woman in disbelief. "You *did not* swap baking soda for heroin."

Gwen grinned. "I sure did. Hunched over so the cameras wouldn't see and swapped all two kilos of it."

Giselle slumped her back and stared at the sharp angles of Gwen's face. Then she started to giggle. "And that worked?"

"Ridiculously well." Gwen giggled, too. "The majority of thefts from evidence rooms are committed by law enforcement employees themselves. So, yeah. They're probably still looking at each other sideways, trying to figure out which one of them is the culprit."

"Oh, my God." Giselle was laughing now, slipping down off the tub, landing on the floor next to Gwen. "That is the most ridiculous thing I ever heard."

Gwen was laughing too. "I'm glad you see it my way."

"Wow," Giselle said. "Is that how it works? I mean, I've never even seen heroin. That's all you do, and then everybody is fooled?"

"That was the thing," Gwen said, sobering herself up. "It wasn't supposed to work as well as it did. The H they caught Zivi with was uncut. Sticky, with a yellow tint, almost brown in places. And coarse. So, I assumed that eventually any moron would see the difference and order it retested. But no one did. I guess it was just paranoia on my part, thinking that everyone and their mother would be going back to check on my particular evidence and would then notice that something was wrong. But it makes sense. There are shelves and shelves of all kinds of stuff back there. Anyway, I had to wait until they were setting up for trial for someone who had seen the stash before to go back and re-tag it. That's when they finally opened their eyes and freaked out. So yeah." She nodded. "I'd say it worked."

Giselle struggled with an appropriate way to express her gratitude. "Thank you," she said, staring at Gwen. "That was really brave of you."

Gwen rolled her eyes. "First of all, I did it as much for me as for him. And secondly," she glared sharply at Giselle, "if you're going to get mushy and sentimental on me, you're gonna make me sorry I told you in the first place."

Giselle did not want to ruin the sudden offering of goodwill. "Agreed," she said, and looked away. The room was still until Giselle could no longer bear the silence. "What did you do with the real stuff?"

"Ah," said Gwen, looking pleased and mysterious. "Now *there's* the ten-million-dollar question. Turns out, I'm leaning against my only witness. If only this toilet could talk, oh the tales it could tell." She smirked. "Then the DA would have quite a case."

"Wow." Giselle shook her head in disbelief. She didn't know what else to say.

"So that's why." Gwen's voice cracked and Giselle fished a tissue out of her pocket and tried to give it to her, but Gwen shooed her away. "So that's why I told you. So that if I ever seem to be tottering, to be changing my mind, you are to dangle this secret in front of my face and tell me that you're going to take it to the police. It's my gift to you. It's your leverage, so that after you walk out of here today, I can never change my mind."

"Change your mind about what?" Giselle whispered. Then she held her breath, afraid that any deviation in air pressure caused by exhaled molecules might somehow cause Gwen to rethink what she was thinking. Because Giselle now knew. It was crystal clear. Nevertheless, she had to hear it. Because it would never truly be true until Gwen said the words herself. Out loud.

"I'm giving her up." Gwen's voice trembled. "Giving her to you and her father." Gwen smiled and her tone softened. "Don't worry. This is no spur of the moment, rash, knee-jerk decision. In a way, I guess I always knew it would come down to this. I've been thinking about what I was going to do for a long time now."

She looked at the wall in front of her.

"I could never harm his child. I tried to explain that to him. But he didn't believe me."

Gwen looked back at Giselle. "You know, it's funny. I guess when you've been a bullshitter all your life, no one believes you when you finally tell the truth. Anyway, for the past three months I knew the two of you had her. He made sure I knew. With his silly little wave. So, I knew she was safe. Hell, I knew she was much better off with the two of you than she'd ever be with me. That's why I didn't push it. Instead, I played the press. Played the detectives. What did you think? Otherwise, I could have just called him. I could have found out where you guys were in a second. So, *Giselle*. The bottom line is that there is nothing spur of the moment about it. Please understand. I'm not *that* heartless. It's just not my time. I have some major issues I still need to work out. Then maybe, someday, it will be my turn." She shrugged. "Or maybe not."

Giselle tried to speak, but Gwen got there first.

"Don't worry," Gwen said, smiling the prettiest smile Giselle had ever seen. "Everything is going to be all right." Then she took the baby and placed her in Giselle's lap. "I promise," she said and squeezed Giselle's hand. "Really, I do. I promise."

Giselle inhaled the familiar scent of baby shampoo in Nell's hair. She let the weight of a thousand worries lift from her weary bones until she felt as if she would float up to the ceiling. The world came barreling back at her. She had to cover her eyes against the bright sunshine bursting in through the bathroom window. She heard traffic clamoring below on Central Park West, heard the sound of children screaming in the playground across the street. Giselle wanted to celebrate. She wanted to sob uncontrollably, to shout for joy, to scream, to whoop, to jump up and down, to turn a cartwheel. But she did none of those things. There would be plenty of time to celebrate. Now was not the time.

This was the time to be caring toward a person who had endured unspeakable pain. A person who had spent the vast majority of her life inflicting endless mental and physical torture upon herself. Giselle knew she must respect Gwen for the entire person that she was, accept her history and each of her experiences, because it was all of that which had combined to bring them together to this place. To this bathroom floor where she had given up so much, in such a wonderfully selfless, yet completely selfish, decision.

She turned to Gwen. Touched her hand. "Well, Nell and I thank you. Now we are officially a family."

"*Nell?*" Gwen snorted. "Nell is a *terrible* name. I named her Cassie and that's what I'm calling her."

"It's Nell," Giselle repeated, amazed by the confidence a little knowledge had bestowed upon her. Suddenly, Giselle was no longer afraid of Gwen. For the first time, she was speaking as an equal. "Her name is Nell." And Gwen nodded her acceptance.

Nell attempted to shove her entire fist into her mouth. She seemed to understand all eyes were upon her and she smiled.

"Do you think—" Gwen began. "Oh, never mind."

"What?"

"It's just that ... no, it's stupid."

"No," Giselle said. "Now you have to say it."

"It's just that..."

"*What?*"

"It's just that I need to shower and I'm really hungry. Do you think you could, I mean are you willing ... What I'm trying to say is, will you ... wait for me? And then, like, maybe we can grab some lunch?"

"Oh. Well, um," Giselle hedged. "I'm not exactly sure." She had successfully wrested Nell from Gwen's clutches; she would be an idiot to risk some unforeseen scenario where everything got turned back upside down. Zivi would tell her to just walk away ... or better yet, run. "How 'bout you shower," she finally said, "and I'll think about it?"

Gwen tried to do her crying under the pounding flow of cold water. She tried as hard as she could to feel the appropriate anguish at relinquishing all parental rights to the child she had nurtured inside her body for nine interminably long months. The torment she thought she was supposed to feel. But the hurt didn't come. There was no grief. Only a deep, deep, down to the marrow, all-encompassing sense of relief.

This meant, of course, that emotionally she was damaged goods. This fact was not news. The loss of passion for all things large and small, important things and insignificant ones, had settled over her sometime in her eleventh year.

She knew the potential to feel was there, that she had always kept the ember alive at the bottom of her heart, never letting it totally extinguish. He had taken everything else from her. She was not going to let him have that, too.

She got out of the shower. Dried herself off. Did the best she could with the concealer and the rest of her makeup.

Maybe someday. Like if she ever went back to that stupid shrink.

She stood sideways in the mirror and flattened her skirt across her belly. Thankfully, she had puked up the Chinese food from the night before, so she wasn't retaining water. Her stomach was relatively flat. Not as flat as Giselle's. But still. Flat for her.

She shut off the light, opened the bathroom door and strained her ears. But beyond the usual cacophony wafting up from the street, there was nothing to be heard. The ominously familiar emptiness, the loneliness and the sadness, crashed down upon her.

Giselle had left with Nell.

Gwen was all alone.

She tried to shake it off. Told herself she could handle it. Stood up straight, chin defiantly in the air. She would go down to the corner grocer and buy gallons of peanut butter cup Häagen-Dazs, pounds of M&Ms, bags of Oreo cookies.

Gwen took one step, and then another, down the hallway to the living room. But she already knew what she would find. The silence was proof enough. Giselle had gotten what she wanted and had abandoned Gwen to return to her charmed existence with her boyfriend. Gwen's body ached with pain and sadness, knowing it was so. She tried to conjure up the hatred and resentment that were so familiar to her, but the feelings would not come. Instead, she was completely gutted. As dead and despondent and broken as she had ever been in her entire life.

CHAPTER THIRTY-EIGHT

DELVECCIO AND MCMILLAN

"Oh, that's just perfect," said Brian McMillan. "Would you look at this."

Giselle turned down 89th Street and disappeared out of sight. The two detectives slowly rose. Brian McMillan's knees creaked as he hobbled out of the park and the two headed back to the 83rd Precinct.

"I gotta tell you, Gary. I'm glad I'm retiring. I'm too old for all this running around."

"I know you are."

"When I go, you're gonna be lead on this case. Have you thought about next steps?"

DelVeccio pursed his lips. "Remember how she told the hospital nurse she didn't want to put the father's name on the birth certificate, but told us the baby came from her penchant for drunken sex with anonymous men?"

"Yeah."

"How she conveniently couldn't ID or remember the names of any of them? Not a single one?"

McMillan nodded.

DelVeccio shrugged. "The guys I have parading her picture

around every bar in town? So far, not one bartender remembers her face. My gut is telling me her story doesn't line up."

"Interesting."

"I think she knows who the father is and she's not telling. I'm gonna start leaning in harder on her. I'm gonna make it happen."

CHAPTER THIRTY-NINE

GISELLE AND ZIVI

When Zivi woke from his terrifying nightmare of abandonment and apocalypse, where only the cockroaches survived, Giselle was standing in the room relocking the locks, re-dropping the deadbolts, resurrecting the barrier. He struggled to rise up from the floor, but his legs were wedged between the coffee table and the sofa, and when he tried to move they were stiff and brittle and he smashed his knees into the sharp corner of an engineering tome, the pain so complete it made him fall backward, seeing spots and groaning in agony.

He looked up helplessly; she was trying to talk to him, he could tell because her lips were moving, but he did not want to hear her. He did not have time to listen to her, because what he had to say was much more important. He inched his way out from the claustrophobic space between the books and the sofa, tried to stand but his injury prone, hyper-extended, Systema-karate knees collapsed beneath him, so he crawled to her feet and wrapped his arms around her legs.

"Zivi," she said, but he would not be put off.

"No, Giselle. No. You have to listen to me. He spoke into her thighs. "I was just trying to make things right. I never wanted to do anything to hurt you." He breathed in the damp, perspiration infused patchouli lotion on her skin. The scent of his woman. "What I did was wrong. But you were so upset, so sad. I wanted to give you back the baby we lost. To make you happy again. And I knew I could do it. Because she was my baby. *Is* my baby. That's why I did it. It's all I wanted to do. I wanted to give you my baby."

"But—"

Zivi shook his head to stop her from speaking.

"All I wanted was to give her to you as a gift and be a family. The two girls I love. I wanted to do what was best for you and what was best for my baby. But I see now. I can't force her on you. Because you're right. She has a mother." He sighed. "The thing is, she is such a *crummy* mother."

"Zivi—"

"But here's the thing," he interrupted her again. "Just now, today, when I—I thought I lost you, but Gissy, I can't lose you. I won't lose you. So, we have to give her back. Like you said. It is right thing to do. It is just that," he tugged at his hair, frustrated, "I wish there was ... but I know there is not ... I can see that now ... It is just that I know Gwen will be such a terrible mother and she is such a terrible person."

"Well, I don't know about that," Giselle said, as if she had some reason to know.

"Don't know about what?"

She took his hand and led him to the couch. "Well, not the terrible mother part. I'll give you that one. She *would* be a terrible mother. It's the terrible *person* part I have a problem with."

"How can you say that?" His heart thumped. "You don't know Gwendolyn."

"Oh, but I do."

"*Giselle.*" Paranoia began to move up from his feet toward the bottom of his stomach. "*No.* You don't."

"Oh, *yes.* I do."

"You're making me nervous. There is nothing about Gwen Black you should know. So why are you telling me she is not a terrible person?" His bodily functions seemed to short-circuit. He shifted his abdomen uncomfortably, to ease the sudden pressure of the falafel sandwich.

"Because I met her."

"*Nyyeettt!*" His heart felt suddenly enlarged and he imagined himself a feeble old man just seconds before succumbing to a massive heart attack.

"I did. I met her," she said matter-of-factly. "And we had a very long talk."

"No, you did not!" He was certain his heart had ceased pumping. "I won't allow it!"

"And I'll tell you something else."

"What?" Now he was afraid, because he knew she was telling the truth.

She shrugged. "She's very ... *interesting.* Rather complicated."

"*Nooo.* She is not complicated. She's a ... a wild animal."

"Yeah, well." Giselle shrugged. "I tamed her."

"So, what? You two made a plan? That's what this is about?" He struggled to make sense of what she was trying to tell him. "Did you make an arrangement for the handover? For when she'll take Nell?"

"Oh, but she's not. I'm Nell's mother now."

And now Zivi knew he would surely die.

"*Aaaggghhh!*" he groaned. "Don't you see? She's setting me up!"

"Oh, no! No, no, no." She smiled. "Don't be ridiculous. No one is setting you up."

Zivi was flabbergasted. *Flabbergasted*. It was all so *deeply complex*, so *immensely difficult*. How could she possibly, ever, *ever* believe that what she was telling him was true? "She told you that?" He was incredulous. "And you believed her?"

"Of course. She promised me. And yes, I believe her. All she needed was another woman. Another woman she could talk to. That's all it took." Again, Giselle shrugged. "The whole thing is all very simple."

"No. It is not *simple*. It is not *simple* at all. She had me to talk to and all I got out of her were threats to turn me in for kidnapping."

"That's because you're a man. No matter how much you talked to her, you never understood her." Zivi frowned and Giselle waved away any notion that she and Gwendolyn had formed a connection. "Anyway, the reason I didn't call you all day is that I had to tell you all these things in person." She put her hand on the side of his face. "I needed to see you when I told you."

"Yeah." He laughed. "I guess the phone was out of the question."

She looked at him and grinned, proud of what she'd accomplished. "I knew you'd agree. So, remember how you told me she runs the hill at West 90th every morning at 7:15?"

As she detailed what had transpired that morning with Gwendolyn, the reality of what she had accomplished left him a little shaken. He may have been instrumental in pulling her out of her devastating, crushing, loss-of-a-child depression, but then she had gone ahead on her own and achieved the monumental goal that had eluded him. Of course he was proud of her. But surely *he* would have done the same if he just had a little more time. He hugged and kissed and smiled at her enthusiastically anyway, because it was, in the end, the result that mattered.

And then it was his turn.

"Today is a very big day in another way," he said, running his fingers through his hair. "Because I have a gigantic surprise, too." He smiled slyly, because not long ago he had promised no more secrets. "I decided not to tell you because I didn't want to get your hopes up." He swallowed. "Months ago, my parole officer told me about a grant. I didn't know if I should, because, well, because it was with Columbia. Columbia Graduate School of Engineering. But he convinced me I should try for it. *Columbia Graduate School* of Engineering."

He got up and started pacing.

"They offer a scholarship. They give it only when they have someone worthy, a person who deserves it. Otherwise, nothing. They're really, really careful with it."

He sat back down next to her.

"See, it's a scholarship for felons, guys with a record. To give us a chance to make it in an honest way. So, I applied. And I interviewed. Like, ten different times, with twenty different people." He looked at her sideways. "I wanted it so much, baby. I was just hoping and praying, and, well, I got the email. Giselle, they gave me full scholarship."

He had tears in his eyes. "Gissy," he whispered. "I'm going to Columbia University on a full scholarship. For architecture. Just like I always dreamed. And now it's time." He took her hands. "No more saying *no*. I love you so much, *beba*. We're in this together, you and me, baby. Now and forever. You *have* to say yes."

The truth was, Giselle did not want to marry Zivi. She had no desire to commit herself to anyone at the altar. She had seen how badly it had ended for her parents and had no wish to tempt fate. In contrast, the marital disfunction Zivi grew up with caused him to dig in, cementing his conviction to defy his father and embrace the tradition wholeheartedly. They'd had this conversation countless times before. Today, they both brought something new to the table.

Giselle was still riding the high, empowered by having convinced Gwendolyn to relinquish Nell and acquiring the truth behind the heroin tampering. She had just arranged an unimaginably successful agreement with a very formidable adversary. She suddenly appreciated that she was an intelligent and capable woman. Not to mention, an adult. She was not a baby. Not Zivi's. Not anyone's. And she was sick of being treated like one and mindlessly doing everything Zivi told her to do.

She stared at Zivi and did a quick inventory of their lives together. Sure, she loved him, but frankly, he had done some pretty horrible things. He slept with Gwendolyn for nearly the entire time they'd been together. And, as if she was an idiot, he was now trying to pass it off as a good thing. And he had been a drug dealer! And, *for God's sake*, he kidnapped Gwen's daughter! Although, to be honest, she shared culpability. She had enjoyed the drug dealer lifestyle. She could have cut it off sooner. She knew Nell was abducted. She kept her, nonetheless. But Giselle believed she had paid the price. Losing Madison was karma for those outrageous transgressions.

And the truth was, although she was happy about Zivi's scholarship, she was also pretty damn annoyed. This had been in the works for months. Couldn't he have waited one more day to tell her, instead of stealing her thunder? So, yeah. She still loved him, probably, but at that moment she needed to take a breath from the enormity of it all. And then another minute to forgive and forget it all. Yet again. Right now, she certainly was in no mood to say *I do*.

"You know how I feel about that, Ziv," she finally answered. "I'd like to just keep things the way they are."

Up until that moment, Zivi had been riding his own high.

But suddenly he was royally pissed. He had been accepted to Columbia, fucking *Columbia,* on a *full scholarship,* and she wasn't down on bended knee? Both literally and figuratively? Plus, now that he thought about how disrespectful she was being, she had also defied him, spat in his face, by running away to talk to Gwendolyn, *his* Gwendolyn, after he unequivocally told her not to. And unforgivably, she embarrassed him in front of that piece-of-shit girl friend of hers and the brain-dead boyfriend. And now, the ultimate humiliation. This needy woman had the audacity to say *no* to his marriage proposal.

He didn't think so.

What was it that his mentor Big TaTa had said? *Trust me, my kuzen. Nothing good comes of giving them too much power.*

"*Nyet.*" He said. "Enough of the bullshit. You do not have a choice. Now we have secrets. Gwen may be out of our way, but we still have Nell. She is our secret, yes? We *must* stay together. Today it is about more than love, *beba*. Now we are blood brothers. *Članovi bandi.*" He paused and looked her up and down. For the first time, it wasn't sensual. She felt like a possession, a bright shiny object Zivi wanted to own.

"Why are you speaking to me like that?" She pulled her shirt tight around her torso. "Stop staring at me." She leaned away from him. "You're freaking me out." His once sexy smile was suddenly greasy. Smarmy.

"Speaking like what? Real me? Bosnian gangsta?" He chuckled as she looked at him in horror. "Okay, okay. I get it. You are used to American White Bread Zivi. But now is reality. You remember Osmani, eh? You recall Gavric? You need me, Giselle. They threatened your life, yes? You need me to protect you. And in exchange, I require commitment, *beba*. Do you not see?"

He reached out to jab her breast. She shoved his hand away in disgust.

"What do you think you are doing, eh?" He laughed in her face. "My *kuzinas* are everywhere." Then he turned deadly serious. "Time to wake up, *beba*. You can never leave me."

At that moment, Giselle saw her future unfurl before her. She was trapped. She would never escape his past.

"Baby? You hear me, yes?"

CHAPTER FORTY

Everything was set in motion with a call from one cheap prepaid disposable phone to another.

Big TaTa called Zivi on a burner he picked up six months prior in Mexico. The minute they hung up, the phone was destroyed. He didn't become a crime boss and then reinvent himself as a real estate mogul by being sloppy.

Big TaTa had presented Zivi with an amazing opportunity. It could set Zivi up on a new path for the rest of his life. Big TaTa was interested in adding a huge dilapidated property to his portfolio. A single building occupying a full city block near Madison Square Garden. Bigger and with more potential upside than any other project he had ever attempted. The exterior was landmarked; nothing in the interior could be salvaged. The outlay of capital required before he saw a return would be enormous. Big TaTa wanted to confirm that in his excitement he hadn't lost financial perspective. He needed someone with Zivi's exact skillset— budding architect, plus seasoned super—to evaluate the feasibility and cost estimates before he could make an offer. Would Zivi be interested in taking a look? It had to be that very day. At exactly 2pm. Big

TaTa was a busy man and that was the only window he had for weeks.

When Zivi arrived precisely at two, the rear door to the basement was propped open just as Big TaTa had promised. Zivi followed Big TaTa's directions through the dark, musty labyrinth of hallways composing the cellar. Big TaTa had insisted on meeting in the boiler room. Zivi had been conducting an inspection for at least ten minutes before he saw the twisted foot protruding from behind the water heater. Just as he bent down to get a closer look, the swat team descended.

"ON THE GROUND! HANDS WHERE WE CAN SEE THEM! NOW!"

Zivi had been in the interrogation room for hours. He had been through all this before. He wasn't flustered by the good cop/bad cop routine. He accepted their offers of bitter precinct coffee and stale cheese sandwiches. He continued insisting on speaking to his attorney Gwendolyn Black, who they assured him was currently unavailable, but they were glad to provide him with a different legal aid attorney. Zivi declined. He would wait.

He was just returned from a bathroom break when two new dicks, Detective First-Grade Brian McMillan and Detective Gary DelVeccio, were waiting for him.

"Petar Zhivinovsky?" the tall sweatpants one said. "I'm Detective DelVeccio. Got an ID on the dead guy. Wanna take a guess?"

"How the fuck am I supposed to know? And how many times do I have to spell it out for you people? I want to speak to my lawyer. Gwendolyn Black."

"She's unavailable right now," the short, disheveled one said.

"Then I'm not talking." Zivi crossed his arms over his chest and slouched down in the hard metal chair.

"That's fine." Sweatpants nodded. "But I assume there's nothing wrong with your ears, so listen up. The dead guy you were found with, alone in a remote basement corner of a locked vacant apartment building, was a most wanted, serial child molester."

Short slob leaned in. "Gwendolyn Black's stepfather," he said.

Zivi stopped breathing. "*What?*"

"When we told her that her stepfather was murdered and you were found with the body, she was speechless." Short slob locked eyes with Zivi. "But then she said it made sense. She claims you've been stalking her. That you're obsessed with her."

"That is, that is absolute *bullshit!*" Zivi shouted. "She's out of her fucking mind. She's trying to frame me! Frame me for something I didn't do!" He couldn't believe this was happening. "This is insane! Call my wife! Now! She'll tell you! That Gwen was obsessed with *me*. Not the other way round. And, and she's a criminal! Gwendolyn Black is a criminal! She destroyed evidence! In my last case! She tampered with heroin. My wife knows how! She told my wife all about it! Ask my wife! She'll tell you the truth!"

Three days later, the morning was again bright and sunny, but Zivi wouldn't have known it, having spent those nights behind bars. When they brought him back to the interrogation room, sweatpants and short slob were waiting, although today they'd donned dated suits.

"Regarding the heroin tampering," the tall one said, getting right back to it. "We spoke to your wife."

"No!" Zivi slammed his fist into the table and jumped out of his seat. "She is MY wife. You do not speak to her without me present!" The two uniformed cops in the corner handcuffed him and then secured the cuffs to the steel table, which was in turn screwed to the floor.

"We can and we did." One rabbit punch to the back of the head and Zivi knew he could kill short slob in a second. "It was a lengthy discussion. We covered a lot of topics."

DelVeccio nodded. "We spoke about the heroin. She doesn't know what you're talking about. She says she met Gwendolyn only once, after the two of you had a huge fight about her, to apologize for you harassing her."

"She said *what*? What the *fuck*?"

"There was no discussion of any heroin. Your wife also confirmed what Gwendolyn said about your obsession with her. Said it's been a matter of contention in your relationship since the beginning. Your wife says that you were in love with Black for years. That it turned into an obsession. You stalked Black. And when she rejected you, your obsession turned to hate."

"I want a lawyer," he growled.

"All in good time," McMillan said calmly. "You don't have to say anything. Nothing at all. But you might want to listen." He nodded at DelVeccio.

"Your wife was quite afraid to talk to us," DelVeccio continued. "It took some time for our female counselors to gain her trust. Typical in domestic abuse cases."

"Domestic...?" Zivi repeated. "You are out of your minds."

"Your wife testified under oath, in front of the grand jury, that your hatred of Gwendolyn Black had become overwhelming. Obsessive. All-encompassing." DelVeccio nodded at McMillan.

"She stated that after careful planning," he continued, "and stalking Gwendolyn until you knew her routine, you kidnapped her baby."

"I did not!" Zivi screamed. "That baby! She's my—" he stopped short. He needed a lawyer.

"Your wife testified that you murdered Ms. Black's daughter and then took her to," and here DelVeccio paused dramatically to check his notes, "Dunkhill Funeral Services, where the poor infant was cremated. Had to get a warrant. The director was uncooperative. Sloppy records, but they showed that you did in fact have a female infant cremated around or about the same time as Ms. Black's baby was kidnapped."

Zivi looked from one detective to the other. "My wife did not say that," he growled. "She did not say any of that. I want to see her. He banged his cuffed fist on the table. "I want to see her, *now*."

"Well, she does not want to see you."

One month earlier, before Big TaTa killed Gwendolyn's stepfather and called Zivi to frame him for murder, Gwen and Giselle had the conversation that set the plan in motion. Among other things, they discussed the least painful way to inflict extensive bruising on Giselle's body. To be convincing, they had to ensure the bruises were in various stages of resolution when it came time for Giselle to testify, yet not to be so numerous as to trigger Zivi's suspicions before he was arrested. Gwendolyn had to repeatedly assure Giselle that a host of contusions would be sufficient. Giselle, wanting to eliminate any possibility of doubt, had advocated for breaking her own nose. Eventually they compromised. Once he was gone, she would use a rock, easy enough to dispose of, to smack herself in the face.

Giselle's cowering performance before the police

psychologists had everyone convinced she feared for her life. None of the District Attorneys assigned to the case had the stomach to bring charges of aiding and abetting against her for her knowledge of the abduction and murder of Cassie, Gwendolyn's child. In exchange for her testimony against Zivi, she would not be charged. An intentionally poor makeup job barely covered her bruised and swollen purple eye. That visual, in conjunction with the corroborative testimony of Sabrina Wellington, left the grand jury in tears.

CHAPTER FORTY-ONE

I have been here a thousand times. I know what to expect and yet the smell still knocks me off my feet. A fetid soup of piss and shit and onions and sardines. The stagnant fog of unwashed bodies housed in windowless cells without ventilation, all competing with the piercing stench of bleach and ammonia. I am here for one last conference with a former client following his trial, before he is sent to Green Haven Correctional Facility, the supermax where he will live out the rest of his life. I don't believe I owe him anything after what he did, but I have agreed to tell him why we did it. For me, I will get a certain amount of pleasure knowing he will be ruminating over this conversation every one of his remaining days. For her, so he understands it's all about karma. Nothing personal. I am willing to be the messenger. I am not nervous to see him again. I am actually kind of excited.

I have requested a private meeting room. For obvious reasons, I do not wish to be overheard. He was once a handsome man, Petar Zhivinovsky. And if things had worked out differently, if he had set out on a different path, he could have been a movie star. A real heart throb. He is already seated when

I arrive, his hands and feet shackled to the table, also by my request. Although his face is unmistakably his own, it reflects the ravages of prison life. Wrinkles are etched across his forehead, furrows between his eyebrows. Gray pouches hang beneath his eyes. He has the making of jowls. A ragged line across his cheek will eventually scar over. And of course, his long flowing locks have been replaced with a buzz cut. All in the two-and-a-half years since his arrest and the three days since the jury returned its verdict. They will be shipping him off soon.

"To what do I owe this pleasure?" His smile reveals half a front tooth.

"Came to say goodbye," I answer, "And she wants you to know why."

He nods. "She was always very considerate."

"On that we can agree. But give credit where credit is due." No need for chit-chat today. "This whole thing was my idea. Do you have any clue how tedious it is pretending to be the desperate mother of a missing baby? I could not spend the rest of my life with the fate of Cassie unresolved. To play that part forever? Why should I have to go through that? And then, to have law enforcement throw all their resources at solving this thing? And those detectives? They actually do have the capacity to figure it out. And where would that leave me? So, yes. For me, Cassie had to die. Giselle had the way to make that happen with the cremation story."

He nods.

I smile. All that is blatantly self-evident. I'm sure he understood it long ago. I'm not too sure he has the insight to unravel the rest.

"And Giselle's requirement?" I continue. "To get rid of *you*. She said she didn't want to get married, but you wouldn't listen. Couldn't get it through that thick head of yours that for her, things were just fine the way they were. You needed to *own* her.

Do you even comprehend that she's come to hate you for that? Eventually, I realized her predicament because yes, despite the fact that you forbade her to contact me—or maybe even because of it—we stayed in touch. It's important to her to keep me updated on the baby. You know, she is really a very good woman. You never deserved her. But I digress." I pretend to wave away the tangent, but it is all intentional. To twist the dagger. To let him know that things went on behind his back. To remind him of what he lost. To make sure he doesn't forget that life will go on without him. "Anyway, back to business. We came to an agreement, she and I. I promised I would guide her through this whole ordeal. If she testified that Cassie was cremated, not Madison, she could finally be free of you."

"Okay," he says slowly, taking time to digest the information. "Understood." I see his wheels spinning. "But why go through the trouble of framing me for Daddy's murder? Seems rather gratuitous, no?"

"My deal had to work for her. Sure, we could easily have made you disappear by using the cremation criss-cross. But, to be acceptable to her, she needed you off the streets when she went to the police. She's afraid of what you are capable of." I do my best impersonation of his stupid, fucking, opportunistic Bosnian accent. "'*Look at me! I am Macho man. I speak of violence and hate. Do not get stupid ideas, wife, or članovi bandi will come and get you!*'" I sneer in disgust. "Remember that incident with the cop the day you went back to your old neighborhood and escaped on the subway? Sixteen broken bones. You think she couldn't figure that out? Just because there were no witnesses and not enough evidence to charge, doesn't mean they didn't believe her when she told them you did it. You nearly killed a cop. *Ergo*, God knows what you would do to her. So, what reason do you think she could give the authorities for waiting so long before finally coming forward with everything she knows? That she was scared to death of you. Obviously."

"Obviously," he agrees.

"If she went before a judge and claimed spousal abuse, maybe she'd get a restraining order, which you'd never comply with. Regardless, you'd be out on the street in a day. Maybe two. So, what to do? How could we arrange to keep her safe? It was a conundrum. And then, bingo! Guess who conveniently waltzes into town?"

"Oh, *fantastično*," he says through his disfigured smile. "Let me guess. The fucking 'K' word again."

"Exactly. You catch on quick. Karma. Kismet. Pick your poison. Yes, I heard through private channels that my stepfather was back in NYC. The guy who raped me multiple times a week for years. It's not like me to hold a grudge, but the dude did rip my childhood from me, stick me with a debilitating eating disorder, and leave me with an obsessive compulsion to over exercise."

You are dirty. You are disgusting. You are worthless. I take a second. The last thing I want is to give him the satisfaction of seeing any emotion. So I take a slight pivot.

"You're not the only one with whom I've racked up favors. Big TaTa would not be freely walking the streets in today's glorious sunshine if it wasn't for me." The tips of his ears go red. He was not expecting this one. "And Big TaTa is a man of honor. He was in my debt, and when I called in my chit, he was a gentleman and obliged."

His nostrils flair.

"So, there it is. Cassie had to die. Giselle had the way to make that happen, with the cremation story, and I had the way to make you disappear before she went public by framing you with stepdaddy's murder."

I pause. "And let us just spend ten seconds going back to the part when you claimed I was Nell's biological mother." I lean into him. "On what *planet*," I hiss, "did you think I would ever consent to the collection of my DNA after you *kidnapped and murdered my baby?* And in what *universe*," I curl my lip at the absurdity of the request, "did you imagine Giselle would ever consent to a DNA sample from the child *she gave birth to*, because her physically and mentally abusive husband claimed that *I* was the birth mother of that same child? You understand that sounds insane, right? And then your lawyer requested a compulsory DNA collection order?" I lean back, not even trying to hide my contempt. "How did it feel, having your old buddy Judge Warner laugh you right out of court?"

The muscles in his jaw clench.

I begin to rise and then pretend to think better of it. "Oh!" I snap my fingers and retake my seat. "One more thing she wants you to know. She is making a huge splash in the gallery scene. Had a tremendous opening. I'm not saying I understand her work, but apparently the experts do. Her paintings are going for six figures each. She really is a huge success without you." I smile. Watch him carefully. So I can report back to Giselle later this afternoon. "And that new boyfriend of hers? Looks like she's finally found the love of her life."

Zivi leaps four inches out of his seat before the restraints snap him back into place.

"Everything all right in there?" comes the guard's voice through the intercom.

"Everything is *just peachy*," I answer. Then I really do get up. Turn away from him for the very last time, stand before the locked door, and wait to get buzzed out.

THE END

ACKNOWLEDGMENTS

I am a ravenous consumer of fiction, and I especially enjoy reading the acknowledgments. The author always explains that it really does take a village and inevitably thanks an outstanding list of special people who helped them realize their dream. And now, pinch me, because here I am, with my own village and an outstanding list of my own.

Thank you to Betsy Reavley, maker of dreams. You took a manuscript that was as good as I could possibly have made it and had a vision to make it far superior to what it was.

To my editor bar none, Rachel Tyrer. Thank you for your brilliant eye for detail, helping me execute Betsy's vision in a way that is so much richer than I could have ever achieved on my own.

Thank you to my agent, Lindsay Guzzardo of Martin Literary Management, who held my hand as a newbie through this whole process, believed in my manuscript, and with her razor-sharp insights and the magic of the 'delete' button, helped make it so much stronger than it was before.

To Hannah Deuce and her talented team for bestowing upon me their creative magic. Thank you.

To Tara Lyons and her crew for keeping me organized and as a result, sane. Thank you.

Becca Heyman, Reedsy editor extraordinaire, who got this whole thing started. When I was first dipping my toe into this whole literary thing, you were the first to tell me *Yes! You can do this!* For that I will be eternally grateful.

To my dear friend Kathleen Kubic, I'll never forget the day you said, *I have a writers' group. I think you'd be a good fit.* You truly got this ball rolling. You, and the rest of Salon 20, Ellen Belitsky, Arlene Shapiro, Annie Letzter, and Lynn Lehrfeld, have been by my side this entire journey. When this baby was twice as long, meandering through a thicket of unnecessary asides, backstories and explanations, you hung in and critiqued every extraneous word.

To my girls, Kailie, Ariana, and Marne. This is it. This is what Mom was doing all that time at the kitchen table.

A special thank you and endless gratitude to my husband, Ira. You gave me the time and space to pursue what I love. Writing is now part of my blood. If we had a nickel for every time you said, *What are you doing?* and I responded, *Working on my book,* we'd be very wealthy.

People often ask me where I came up with the idea for *A Kidnapping in New York*. When we had our first child and lived on the Upper West Side of Manhattan, we had a baby nurse obsessed with the notion that everyone was out to kidnap her charges. She soon moved on, leaving me with a head full of nightmarish images of the evil that lurked around every corner. Shortly thereafter, as I jogged with my infant in her baby stroller, roadies were setting up for a concert later that evening in Central Park. I suddenly had a harrowing vision. From that moment on, the novel pretty much wrote itself.

And finally, to Apricot, Rhoey, Lily, and now Willis. Each of you have slept by my feet for countless hours, oblivious to what I was doing, yet tirelessly committed to seeing it through. You have enriched my life more than you will ever know. (Except for Lily. She knew.)

ABOUT THE AUTHOR

Having lived and worked in New York City, Jackie White now enjoys more relaxing times residing in a charming village along the Hudson River and hiking in the Green Mountains of Vermont with her husband and her Great Dane. Once a corporate lawyer, Jackie replaced her treatises for storytelling. In addition to being a novelist, Jackie writes on topical issues for her local newspaper.

A NOTE FROM THE PUBLISHER

Thank you for reading this book. If you enjoyed it please do consider leaving a review on Amazon to help others find it too.

We hate typos. All of our books have been rigorously edited and proofread, but sometimes mistakes do slip through. If you have spotted a typo, please do let us know and we can get it amended within hours.

info@bloodhoundbooks.com

Printed in the USA
CPSIA information can be obtained
at www.ICGtesting.com
CBHW060957091124
17174CB00030B/333